HOW TO RUIN YOUR EX'S WEDDING

A ROMANTIC COMEDY

DENISE WELLS

Cover Design: Opulent Designs

Editing: Missy Borucki

Proofreading: Jenn Wood, All About The Edits

Publicity: Linda Russell, Foreword PR

All Around Awesomeness: Rachel Radner

❀ Created with Vellum

For Gabriella S-B., Jaime R., Rochelle W., and Susan H. - the best support system a girl could ask for.

You know you're in love when you can't fall asleep
because reality is finally better than your dreams.

— DR. SEUSS

ALSO BY DENISE WELLS

<u>STANDALONES</u>

The Three Way, a steamy novella in the **AB Worlds Valentine's Day Series**

Forever Wicked, a steamy novella in the **AB Worlds Halloween Party Series**

Summer Shivers, a romantic thriller in the **Summers in Seaside Collection**

Overdrive, a steamy enemies to lovers romance **in KB WORLDS - DRIVEN COLLECTION**

Pour Decisions, a romantic comedy novella in the **Girl Power Collection**

How to Ruin Your Ex's Wedding, a romantic comedy

I Heart Mason Cartwright, a romantic comedy

Love Off The Rocks, a romantic comedy short

Rebel without a Claus, a steamy, gay romantic short

Breaking Dylan, a coming of age story

<u>AGENTS AND ASSASSINS TRILOGY</u>

Fearless - Book One, a steamy romantic thriller

Careless - Book Two, a steamy romantic thriller

Ruthless - Book Three, a steamy romantic thriller

<u>SAN SOLOMAN</u>

Keeping Kat, a steamy second-chance firefighter romance

Romancing Remi, a steamy enemies to lovers romance

Loving Lexie, a steamy cowboy enemies to lovers romance

Seducing Sadie, a steamy firefighter romance

Trusting Tenley, an emotional second-chance at love romance

ANTHOLOGIES

High EX-Pectations, a romantic comedy short in the **Imperfect Date Anthology**

CAUGHT UNDER THE MISTLETOE - A Holiday Affair to Remember, a romantic comedy holiday short

STORYBOOK PUB CHRISTMAS WISHES - Mistle Oh-No, a romantic comedy holiday short

STORYBOOK PUB - Breezy Like Sunday Morning, a romantic comedy short

LIMITED RELEASES

GIRLS JUST WANNA HAVE FUNDAMENTAL RIGHTS - Charity Anthology

SEEDS OF LOVE A Charity Romance Anthology to benefit Ukraine - Charity Anthology

HOT AS F$#K SUMMER ROMANCE ANTHOLOGY - SULTRY SUMMER NIGHTS

LOCKED AND LOVED: An Isolated Romance Collection

SUMMER WITH YOU: Summer Shorts Collection

JUST A LICK Collection

LOVE LETTERS Collection

STOCKING STUFFERS Anthology

INTRODUCTION

I shoot war zones, not nuptials.

But when my ex-wife lands a starring role in the wedding of the year, it's tempting to change things up a bit.

Who's better than me to follow her around before and during the big day, capturing every picturesque moment, snapping every detail as they join together in wedlock? No one.

Not to mention, she still owes me for destroying my prized vintage camera during our divorce.

As the saying goes, revenge is a dish best served cold.

HOW TO RUIN YOUR EX'S WEDDING

PROLOGUE

KEEPING TABS -
SEASON ONE, EPISODE EIGHTEEN

ANNOUNCER VOICEOVER: Tabatha and her husband, Pax, are enjoying a rare date night at home with nothing but the near-hidden cameras and producers watching them. Such is life since they agreed to allow their lives and marriage to be broadcast via an online streaming service. And, once you get used to having cameras around—all day, every day—it becomes normal and much easier to forget they're there.

Tabatha buries her head in Pax's chest and covers her eyes. Her long red hair cascades down, hiding her face.

"I can't watch," Tabatha says. "I just know Mary will be eaten by zombies and I don't want to bear witness to it." A light squeal lends credit to her statement.

"Hey, Tabs? It's okay to look now." Pax chuckles, and tightens his arm around Tabatha's shoulders for a brief beat before resting his arm along the back of the couch again. "She's still alive. Bill sacrificed himself so she could live."

Tabatha spreads her fingers slowly to peek between them. "Ohmigod, really? So now Bill is dead?"

"Sadly, yes." Pax turns and kisses her forehead before returning his attention to the movie.

> *TABATHA VOICEOVER: Even from the safety of our living room, the threat of zombies feels real. And Bill and Mary like friends, even though they are only characters in a movie. And movies are fake. I would know, I starred in them as a kid. Besides, growing up in the land of make-believe isn't all it's cracked up to be. Sure the fame and the money are great, but you are forced to exist in a constant state of suspended belief with unrealistic expectations of how the world works. Like now, I know that only the character Bill is dead, not a real person. But that doesn't stop me from mourning his passing anyway.*

"What a sacrifice." Tabatha sighs. "I can't believe he would do that. That's so romantic. Giving your life for someone you love is, like, the ultimate gesture."

"That's not romantic," Pax scoffs. "Bill's a (BLEEP) idiot."

"It is romantic. It is," Tabatha says. "He saved Mary's life."

"Baby, who cares?" Pax counters. "If she's not complaining, she's screaming and crying. All she's done through the entire movie is slow Bill down. She lost the keys to the car, can't aim a gun to save her life, literally. Not to mention she dropped their entire food supply in the river, and it washed away. Mary's life wasn't worth saving. Definitely not by sacrificing his own."

Tabatha sits up and leans away from Pax.

"Of course it was," Tabatha says. "He loves her."

"Pfft." Pax's eyes don't leave the screen.

"It's the ultimate gesture of love." Tabatha crosses her arms over her ample chest.

Pax looks at her, his dark eyes wide. "*That's* the ultimate gesture of love?"

"Yes! He's putting her life above his own. Showing her that she is the most important thing in the world to him. Even over himself," Tabatha says.

PRODUCER VOICEOVER: *Do you really think that Bill should let Mary be eaten by zombies?*

PAX VOICEOVER: *(BLEEP) I don't know. No, probably not. I mean, regardless, it's a stupid thing to be arguing about.*

PRODUCER VOICEOVER: *You really think so? I don't know, man, if it were me and my woman was wanting me to throw myself to the zombies just so she could live, when we both knew she'd die anyway, I'd be pissed. That's just not rational thinking.*

PAX VOICEOVER: *But it's not Tabs and me, it's Bill and Mary. And they aren't real.*

PRODUCER VOICEOVER: Is it though? Is it really Bill and Mary that you and Tabatha are talking about? Don't you think that every time these scenarios come up, your responses are based on reality and what you would do in a similar situation?

PAX VOICEOVER: Mine weren't based on reality. Oh, hell, maybe they were. I didn't think about it like that. And if I'm thinking about it like that, then so is Tabs. Which means she thinks I should throw myself to the zombies?

PRODUCER VOICEOVER: Exactly. And if you ask me, that's a really messed up thing to do.

"I go back to my earlier statement," Pax says, turning back to the TV.

"Which one?" Tabatha asks.

"That Bill is a (BLEEP) idiot," Pax replies.

Tabatha curls her lean body into a ball before asking, "What are you having a hard time with, that he loves her that much or that her life wasn't worth it?"

Pax hits pause on the movie and looks at Tabatha, shrugging his broad shoulders. "I don't know. Both," he says. "He should have just let her go."

"Let her go? As in let her be eaten by zombies?" Tabatha asks.

TABATHA VOICEOVER: I'm shocked when he says this. I've always thought of Pax as more of a knight in shining

armor, not a man who'd sacrifice women and children to save his own skin.

"Exactly," Pax says. "But now he can't because he's dead. And it was pointless because she is going to die anyway."

"You don't know that—she could end up saving the world."

"She can't run for (BLEEP). She keeps looking back and falling down. She has no weapons. They're going to catch her any second. No way someone like Mary is saving the world," Pax says.

"Why? Because she's a woman?"

"No, because she can't outrun a bunch of idiot zombies. It would be like you trying to do the same. You've got a beautiful body, baby, but you and I both know your stamina is for (BLEEP)."

"You don't think I can outrun the zombies?" Tabatha asks.

"Beautiful, I *know* you can't outrun the zombies. And I'll be sad to see you go." Pax smirks.

"Wait, are you saying you wouldn't sacrifice yourself to save me in the zombie apocalypse?"

"Damn right that's what I'm saying." Pax points the remote to the TV to start the movie again.

Tabatha pulls his hand down. "Hold on a second."

Pax looks at her and sighs. "Yes, dear?"

"Just to be clear, you would let the zombies get me and you would just keep running?"

"Hands down, babe. I'm the better choice between the two of us when it comes to the salvation of the human race by outrunning zombies."

"And I'm dead?"

"Sad, but true." Pax smiles.

Tabatha doesn't smile back, instead narrowing her green eyes at him.

"Okay." She draws the word out slowly. "I'm dead, who do you re-populate the world with? Since apparently you're the only one who can save it."

Pax shrugs again. "I don't know. Some chick that runs faster than you."

"Faster than me." Tabatha pauses. "Do you even mourn me when I'm gone?"

"Ain't got no time for mourning, babe. I'm zigging and zagging around the undead, carousing for female sprinters."

"Seriously?"

Pax laughs. "Yeah, seriously."

"Unbelievable," Tabatha says.

"Oh, lighten up, you aren't actually mad about this are you?"

"Yes, I am."

"Jesus, Tabby. Come on."

"What? You're leaving me for dead and moving on to someone else, who's more *physically fit*."

"Because she can take care of herself. Not because I like her better," Pax explains.

"Uh-huh."

"Tabatha. Don't start."

"I'm not starting anything, Pax. I'm just letting it sink in that future you callously tosses future me aside when push comes to shove."

"It's a movie, Tab."

"It was a serious question, Pax."

"About *outrunning zombies*?"

"Yes."

"Wow. Okay, fine. Have it your way. Be pissed about it." Pax waves his hand.

"I will," Tabatha says. She falls back against the couch cushion and huffs. She does not lie her head back down on his shoulder or curl back into his chest.

Pax restarts the movie.

> *TABATHA VOICEOVER: I can't stand sitting next to him right now. I feel betrayed and unimportant. I get that the conversation started as a result of a fake plot in a movie. I'm not a lunatic. But fake him isn't even going to try and save fake me. He couldn't even pretend for the sake of the argument. That hurts my feelings.*

Tabatha stands to leave the room.

"Where are you going?"

"To bed," Tabatha says.

"The movie's not over yet."

"Don't care."

"Jesus." Pax sighs loudly, mostly for Tabatha's benefit.

> *PAX VOICEOVER: Yeah, I know that loud sighs are passive-aggressive, but I don't care. I want her to know that I'm annoyed, but I don't want to continue this fight. I want to finish the movie.*

Tabatha takes her time getting ready for bed, expecting that at any moment Pax will come upstairs to apologize. She lies in bed alone. Eventually realizing he must have started watching something else since the movie should have been over.

> *TABATHA VOICEOVER: So, I do what any level-headed woman would do in my situation. I pull sheets and a blanket from the linen closet, then set them, along with his pillow, in the hallway. Next, I close the bedroom door softly and barricade it from the inside with a chair. Because if he can't even be bothered to spare my life during a major world-changing event, then I can't be bothered to share a bed with him.*

～

**KEEPING TABS -
SEASON ONE, EPISODE NINETEEN**

> *ANNOUNCER VOICEOVER: Tabatha and Pax have been fighting since date night, not able to get past the sore*

feelings that surfaced during the argument. Tabatha, expecting an apology from Pax, has gotten increasingly upset when that hasn't happened. Confused by Tabatha's cold shoulder, Pax has taken to retaliating by staying out late. Tonight, in this special one-hour episode of Keeping Tabs, we will see how they handle this strife in their relationship.

PRODUCER VOICEOVER: So, Pax hasn't even talked to you since that night?

TABATHA VOICEOVER (CRYING): No. And he's been out late every night since then. I don't know where. I don't know with who. (BLOWS HER NOSE) I don't know what to do.

Tabatha's red curls are pulled up into a messy bun, green eyes red and swollen, and plump lips turned down in a frown. The usually picturesque Tabatha looks a wreck in distressed jeans, white tank top, and flannel shirt, curled in a ball in her interview chair.

PRODUCER VOICEOVER: Do you think you need a break?

TABATHA VOICEOVER: You mean, like, from the show? Or from Pax?

PRODUCER VOICEOVER: Maybe both. I'm worried about you Tabatha. If this were my guy, I'd definitely be doing something to teach him a lesson. But that's just me. What do you think you should do? I hate to see you crying all the time.

TABATHA VOICEOVER: What would you do to teach your guy a lesson. **(SNIFFLES)**

PRODUCER VOICEOVER: Well, first, I'd be throwing him to the curb. No one, and I do mean no one, ignores me for days, doesn't come home till late, **and** *sacrifices me to zombies without some sort of payback.*

ANNOUNCER VOICEOVER: Taking the producer's advice to heart, Tabatha throws Pax out of the house, thereby teaching him the most important lesson of all: you don't sacrifice the ones you love. She starts by changing the locks on their coastal townhome, and then sets out to toss all his belongings onto the front lawn, in no particular order of importance. Which is what Pax arrives home to a short time later.

"Tabatha Baldwin! What in the ever-loving hell are you doing?" Pax yells.

PAX VOICEOVER: I have flowers for her. An apology for my part in our fighting all week. I don't want to argue any more. I miss my wife. That is until I see she's tossing all my things to the front yard.

"Are these my clothes on the front lawn?" Pax shouts. His handsome face is red with fury.

"Do they look like your clothes?" Tabatha yells back. She turns to the closet to grab another armful of Pax's things and toss them out.

"Yes! You mind explaining?" Pax's voice bellows through the courtyard where they live.

PAX VOICEOVER: Of course I forget the (BLEEP) flowers in my car. Not that they would have made a difference at this point.

Tabatha leans against the window sill and looks down at her nails. "I do mind, actually. I'm busy right now."

Pax audibly growls at Tabatha, throws his hands up in the air, and turns in a circle.

Tabatha smiles.

"Well, jeez, sweetheart, do you think you could speed things up a bit, then? I mean, (BLEEP), if you're kicking me out I'm going have to pack my things in my car, find a place to stay, unpack everything . . . it's going to be a busy evening for me," Pax yells to her.

"Don't you dare make fun of this, Paxton!"

"Oh, dragging out my full name, Tabs?" He sneers. "You sound just like my mother."

Tabatha narrows her eyes at Pax.

"Hey, whaddya know," Pax says. "Now you look like my mother too."

Tabatha's eyes widen.

TABATHA VOICEOVER: He did not just say that. Did he? Comparing me to his mother in any manner is not a compliment. But saying that I look like her is unforgivable.

"And you wonder why I'm doing this, when you say things like that." Tabatha rolls her eyes and drops a few more items at Pax's feet—toothbrush, electric razor, framed picture of his dog from when he was a kid.

"It's not like I'm surprised," Pax says as he walks around, picking up things. "It's only, what? The most dramatic thing you could come up with? Besides, you've threatened to kick me out before, the only difference now being you're actually trying to do it."

"It's so typical of you to throw something like that back in my face later. Maybe if you weren't such an (BLEEP) all the time, I wouldn't be kicking you out," Tabatha yells.

"I didn't even do anything!"

"Exactly! You had the opportunity to do the right thing and chose not to. Not saving me from the zombies? Not okay, Pax. Now I'm forced to be the bad guy once again by taking a stance. So, here's three pairs of shoes and some jeans. I hope you and the zombies enjoy them!"

"Hey," Pax calls out to her.

"What?" Tabatha leans out the window.

"You mind unlocking the front door so we can talk about this?"

"Oh no." Tabatha opens her mouth, covers it with her fingers, and blinks rapidly. "Can't you get in the house?"

"My key won't work."

"Hmm, pity."

TABATHA VOICEOVER: I break his golf clubs next, dropping them one by one out the window. Which probably won't even bother him much. Except, they were a gift from his best friend, Gregor, to try and get him to pick up the game.

Tabatha leans her head out the window. "And let me tell you, it is much harder to break a golf club in reality than it looks on TV."

"You really want to be divorced before we've even been married a year?" Pax asks before she has a chance to duck away again.

"Damn right, I do!" Tabatha screams. "I can't stay married to you for a second longer!" She slams the window.

"Tabs!" Pax yells at the closed window. Tabatha does not return. Pax picks up a small rock and tosses it at the window. "Tabatha!" he yells again. "I know dramatic is your second language, but you better be serious about this."

Nothing happens.

PAX VOICEOVER: She had the locks changed; I can tell by the shiny new deadbolt. So, I ring the doorbell, holding my finger against it and letting it ring repeatedly and wait to see what she does next.

Tabatha opens the upstairs window a moment later and leans out.

"What do you want?"

"I'd like to come in my house."

"No." Tabatha looks down at Pax. "And it's not your house anymore. I'm kicking you out."

"Tabatha, (BLEEP), I'm not playing games."

"Neither am I, Pax."

"Is this still because of the (BLEEP) zombie fight?"

"Among other things, yes." Tabatha crosses her arms over her chest, her face immobile and pert nose pointed in the air.

> *PAX VOICEOVER: I'd like to punch that nose; you know, if I were the kind of guy to actually hit a woman. But I'm not; doesn't mean I don't fantasize about it just a bit sometimes where Tabs is concerned. That and booting her luscious little (BLEEP) right off the edge of a big cliff and wait for her to splat at the bottom. Oh, sorry, that's a little graphic isn't it? Let's switch that to dead. Sometimes I fantasize what it would be like if she were dead.*

"Un-(BLEEP)-believable," Pax says.

"Yes, it is." Tabatha resumes throwing Pax's belongings out the window. Hair products, shower gel, razor blades, clothes, jackets.

> *PAX VOICEOVER: At this point, I'm just happy she hasn't gotten to any of my camera equipment. So, I breathe easy, you know? That is, until she dangles a camera bag out the window. And it's the Hasselblad bag.*

"I swear to god, Tabatha. If you drop that and it breaks. I will never forgive you," Pax yells.

Tabatha looks at the bag. Then Pax. Then the bag again.

And drops it.

"Nooo!" Pax dives toward the bag, and barely misses catching it. The bag lands on a pile of clothes. Pax takes it in his arms, cradling the bag like a baby. He opens the bag to find it empty. "Thank god," he mutters to himself. "I didn't think she would stoop that low."

PAX VOICEOVER: I swear, it's like my life flashed before my eyes as I was going for it. The most horrific thing I've ever experienced by far. Even though camera bags are heavily padded, I never take chances with my cameras.

"Catch," Tabatha calls from above.

Pax looks up.

Tabatha tosses the camera.

PAX VOICEOVER: But I was wrong. She would go lower than that low. I watched like a movie in slow motion as her fingers opened from where they held the strap and the camera started to fall through the air. I couldn't move fast enough to get the camera. It landed on the edge of the concrete. And in a matter of seconds, it went from one whole, to hundreds of tiny pieces bouncing along the walkway. Even if I had one hundred years, I couldn't put it back together again.

I never thought Tabatha would be capable of such a thing. Something so malicious, so unkind. She knows how much that camera means to me. It would be like if I took one of her . . . I don't even know what would compare. But once I find it, I'm going to (BLEEP) destroy it.

"You want a war, woman? You got it!" Pax roars.

Tabatha does not hear the ladder at the window. And she doesn't see Pax until he's halfway inside the room.

"How'd you get a ladder?" Tabatha asks. She stands and backs up until she runs into the wall.

"Oh, wouldn't you like to know?" Pax sneers and advances on her quickly.

"Kind of, yeah. If we owned one, maybe you would've been a little more *handy* around the house." Tabatha tries to dodge his grasp by moving to the right.

"We own a vacuum, didn't turn you into a decent housekeeper." Pax is quick on his feet. It seems no matter which way Tabatha turns, he will still be able to reach her.

"How dare you!" Tabatha screams.

"Oh, sweetheart, I haven't even started to dare." Pax continues to advance toward Tabatha until the two are nearly nose to nose.

"Get out, Pax."

"Make me." Pax crosses his arms over his chest and widens his stance, looking imposing.

Tabatha visibly shivers.

"Are those my socks? You're cutting holes in my socks?" Pax narrows his eyes as he sees what is in Tabatha's hands. He turns and opens her closet before she even has a chance to answer. Pax pulls her favorite Yves Saint Laurent dress out and rips it in half.

"*Ohmigod*! What is wrong with you?" Tabatha cries.

"With me? Oh, I'm just getting started, baby!"

PAX VOICEOVER: I try to think of the most disgusting, most repulsive thing that I can possibly do to her. And then it hits me. Piss and Prada.

Pax grabs her Prada bag next.

"No!" Tabatha yells.

TABATHA VOICEOVER: I watch, with total revulsion, as he undoes his pants, pulls out his (BLEEP), and pisses in my bag, whistling as he goes. Whistling! I lunge for the bag. I have to. I don't even care if I get his piss all over me. Because, Prada.

Pax turns so his back is to Tabatha, then swivels to and fro as she tries to reach around his sides to grab it. He finishes up, tucks himself back in his pants, and tosses the bag aside. Urine splashes up and around when it lands.

Tabatha takes off her shoes, jumps onto their bed, and throws one at him.

The shoe bounces off Pax's forehead, nicking his skin.

"Ow!"

"That's right, you big lug. Ferragamos are fierce."

"(BLEEP), Tabs! That (BLEEP) hurt."

Tabatha looks around, as though searching for something else to destroy. She makes a move for Pax's grandfather's Pulitzer Prize-winning photograph. An original print from The Battle of the Bulge in World War II. He treasures it. Maybe even more than his cameras.

"Don't do it," Pax warns.

Tabatha takes it from the wall and tosses it to the side, like a frisbee. Both watch as it crumbles to the floor, frame and all.

TABATHA VOICEOVER: The minute I do it, I know I've gone too far. I see the devastation on Pax's face and I instantly regret my actions. It's one step too far. Well, one step beyond the Hasselblad, another that I also should never have taken. But it's too late to take it back.

"You (BLEEP). Do you hate me that much?" Pax asks.

"I'm not sure how to answer that, Pax, other than to say, *yes*!"

Pax stalks toward Tabatha.

Tabatha hunches down, her stance wobbly on the mattress, arms out to the side for balance, ready to bolt in either direction. But Pax is a big guy and his arms more than span the width of their California king bed. Pax grabs Tabatha's hand and yanks her toward him, then he tosses Tabatha over his shoulder like it's nothing.

"Put me down!" Tabatha cries.

"Not a chance, babe." Pax spanks her. Hard.

TABATHA VOICEOVER: I'm not going to lie, it made me cry when he spanked me. But at the same time, it was such a turn-on. Which is why I cry. I literally disgust myself by still wanting him. Even now. But no way will I let him see me tear up.

Tabatha pounds on Pax's back the entire trip down the stairs, but to no avail. Pax opens the front door and dumps Tabatha in their front yard.

Literally.

On her ass.

Claps his hand together in an all-done motion and turns to stride back into the house. The door is shut, and the new lock turned before Tabatha even has a chance to get to her feet.

PAX VOICEOVER: I'm halfway up the stairs in the house before I remember I left the ladder outside against the window. Because, I'm a (BLEEP) idiot.

Pax takes the remaining stairs two at a time. He reaches the master bedroom right as Tabatha tumbles through the window.

Tabatha stands and flips her long red hair over her head with her forearm, huffing as she goes.

Tabatha's eyes narrow.

Pax looks at her, in her bare feet with her hair awry, reddened cheeks, and dress that is ripped slightly at the bodice. He chuckles.

"What's so funny?" Tabatha asks.

"You remind me of the women on one of those historic romance covers you love to read. The fierce and beautiful, disheveled woman fighting a pirate, or baron, or whoever the hell she would fight before she (BLEEP) him."

"They only did that because they were in love. And complimenting me will get you nowhere."

"You thought that was a compliment, Tabs?" Pax sneers.

Tabatha straightens and points her nose in the air. "You said fierce and beautiful."

"So, I did." Pax moves toward her. Tabatha backs up to the wall behind her. "And you are both."

> *PAX VOICEOVER: Because there are times, like now, that I can forgive Tabatha in an instant for something otherwise unforgivable if it means I get to (BLEEP) her. Maybe not completely forgive, but definitely forget for a while. It's part of her charm, the ability to make me forget all the bad and retain only the good.*

Tabatha's breath catches as Pax reaches up to push her hair behind her ear, running his fingertips along her cheek in the process. Tabatha leans into his touch, despite herself.

> *TABATHA VOICEOVER: I hate that he has this sexual power. Like an electric current that snakes its way between us.*

"We may suck at being married, babe," Pax growls into Tabatha's ear. "But we have never sucked at (BLEEP)."

> *PAX VOICEOVER: And even better than that? Hate-(BLEEP). Because just as quickly as I forget, I choose to remember. She killed my Hasselblad. And destroyed my grandfather's Pulitzer (BLEEP) Prize-winning photo-*

graph. The original, not a reproduction. So, yeah, I hate her. With every fiber of my being, I despise her.

Pax leans in and captures Tabatha's lips with his. Within seconds she has her arms wound around his neck and is moaning into his mouth.

TABATHA VOICEOVER: I may hate him with everything I have and everything I am. But I still die for his touch.

Pax reaches around and grabs her ass and squeezes hard, tightening his hold as Tabatha's body melts into his. Until the two are a writhing mess of hot breath and long moans.

Tabatha pulls away. "Just so we're clear, I hate you. This changes nothing."

"Ditto, babe."

ANNOUNCER VOICEOVER: And the rest, as they say, is history.

1

TABATHA

"In other news, actress Tabatha Seton (formerly Baldwin) has announced her engagement to tech genius, Hunter Simpcox, who just sold his social media app, Face-to-Face, for a cool twenty-five million dollars. This will be the second marriage for Seton, who was previously married to award-winning photographer, Pax Baldwin. The two were married after a tumultuous multi-year courtship, before citing irreconcilable differences and splitting for good close to ten years ago. This will be the first marriage for Simp-cox. No word yet on when the nuptials will take place or where."

I use the remote to switch off the TV, taking a moment to admire my five-carat, cushion cut diamond with platinum pave band engagement ring. Loving the way it sparkles in the overhead lighting of our den. I am somewhat pleased with the news clip. I would have rather they not mention Pax, but I suppose it's better to have media attention with Pax than no announcement at all.

"Hunter," I call out to my fiancé. "Did you see the news clip about the engagement?"

"I did," he says, coming in to the room. He takes me in his arms and kisses me once on the lips. "They said I was a tech genius."

"Well, you are." I smile.

"One sold app does not a genius make," he says.

"It does when you sell that app for twenty-five million."

His eyes shine. "It's a lot of money, isn't it?"

"It is," I agree. He likes to talk about his money. I think it makes him feel important. My mother would do the same thing as my stage manager. She'd grown up poor, so I think once she finally had money—mine—the need to talk about it helped to make it more real. At least that's what my therapist says.

It's the same with Hunter. The more he talks about it, the better it is for him and the more he believes it's real.

"More money than you've seen?" he asks.

"Yes, I believe so," I say, because he also likes it when he can impress me. "What time are we meeting for lunch?"

"How about twelve-thirty?" he asks.

"That's perfect. I'm off to my yoga class, see you in a couple hours."

"It will be hard for you to improve upon perfection, my queen," he says, referring to the yoga and me. "Until then." He kisses my cheek and is out the door. I'm not far behind him.

I kind of hate it when he calls me *my queen*, but I've never told him. Hunter can be delicate when it comes to any form of criticism or what he perceives as criticism. So, I refrain because he is good to me, we never fight, and he wants to marry me.

We met a little over a year ago. I was a guest judge on a reality talent show and his niece was a placing contestant. He was visiting LA for a few weeks and asked me out for coffee, and then dinner. It was at dinner he admitted he was a long-time fan of mine.

I started as a child actor with a TV variety show *Tabby is so Gabby*. I solo-hosted the show spanning from age seven until we could no longer hide that I'd grown breasts. Then I had a string of hit movies as a pre-teen. The variety show made me a household name, but the movies made me a star. My mom worked me every day, as many hours as she could. I was burned out by seventeen, and in true teenage melodramatic fashion, I had a monumental breakdown.

After a stint in a *relaxation facility*, Mom moved us to Washington. We bought a house in the suburbs and pretended to be normal, living off endorsements, my fledgling makeup line, and residuals from syndication. That's how I met my ex, Pax Baldwin. The good-looking boy who lived next door. But he's a story for another time. Or not at all. Because my life works better when I don't think about Pax.

I attended a public high school in the Seattle suburbs, tried my best to fit in, met my best friend Crystal, and pretended I was equipped—emotionally and otherwise—to be normal and live a regular life. I'd thought the move to Washington took me out of the industry forever, so no one was more surprised than I when my (ex) agent called a few months after my high school graduation with a movie offer.

By then, Pax and I were practically engaged, so I left my mom at home and he and I flew to LA to see about the role. It was almost as though it had been written about me. Child/teen actress who has a breakdown and moves away, then tries to make a comeback. Granted, I wasn't the one trying to make the comeback, it was more the comeback trying to get me to make it happen. I did the movie and launched myself right back into the spotlight.

Pax and I moved to LA permanently, causing my mother and me to become estranged. It wasn't a big jump for Mom and me, we'd not been getting along already. Pax worked on his photography career and I started trying to write and produce a pilot in between movies. The pilot was about my life but focusing on me as an adult. One year turned into two, and pretty soon we'd been in LA for almost four years.

It was at an industry party that we met the talent scout for a major online streaming service that often produced its own shows and movies. We'd just gotten married and were all starry-eyes and positivity. After interacting with Pax and me for an hour, the scout said we needed to have our own show. We laughed it off at the time. Six months later, it became a reality.

Of course, there was only one season of *Keeping Tabs* that aired, because once I kicked Pax out and we didn't reconcile, the concept was pointless. I didn't really want to act after that, and no one was interested in my pilot, so I just kind of drifted for a while. Not literally, just mentally. Somehow, I always ended up at the right place at the right time and just before the divorce, I was able to put my name on a clothing line that's in all the major department stores. Shortly thereafter, my makeup line from when I was a teen got a total revamp.

That kept me busy for a while, until it didn't. Being a face or figurehead doesn't take much effort, so when the offer to guest judge on a reality talent show came up, I jumped at it, met Hunter, and now I'm here.

I moved back to the Seattle area to be with Hunter about a month ago, after maintaining a long-distance relationship for almost a year. Deciding, once again, to leave show biz and just keep my focus on the clothing and makeup lines. Both provide enough financially that I don't have to work aside from them if I don't want to.

Hunter lives, rather we live, in a small suburb outside of the city, which he says is the new Silicon Valley. The area where we are is very green and scenic, with a mountain feel. The downtown area boasts a decent green grocer, small boutiques, and a great yoga studio. And it's only a ten-minute drive from downtown Seattle.

I hop in my car and head down the hill into town. The roads are wet and the sky gray, but the air smells clean. Which is probably my favorite thing about moving from California back to Washington, it always smells good here. Where California has sunshine and palm trees, Washington has evergreens and fresh air.

Crystal and I meet for yoga three times a week. Best friends since high school, she was literally the only girl who would talk to me. But it worked because we totally hit it off and have been near inseparable since, even though we are opposites in almost every way. She's short and curvy with shoulder-length, shaggy, dark hair and a sexy America Ferrara vibe. I'm taller and more a cross between Julia Roberts in *Pretty Woman* and Molly Ringwald in *Sixteen Candles*. Mostly legs, teeth, and hair.

Crystal and I pull into the parking lot at the same time as one another. She waves frantically, as though I don't know her car, or that she'll be here, which makes me laugh. In the last few years, our lives have gone in opposite directions. Prior to that, she came and hung out with me in LA for a few years. I paid her to be my personal assistant, but that mostly meant that we hung out and goofed off.

About three years ago, she decided to "get her life together" —her words not mine—move back to Washington, and focus on establishing a career. She became a medical device rep, which is how she met her doctor husband, Michael. He asked her out, they eloped six months later, and now she's a deliriously happy stay-at-home mom with twin eighteen-month-old girls. I would kill myself if I had her life.

"Hey, fancy pants," she says as she gets out of her car, the nickname she's had for me since high school. I was fancy pants because I'd come from Hollywood.

"Hey, baby mama." A new nickname I've adopted for her since becoming pregnant and having babies. Prior to that, I just called her C. Obviously she's the more creative one between us.

We hug and head into the studio.

Most times I don't get a chance to talk to her until after our class. Today is no exception. She usually hires a babysitter for three hours so we can get coffee after yoga and catch up on things. Like we're doing now.

"Have I told you how happy I am that you're back?" she squeals. Yes, squeals. It should be annoying, but it's not. Crystal has an adorable squeal. It goes right along with everything else about her, also adorable.

"Me too," I tell her. And I am. LA gets old after a while if you aren't in the thick of it—acting, auditioning, preening for the paparazzi. Not actively going after movie roles is the epitome of not being in the thick of it.

"How goes wedding planning?" she asks.

"Barely begun, but not bad," I say, taking a sip of my Americano, wishing I could afford the calories of creamer. But with wedding dress shopping around the corner, I need to watch my intake.

"Have you thought about locations yet?" Crystal asks, pulling the lid off her cup and scooping out whipped cream with her finger.

I'm jealous.

"No, not really," I say.

"What do you think of Court in the Square? Michael and I went to a medical mixer there a while back, it was amazing."

"I don't know. Hunter wants fancy, and I think I'm still undecided."

"Definitely Fremont Foundry. It's fancy as fancy gets."

"It's to be expected, right?"

"Absolutely, when tech genius takes fancy pants as his bride, people expect shiny and spectacular."

I laugh at that. Crystal is the only person I seem to be able to laugh at myself with. And only because she instigates it. With everyone else, it's all seriousness all the time. Including me with myself.

"What about dresses?" Crystal asks. "When do we go dress shopping?"

"I need to lose ten pounds first." My weight is a sore subject between us. I've always been a bit preoccupied with how much I weigh, how I look. I am an actress after all, and my face and body are constantly photographed. Plus, Hunter's constant observance of my weight adds pressure too. And the camera adds ten pounds. Since pictures and video from this wedding will be seen on television, in magazines and all-over social media, not losing ten pounds isn't an option.

"Are you kidding me? From where?"

"My ass, my stomach, my upper arms. I'm hideous right now, Crystal. I've totally let myself go since I stopped acting."

"Tabs, your body is amazing. The envy of many. You work out like a fiend, totally watch what you eat, have perfect dimensions. Don't think I didn't notice you sipping on plain black coffee there—yuck, by the way. You do not need to lose any weight."

"Not all of us have breastfeeding as a means of weight reduction," I complain.

"Well, not just breastfeeding but running after two little monsters all day. Did I tell you, we started weaning them this past weekend?"

"Really? How's it going?"

"Good, I guess. You know it skeeves me out they can ask for it now, right? So, it needs to be done. Plus, both have full mouths of teeth. Which just seems like a disaster waiting to happen. So, yeah, gonna be denying the girls the boobs. Michael will be happy to have them back to himself without the surprise milk squirt once I dry up. And we've been breast-feeding only at night for a while now, so it's not like they are going cold turkey."

"You make them sound like junkies."

"They are. Twenty-seven-pound junkies, jonesing for a fix every night at seven o'clock. Speaking of babies and junkies, what's Hunter going to do now that he sold his tech-baby?"

"Well, first he wants a great big splashy wedding." I smile.

"Do you feel weird doing that your second time around?"

"A little," I admit. "But he really wants it and it's a small thing to do for him. He's paying for it all and has already hired a coordinator. Outside of making a few decisions, it's looking like all I will really have to do is show up."

"He's already hired a coordinator? Wow, who is it? Do you like her?"

"I haven't met her yet. He hired her on his own—"

"You okay with that?"

"Yeah, I think I am. This whole big wedding thing isn't as important to me as it is to him, so I'm happy to let him take the lead on whatever he wants." Plus, he said the less work I had to do, the better. That my days should be spent by the pool eating grapes and lounging. If he has his way, I'll never work another day in my life.

"That's really nice of you," Crystal says. "Most women would have a fit that he made the decision without them. So, who did he pick?"

"Liza Littleton."

"Oh, she's really good."

"I know, her reputation is impeccable. How can I complain?"

"Yeah, you really can't."

The conversation stalls for just a moment. But it's that comfortable silence you can only have with the closest of friends.

"Hey, how's the book coming along?"

"Ugh. Not well." I'm writing a book about my life as a child star. Well, I'm telling my story to a ghostwriter who is writing the book. For which I am grateful. Remembering the stories and retelling them is hard enough without having to also figure out how to make them entertaining. "The writer keeps trying to make it this salacious story of stage moms and demanding directors, parties and drugs, sex and alcohol, with Pax and me as star-crossed lovers thrust into the middle of it all."

"I'd buy that book." Crystal winks.

I laugh at her. "Me too. But that's not the story I want to tell. That's every child actor's story, pretty much. I want to tell a different story, one of a young woman who worked hard and built a solid career after retiring from acting, which brought me to where I am now. No Pax, no stage mom, none of that usual crap."

"I get it," she says, taking a drink of her blended coffee. "But those are two very important aspects of your past and your success. People want to know about the dirty details. Especially since neither Pax nor your mom are in your life any longer and both of those break-ups were so public."

"Everything people need to know about my mom, they can get from *her* books," I grumble. After cutting ties permanently, Mom wrote a tell-all consisting mostly of trumped up stories about what a histrionic—her word, not mine—pain in the ass diva I was. Her book release coincided with one of the movies I did after returning to Hollywood.

It was a bestseller.

She followed it up with a how-to on successful stage mom-ing.

It was also a bestseller.

The irony kills me.

Rumor has it she's moved to Montana and is working on a third book about life after Hollywood.

And Pax? I keep hoping if I ignore that he was a part of my life, he will just go away. So, I refuse to let the ghostwriter include him in the book. Well, try to anyway.

"I never told you this, but I read her book," Crystal says.

"You did?" My stomach sours immediately. I can't believe she would support my mom in such a way. I'm hurt. And pissed. "How—"

"Before you get all wound up"—she reaches her hand over the table to grab mine—"I didn't buy it. I saw it in that Little Library Kiosk on State Street and grabbed it."

I nod. That makes me feel a little better. I try to swallow down the acid already rising in my throat. The coffee makes it worse.

"Do you want a water?" I ask, standing and heading back up to the counter.

"Sure," she calls after me.

I've calmed down by the time I return to the table. The acid is still there, churning in my stomach, but I feel better in my head.

"Don't be mad, please."

"I'm not mad. I was hurt at first. But you didn't buy it or support her in any way like that. And if I'm honest, I can see where someone might be curious about it. I just wish there were more of the truth in it."

"From what I know of you, most of it was real, just embell-ished a bit."

"Most of it?"

"Well, some stuff was clearly made up. Like this one scene where she claimed you threw a temper tantrum and cut up something like fifty thousand dollars' worth of wardrobe for *Tabby is so Gabby* because craft services ran out of chocolate chip cookies."

"That did happen," I say drily.

"Really?" Her eyes grow big, but I can tell by the smirk on her face that she knew that and was just baiting me.

"You're a bitch." I smile.

"Takes one to know one." She smiles back.

I check the time. "Sorry, I gotta go. I need to shower and change before Hunter picks me up."

"Yes, your highness." She smirks.

"Thanks for that," I say. "I know, I need to tell him I don't like the '*my queen*' nickname." I stand, put on my jacket, then grab my phone and yoga mat.

"You know, most women would appreciate being called a queen."

"Yeah, well, I'm not most women."

It's one thing to be worshiped, but it's a whole other thing to be perceived as infallible, which I fear is where Hunter is heading with his ideas of perfection and royalty.

2

PAX

"Yes, baby, Yes. So good. Perfect." I move to the side to get a better angle on her face. "Oh yeah, just like that. Do it again."

God, she's good.

Her head falls back and her chest thrusts out, her breasts on full display trying to squeeze out of the small top covering them. The sun is hitting us from the perfect position and the sand is damp, but not so wet it sticks. Waves are crashing along the shore in the background, the setup can't get any better.

"That's my girl," I tell her. "Keep moving, just like that."

She looks up at me from under her lashes, her blue eyes bore into mine, lips pursed, hands running through her hair, lifting it away from her face.

"There, right there. Oh, that's good."

She stays on her knees, legs parted, skin glistening, looking at me like she wants this. Bad.

She licks her lips and winks at me.

I groan slightly. *Oh, yeah. That does it for me.*

Right there.

I take a dozen or so more shots, cooing to her all the way, before handing my camera off to Ryan, my assistant for the day.

"You are a goddess, E," I tell the model. She stands and someone hands her a towel to wipe off the sand from her legs.

"We got it in that last bunch." I turn to the editorial director and give him a satisfied smile, because those last few shots were fucking fabulous. There are some models I love working with, and Emmanuelle is one of them.

"Fantastic as always, man, thank you," the director says to me, reaching out to clasp my hand in his, then turns to everyone else, clapping his hands to get their attention. "That's a wrap, everyone. Good job. Let's clean it up. Emmanuelle, great job." Emmanuelle preens under the praise. The rest of the group follows in kind, wishing one another congratulations on a job well done with handshakes and half hugs.

Emmanuelle smiles at me before retreating to the wardrobe tent.

"Goddamn, she's hot." Ryan mumbles under his breath.

"Eh, you've seen one, you've seen them all," I tell him, only partially joking. I photograph models in swimsuits all the time and have done this particular calendar shoot nine years in a row. I'm not saying I'm tired of doing it, because that would be ridiculous. As Ryan said, it's hot chicks in bikinis. And it's my bread and butter.

But I can't exactly be famous for shooting pics of bikini models and celebrities when both my father and grandfather were Pulitzer Prize, International Photography, and National News Award winners in photojournalism. Yes, both won all three awards. So, to avoid *tarnishing* the family name with *sub-par* gigs, I created an alias and wore a disguise when I was first starting out. Which turned out to be a smart thing because thanks to the reality show, *Keeping Tabs*, that my ex-wife Tabatha and I were on, my real face was recognizable pretty much anywhere.

I use the name Matthew Hanhauser—my middle name and my grandmother's maiden name—and wear a cheesy disguise that, surprisingly, has not once been questioned: glasses, fake mustache worthy of a 70s porn shoot, and a baseball cap with some shaggy hair attached to the bottom. Matthew takes pictures of models and celebrities, like today. And I, Pax Baldwin, do the more *serious* photo shoots. Not even Tabatha knows I'm Matthew Hanhauser.

I'll admit, it's odd to go from capturing images of war-torn areas in Yemen filled with lawlessness and devastation, to the beaches of Southern California where excess and freedom abound with women posing wearing next to nothing as a means of making a living. It takes a major mind-shift to wrap my head around the dichotomy of the two worlds. And I don't bounce between the two *that* often any more, focusing instead on getting the best shots possible in every situation.

In addition to calendar and celebrity shoots, Matthew is a highly sought-after celebrity wedding photographer. I don't even know how it got started, but it's ballooned into an extremely profitable side business. And I will forever call it a side business, even if I do make more shooting celebs and weddings than I do with *National Geographic* and *Time* magazine covers.

Emmanuelle exits the tent wearing yoga pants and a sports bra. "Hey, Matty, you around later?"

"Should be, why? What's up?"

"I'm around too. You've got my number, use it."

"I might just do that." I smile and wink. I still have yet to understand how women find this getup attractive. The 70s 'stache alone would be a turnoff for me if I were a chick.

She turns and walks away. Ryan and I continue packing away my equipment. "That is exactly why I want to be you," Ryan says.

"You don't want this life, Ryan. It can be lonely, filled with different cities all the time, getting used to new time zones, constantly meeting new people, hardly ever the same girl twice in your bed."

"That's supposed to dissuade me?" He laughs.

"It's not all models and bikinis."

"I know, dude. I know."

"All I'm saying is it can be hard to make connections with people. I have my friends back home, but I'm too busy to make new ones."

"Emmanuelle is your friend." He leers.

I laugh at him. I don't blame him for getting excited. I was the same way with my dad, who was my mentor, when I was his age. Though my dad didn't do a lot of women in bikini shots, the money wasn't in it then like it is now. But when he was first starting out, he did studio shots of pin-ups for calendars. This was before my grandfather won the Pulitzer and the legacy for my dad wasn't quite so daunting like it is for me.

We get everything packed away and Ryan helps me stow it in my rental car.

"You going to call her?" he asks me once we are at my car and out of earshot.

"Probably not," I tell him.

"Why not, dude?"

"Well, partly because if you sleep with a girl too often, she tends to get the wrong idea. And I can't afford to piss off any top models in this industry. Plus, I have an early flight out tomorrow to Seattle. I'm heading home, going to take a few weeks off to regroup."

"Can I have her number?" He snickers.

"Sure, if you ask her for it and she gives it to you."

He rolls his eyes at me.

"Hey, good luck at college in the fall," I say.

"Thanks, man. I learned a lot today, hope to work with you again."

I nod in response, then get in my car and take off. I'm looking forward to room service, scotch, and a big bed all to myself.

Once at the hotel, I carefully remove my disguise. The mustache wreaks havoc on my upper lip. Then I take a long, hot shower, throw on a clean pair of sweat pants, grab a scotch from the mini-bar and pour it over ice, and switch on the news while I wait for my dinner to be delivered.

"And for our top story in entertainment news, actress Tabatha Seton has announced her engagement to millionaire tech genius, Hunter Simpcox. Seton was married for a short time to award-winning photographer, Pax Baldwin, before splitting for good ten years ago. Let's hope she can make this one last a bit longer, am I right? No word yet on when the nuptials will take place or where. And in other news . . ."

I stop my glass halfway to my mouth. They've got a picture of Tabs with the tech genius up on the screen. My Tabs. Rather, my ex-wife, Tabs. The guy looks exactly like one of those nouveau riche douchebags who just got a bunch of money and wants to make sure everyone knows it. My heart sinks.

Tabatha's getting married. To a tech genius douchebag.

Well, good for her.

I guess.

I tell myself it doesn't bother me, except it might. I also tell myself I'm over her, but that's probably not entirely true either. She was my first big love. But we were too young, too stupid, and way too stubborn.

I finish my first drink and pour another. Then call down to room service and ask them to bring a big bottle with my dinner.

I'm going to need it.

~

My flight to Seattle lands on time, and thanks to being in first class, I'm one of the first out the door. I moved back to Seattle after Tabatha and I divorced and eventually bought a place on Puget Sound. It's still home to me over anywhere else, especially Los Angeles.

I take my phone off airplane mode and head through the jetway to the gate, my camera and laptop bags banging against my back and butt as I go. My cell starts beeping almost immediately with voicemail alerts.

I punch the button to hear the first message as I jog down the escalator to the subway/tram that will take me to baggage claim and the taxi stations. Sea-Tac is about an hour from my place in Port Orchard, which is just outside Seattle. Depending on the ferry schedule, I might not make it home for two hours.

My first message is from my business manager. She heard about Tabatha's engagement and wants to make sure I'm okay.

Short of a massive hangover, I'm fine. More power to her and her douchey fiancé.

Second message is from my best friend, Gregor. Same sentiment.

What the fuck? Why do they think I'm going to have an issue with this? It's been ten years since we were together. It's not like I haven't seen other people. I've had plenty of sex, plenty of dates, plenty of action. It's possible that none of them measured up.

It's not for lack of trying on my part. I am very active in my attempts to get over my ex.

I call Gregor back first. "Dude," he answers. "Where you at?"

"I just landed at Sea-Tac. I'm heading home."

"I'm twenty minutes from there, heading north. Want a ride and we can go grab a beer?"

Gregor's twenty minutes ends up being thirty. But it gives me a chance to text my manager and tell her not to worry, and then to check email.

I'm about halfway through all my email, deleting nonsense messages and answering legit ones, when Gregor pulls up, some kind of 70s playlist blaring from the speakers in his Expedition. He's a very large man, offensive tackle for the Seabirds. Six feet five inches, three hundred pounds of solid muscle, big hair, long red beard and mustache. He could easily pass for a Viking—the seafaring kind, not the Minnesota kind. We've known each other since we were kids. In my early days as a photographer he tried to help me get into sports photography, but it didn't pan out.

He gets out of the car, singing and dancing to the music. Lou Rawls. Snapping his fingers, one step forward, two steps back, and a little side-to-side sway while singing about how I'll never find another love like his, and in general making a spectacle of himself.

Which he enjoys doing.

A lot.

For such a large guy, he has an amazing amount of finesse when he moves. He's also a fantastic dancer and singer, which he often puts to good use in one of the pubs he owns in Seattle. They all feature karaoke and dance floors.

He hits the chorus as I'm loading my things into the back of his SUV. Knees bent, hips thrusting, index finger pointing outward and sweeping across the crowd that has started to gather, singing about how we're all going to miss his lovin'. A few people recognize him, beginning to sing and dance along. Most take video, and the airport police blow the whistle telling him to hurry along. He blows a kiss to the crowd and gets back in behind the wheel.

"My man, how goes it?" he asks.

"It's good. I'm tired, happy to be home."

"All those bikini models wearing you out?"

"Yeah man, that's it." I laugh.

"Did you tell Emmanuelle to call me?" he asks.

"I did. She said something about you being a big lug who wasn't worth her time of day."

He puts his hand over his heart and looks at me. "Words wound, man."

"Sorry, bro."

"Speaking of wounds," he says. "You okay with this whole 'Tabatha getting married' thing."

"Of course. It was bound to happen sooner or later, right?" I ask.

"Not if you ask me."

Gregor doesn't like Tabby. At all. His exact words for her are *cold-hearted shrew with the personality of a bull shark.*

He continues talking. "I gotta admit, I'm amazed she found a second sucker. I thought for sure you'd be the only one."

He's not exactly without warrant in his assessment of her. Tabatha was a bit of a diva when we first met her. Not that you could blame her. She went from private tutors, personal assistants, and movie premieres to public school, tract housing, and prom. Even if it was her choice to do so, it was still a hell of a culture shock. And the girls at our school did not welcome her with open arms.

Except for her friend, Crystal. But the snubs turned Tabs hard(er). To say the least. Which is what Gregor is referring to. That, and he thinks she stole me from him. And maybe she did, who knows. Not that I'm a commodity to be had. Problem was, both were reaching new heights in their lives at the same time and relied on me, as their special person, to help them pave the way. Gregor, who was up for a Heisman trophy, which he won, and being first draft pick in the NFL. And Tabatha, with her return to acting after attempting normal teenage life.

"You hungry?" Gregor asks.

"I could eat."

"New bistro I want to try over in Ballard."

"Sounds good."

Anything to get my mind off Tabatha. Not because I'm still hung up on her. But it never feels good when your ex moves on before you do.

3

TABATHA

Hunter pulls up to valet parking and waits for the attendant to open his door. I start to open mine, and the poor guy halts in front of the car, unsure as to which direction to go. I wave him toward Hunter's side and continue getting out. Another attendant appears and assists me. Which, I have to admit, is always nice when in a car that is low to the ground while wearing heels and a pencil skirt.

Hunter straightens his jacket and then offers his arm to me as we enter the restaurant. He holds his head high, his handsome face stoic. He reminds me of a young George Reeves, the original Superman actor, with his slicked back hair and thick glasses. He wants to get married in two months, which seems fast, but for whatever reason, that timetable is important to him. Who am I to argue? Hunter has his quirks, but overall, he's a great guy—solid character, hardworking, good lover, charming personality.

"Table for two by the window, please," he tells the hostess and she leads us to exactly that. Hunter pulls out my chair for me, one that leaves my back to the restaurant. I don't mind. Hunter likes to face people, and I'm used to having my back toward the crowd from my acting days, when I was out but didn't want to be seen. As it turns out, there is a mirror behind his seat that allows me a view of the room anyway.

The server brings us water and Hunter orders a bottle of champagne to accompany our lunch.

"Are we celebrating?" I ask, smiling.

"Every day with you is a celebration, my queen."

My smile starts to falter, but I work to keep it bright on my face. I've got to tell him my feelings on the *"my queen"* nickname.

"I thought we would celebrate choosing a wedding coordinator and a date for the wedding," he says.

Both of which he selected.

"That sounds lovely," I tell him. His chest puffs out at the praise. I already know I won't have more than a glass, if that. First, alcohol is extra unnecessary calories that go straight to my mid-section. Second, I don't like losing control or my inhibitions. Ever.

"A toast," Hunter says, after we've each been poured a glass of the Billecart-Salmon. "To us, and a seamless wedding planning process."

I raise my glass and say, "Cheers." The bubbles tickle my nose slightly as I sip, but it tastes amazing. If I was going to drink a lot, I'd choose this as my beverage of choice for sure.

Our salads arrive—mine with way too much dressing. I try to eat around it, but it's across everything. I'm tempted to wipe the leaves of lettuce off with a napkin. I should have asked for dressing on the side.

"You should wear your hair like that more often." Hunter chomps away at his salad, oblivious to the amount of dressing that is drowning it. "It's very regal."

I put a hand to my hair. It's in a quick chignon today, which, when I do it right, hides that I have any curls in my hair at all. Hunter is not a huge fan of my curls, says they are too unruly.

"Thank you."

"Did I tell you that CompyCat wants to interview me about my next project?" he asks, excited. CompyCat is a very well-known tech blog.

"No, that's great news."

"I'm going to tell them about . . ."

I tune him out, while maintaining eye contact, a skill I learned at a very young age. It's self-preservation. Do you have any idea how many people think they can spout their inane ideas for this, that, and the other when you are a celebrity? It's worse when you're a kid because they just assume you don't have anything better to do than listen to them.

It's not that I'm not interested in Hunter's work, I am. But I don't need to hear about the behind the scenes stuff that goes into it. When it's all finished and pretty, go ahead and tell me what it does. If I like it, I'll use it.

Movement in the mirror behind Hunter's head catches my eye and I glance up.

Gregor Stravinsky.

Pax's best friend.

Otherwise known to me as Igor BigJerksy.

Ugh.

My heart skips a beat in fear that Pax may be with him. But I don't see him anywhere. I see Gregor out and about every so often. It's hard to miss him. He's a giant. A loud, rude, boorish giant. I avoid his pubs intentionally, or places I think he might frequent. To say that we don't like one another is an understatement. It goes back to my high school days, when I first started seeing Pax, and therefore met Gregor.

Mostly because I took Pax's attention away from Igor BigJerksy and he didn't like that. Gregor was focused on three things during high school and at the University of Washington: football, his friends, and his studies. That's it. He didn't date much, so when I *took* Pax from him—his word, not mine—he lost one third of his interests. Which was too much for the big lug to handle.

File that under "not my problem."

Except, he made it my problem. And Pax's problem. And anyone else within a twenty-mile radius who cared to listen.

I responded in kind.

We became steadfast enemies.

Nothing has changed in the last ten years.

Igor BigJerksy is laughing at something the hostess said as she lays a hand on his big tree-trunk-like forearm, flirting.

I roll my eyes.

"What's the matter with that?" Hunter asks.

"With what? Nothing, why?"

"You rolled your eyes when I said we could make it to market in three months."

Shit.

"Oh, um, I'm sorry, darling. I wasn't rolling my eyes at that."

"What were you rolling them at?" He narrows his own eyes at me.

"Uh, I was trying to get a piece of lint off my eyelash without have to touch my eyes."

He nods and continues talking.

The server brings our meals at the same time the hostess shows Gregor to his table, a four-top that is three tables away from ours.

He's eating alone. Huh.

His hulking form takes up most of the space around him and over half the table.

No wonder he has to eat alone. No one else could fit at the table with him.

I turn my attention to my entree— a chicken breast with steamed vegetables.

"It's nice to see you eating healthy," Hunter says, gesturing to my plate. "Helps keep you lean."

I give him a small smile in response. He's right, it does keep me lean. Not everyone can have the metabolism of a teenage boy, like Hunter seems to.

He ordered pasta, which he cuts with a knife and fork before bringing it to his mouth. Before him, I'd never seen anyone eat pasta that way. I find it odd and fascinating at the same time.

My chicken is rubbery. Often the result of asking for a baked breast plain, no oils, no seasonings. And my vegetables are soggy. It's just depressing when a restaurant can't steam vegetables properly. How hard can it be to bake a breast and steam some broccoli?

Sigh.

I set my fork down and dab at my mouth, then reach for my water to take a sip.

Which is when I see him.

My ex.

Pax.

Pax-mother-effing-Baldwin joins Igor BigJerksy at his table and the two laugh about something. Neither have seen me, thank god. And they won't if I have anything to do with it.

I drink Pax in. I can't help it. It's been years since I've seen him in person.

He looks good.

Pax is wearing his typical attire of a vintage t-shirt with low-slung jeans that show off his ass, biker boots, and a leather jacket with his tousled brown hair falling over his forehead. He has the beginnings of a beard and mustache, which are a tad salt and pepper in color and make him look dangerous.

The air whooshes from my lungs.

I try to mentally steady my heart rate.

It's not fair that he still has an impact on me. We haven't been together in forever. I've moved on. I'm engaged to the man across the table, we are drinking champagne, and he and I are happy. Beyond happy, even. I grab my glass and drink half of the champagne down in one gulp.

Hunter's eyes widen as he looks at me. "Thirsty?" He chuckles.

"It's just so good," I enthuse. "Have we had this one before?"

He refills my glass. "We've had it a couple times, and we have a case or so at home. If you like it, maybe this should be the one we consider for the wedding. What do you think?"

I take another large gulp, then burp lightly into my napkin. "I love that idea."

"Remember not to drink too much, my queen. We aren't day drinkers."

I nod in response.

Hunter continues talking about his next project and the team he plans to assemble to assist him. I look just beyond his head to the mirror behind him and watch Igor BigJerksy and his pal Pax spread their testosterone around the room like fairy dust, collecting admiring glances from men and women alike.

Luckily, Hunter hasn't seen them yet. He knows a little bit about my history with Pax, but not all of it. And I'm not even sure if he would recognize Pax if he saw him. It's just that he's a huge fan of Gregor's. Really all Seattle Seabirds, past and present. He has season tickets, hats, jerseys, scarfs, bean-ies, blankets, seat cushions, flags, fingers, a cooler, and lawn chairs. The *man cave* in our house has one wall painted in the appropriate green and blue. The only thing he won't do is put a bumper sticker on his precious Tesla. But he does have one lying just inside the back window so it's still visible without being permanent.

He would want an autograph. And probably a selfie. Which he would then print and have framed to put on the wall of said man cave. Lucky for me, he has friends who go to the Seabirds games with him. It's an all-day event. They tailgate in a nearby lot—Seabirds Field does not allow it on premises —starting at nine o'clock in the morning, and not ending until an hour or so after the game is through.

I love Sundays for that reason. And sometimes Mondays and Thursdays. Don't get me wrong, I adore spending time with Hunter, but I value my time alone even more.

I notice when a woman approaches Gregor and Pax's table and asks for an autograph.

On her breasts.

Figures.

Gregor is happy to oblige. The woman pulls her top down low. Gregor produces a Sharpie I'm sure he keeps in his pocket for this very reason, and signs away. Pax looks politely to the side while the woman exposes herself, laugh-coughing into his fist. And meets my eyes in the mirror.

His face registers surprise for just a moment before he raises one eyebrow in the way that only he can and bobs his chin in greeting. I look away at once and close my eyes.

Stupid. Stupid. Stupid, Tabatha.

I interrupt Hunter mid-sentence. "I'm sorry, darling. Will you excuse me a moment? I'm not feeling well." I stand and place my napkin on the table beside my plate. Hunter half stands and holds a hand out to me.

"Shall I go with you? Do you want to leave?"

I shake my head. "No need to go with me. But I may want to leave if you don't mind."

"Of course, my queen. I will have the food boxed—"

"Not mine, thank you."

"Okay, I'll send for the car and see to the bill."

I smile gratefully as I back away, not looking into the mirror again. Pax's back is to me, but he can still see me in the mirror. And Gregor will be able to see me walking to the restroom if Pax mentions it.

Shit. Shit. Shit.

I make it to the restroom and lock myself inside a stall. My breath erratic and face warm. I don't want to run into him. Either of the hims. I lower myself to the commode and press my face against the cool stone of the stall wall. Bile rises in my throat. I work on forcing it back down, using mild meditation techniques to get everything in my body to still and calm.

I've worked hard to portray a cool and calm woman who does not easily excite, nor fluster. It is in direct contrast to the hothead with a short temper and a diva complex of my youth. I want to keep it that way. With Hunter, I maintain composure at all times. With Pax, I never did.

I leave the stall and run my hands under cool water, then press a damp towelette gently to my face, careful not to smudge my makeup or touch my new eyelashes.

Deep breath.

And a pep talk. "All you have to do now is walk to the front entrance and wait for Hunter. He'll have taken care of the bill, generously donated the remainder of the champagne to the servers, and summoned the car from the valet."

One step in front of the other.

I pull the door open and step into the hall.

Right into the chest of Pax Baldwin.

"Hey, Tabs," he says in that sexy pseudo drawl of his.

Fuckity fuck fuck fuck.

4

PAX

I grab Tabatha by the waist to make sure she doesn't fall back. Her hands come to my chest to steady herself with her elbows tucked in between us. I hear the sharp intake of breath and for a brief moment, I like having her in my embrace.

And then she ruins it.

"Get your hands off me."

"Just keepin' you upright, Tabs," I say, but don't move my hands.

"Don't call me that," she hisses. She hasn't moved her hands either. Her palms slightly curved to form over my pecs. I flex one.

She arches an eyebrow. "Is that supposed to impress me?"

"Did it?"

"You're old news for me, Pax, so I'm afraid not."

She still hasn't moved her hands.

"I hear congratulations are in order."

"Yes, I'm very happy." She doesn't sound happy. I know what Tabatha Seton sounds like when she's happy, and this isn't it. This is a watered-down version of happy, but I'm willing to play along.

"That's all I ever wanted for you, baby," I say, watching her face soften before turning hard once again.

"Yes, well, it's not hard to top what you had to offer, the bar was low."

"Ouch, Tabs. That hurts."

"The truth has a tendency to do that."

"What's the poor sap's name again? Hugh? Howie?"

"His name is Hunter." She sighs. "Hunter Simpcox."

"Right," I say. "*Simpcox*. You know, if I wasn't such a nice guy, Tabs, there's a lot I could do with that last name. Simple-cox. Limpcox. Pimplecox."

"Are you through?" She looks up at me through her lashes, after rolling her eyes excessively. Her expression couldn't be more exasperated.

"Baby, I'm just getting started. Smallpox. Smallcock. Simpering—"

"Please stop. Your words are beneath even you."

I open my mouth to tell her my words can't be beneath me if I'm saying them, but I close it again. We are getting along somewhat okay right this second and I kind of don't want to blow that. Or at least I don't want to blow it much—because I'm going to keep pretending I didn't cyber-stalk the fuck out of the guy when I heard the news—to make sure he wasn't better than me.

He's not.

And I know everything about this dweeb now.

"He builds computers or something?" I ask.

"Hunter is a software engineer. He just sold his app for —"

"Like five billion, right?"

"Twenty-five million."

"Oh, bummer. Well, that's almost like five billion." I chuckle. It's disingenuous as hell. "Still, I'm sure that's enough to keep you in the lap of luxury for a least a couple years, right?"

She pushes at my chest. "Twenty-five million is a lot of money, Pax."

I tighten my hold on her hips, angling my fingers just a bit to graze the curve of her ass.

She still has a great ass.

"I mean, it's not five billion, but yeah, it's a lot."

"You can let me go now," she says, dropping her hands from my chest.

"You sure? Wouldn't want you falling."

"I'm good," she says with a huff as she pushes at me again. This time, I let her go. She stumbles slightly. I can't stop the grin from sneaking onto my face.

"Such a child." She rolls her eyes as she says it.

"Takes one to know one, baby."

"Tabatha? Are you okay?" Hugo-Howie-Hunter Limp-pimple-cock heads toward us, concerned look on his face.

"Fine," she says. "I just ran into someone, not important. Let's go." She takes his arm and spins him around to head back toward the front door.

"Bye!" I yell after them. She flips me off behind her back, making me laugh. It's nice to know I can still get a rise out of her. I head back to our table where Gregor is signing an autograph for a young boy. He ruffles the kid's hair before he leaves and tells him to stay in school and eat his veggies.

I take my seat and a long drink of my beer.

"Was that the *lovely* Ms. Tabatha Seton you had cornered over there?" Gregor uses the word lovely, but what he really means is *horrid.*

"It was indeed," I reply.

"Interesting," he says, drawing the word out and stroking his beard.

"Why?"

"Well, I'm just saying, the day you get back to town and find out about her engagement, we happen to run into her. What are the chances? Hey, maybe it's fate letting you know to reclaim your woman." He scoffs., even though he's a big believer in fate. His favorite chick flick is *Serendipity.*

I, however, am not.

"It's not fate. Pull your man card out of your vagina. She's not my woman. She's engaged to someone else. We've both moved on."

"Bullshit." Gregor fake coughs the word behind his hand.

"*I've* moved on," I say, even though we both know I pretty much haven't.

"Double bullshit." Gregor fake coughs again to prove it.

"Fuck off, dude."

The server brings us each a second beer.

"I took the liberty of ordering another round, figured you'd need it," Gregor says.

"Thanks, asshole, but I'm fine," I say, even though we both know I'm pretty much not.

"Hey, wouldn't it be funny if they hired Matthew to be their wedding photographer," Gregor says. He is the only person who knows about Matthew Hanhauser. "You could photoshop a dildo where the groom's nose should be."

"His name is Hunter," I sneer.

Gregor frowns in thought and bobs his head a bit. "Not a bad name."

"Simpcox," I finish.

Gregor laughs. "Oh, there is so much I can do with that."

"Right? Pimplecock, Limpcock—"

"An Imp's cock. Wimpcock. Skimpycock."

"Exactly. It's a douche name. And he's a software engineer." I use air quotes for the title.

"Just made twenty-five million doing that, or so I hear," Gregor says.

"It's no five billion," I say.

"What does that have to do with anything?"

I shrug, grab my beer, and chug over half, wanting something to ease the angst building inside me. I want Tabby to be happy. I do.

Sometimes.

The other times I want her to burn alive in a fiery death like the wicked witch that she is. The hard truth is she and I don't work well together. We tend to bring out the worst in one another and that's when it's bad. But when it's good between us, it is fucking sublime. And if being apart for the last ten years has taught me anything, it's that I've yet to meet anyone who affects me the way she does. Good or bad.

We met in high school. She was assigned as my lab partner in science class and we became fast friends. Her being famous clicked with me having a famous father and grandfather. Gave us something in common.

It was her first public school experience and she was trying hard to fit in—dying her signature red hair brunette and using a different last name. It worked for a while, she was exposed to the typical mean girl drama of high school. But eventually she was found out. People freaked out about it for a time, but after a few months, she was just Tabatha, the girl who everyone wanted to be or be with.

She was smart and beautiful, with a poise not common in a typical teenage girl. I'm sure due to her past and her acting experience. Before long, she pretty much ruled the school: student body V.P., varsity cheer captain, and she wrote a column for the school newspaper while maintaining a straight A average.

But for someone that everyone knew, she didn't actually have a lot of friends. Outside of me and Crystal, that is. It wasn't until the end of our junior year that I worked up the nerve to ask her to the homecoming dance. That was the night I fell in love with Tabatha Seton for the first time. And over the next few years I fell in love with her over and over. Only to be interrupted by the times that I hoped someone pushed her into a hungry-crocodile filled swamp.

Today, as in literally today, I'm kind of in between. She looks amazing. Way too good for that guy. Tight white skirt that ends just above her knees. Heels that make her legs look miles long, and a low-cut wrap-type blouse showcasing her tits and her curves. When I had my hands on her hips, my fingers at the curve of her ass. If I used my imagination, I could almost feel the tiny strips of fabric holding her panties together.

My guess—if I had to make one—a nude-colored, lacy, thong. She's always been a thong girl, or at least she was when I knew her best. I can't imagine that has changed. Much of her lingerie when we were together was more formality than practicality. Beautiful, sexy, barely there formality.

My phone buzzes on the tabletop with a new message from social media.

For Matthew Hanhauser.

I open my notifications and see a request for an appointment.

A-List client requires utmost discretion.

I roll my eyes. All *A-List* clients say they need discretion, by which they really mean, *"Please leak a few solid shots where I look really good to build hype around whatever I pretend to need discretion with."* I open the message and see the words wedding and two months in the first line. Ugh. I was hoping to take a break from weddings for a while. But, A-List clients pay big bucks and it's not like I have anything better to do.

I'm about to hit decline, when I wonder for just a second if it's possible . . .

The request is from Liza Littleton with Opulence in Stride Event Planning, looking for a photographer for a very high-profile event.

I message back. **What's the event?**

Then turn my phone over and return my attention to Gregor. I hate it when people sit at restaurants, or anywhere really, on their phones and ignore the people they are with.

Gregor is busy talking to the server about the specials, asking in-depth questions that only people preoccupied with food, like Gregor, care about. In addition to playing football, he owns two pubs in downtown Seattle as well as an upscale restaurant. The pubs each serve dishes devised from his own family's recipes, and the restaurant serves fancy shit. He considers himself to be a bit of a foodie at this point.

My phone buzzes again. I turn it over and peek.

Liza Littleton has gotten back to me. **High-profile wedding and pre-wedding planning events. You are our top pick for a photographer. Your reputation precedes you.**

Who are the clients? I ask. I already know my reputation precedes me. I'm a fucking fantastic photographer.

She responds immediately. **I'm not at liberty to say without a contract.**

I grab my phone and start typing. **I'm not even going to take the appointment unless I know who the client is.**

I turn my phone back over.

"What's going on over there?" Gregor asks.

"Just an appointment request." I wave my hand as though it's not a big deal.

"I ordered for you since you were too busy ignoring me to be bothered."

"I'm sure I'll love it, thank you."

"Aw, anything for you, sweetheart," he says, blowing me a kiss.

"So, you keep asking me shit, what's been going on with you over the last couple weeks?" I ask.

"Same old stuff," he says. "Fending off beautiful women wanting to use me for my body." Gregor talks a big game, but deep down, I know he just wants to get married and have kids. The problem is he doesn't want to marry just anyone. Not that it's a problem—that's how everyone should be—but his parents have a fairy tale relationship. They've been together forty years and they still enjoy one another, laugh, date, kiss, can't keep their hands off each other. It's a hard example to live up to. He can barely find someone to do that with forty days, let alone years.

"I thought you were going to do that speed dating thing?"

"Yeah." He winces. "It wasn't good."

"What wasn't? The event? The girls? The restaurant?"

"All of the above. I've never seen so many girls who look exactly the same in my life. You know how every girl used to be blonde?"

I nod.

"Now, every girl is brunette. Same long hair style, with the curls at the bottom that they are always touching to make sure they're still there. Same glossy lips, big cleavage, tight dresses, and crazy white teeth." He shakes his head.

"I thought you liked big cleavage and tight dresses?"

"I do. But it was a little overwhelming. And I felt like no one wanted to get to know me, they just wanted to talk about themselves. As though they already knew me or something."

"Poor famous football baby." I fake pout.

"You know what I mean. I'm not just football, man. I'm a person. With interests."

"I know, you're karaoke and pubs too." I grin.

"Fuck off." He laughs.

My phone buzzes with a new message. I turn it over. It's from my new friend, Liza Littleton.

Just say yes. You won't regret it.

I don't respond.

Fine. Hunter Simpcox and Tabatha Seton. Don't make me sorry I'm telling you.

I move my hand to respond, then pause a moment.

"Remember when you said it would be funny if they asked me to be their wedding photographer?"

"Yeah?" He raises an eyebrow and takes a long drink of his beer.

"Well, what if I was?" I look at him.

He looks at me.

"No," he says, his eyes widening.

I nod as I finish off my beer.

"You have to do it," he says. "No, wait, you can't do it."

"Which is it?"

"You have to do it," he concedes.

"My thought exactly." I pick up my phone to set an appointment with Liza Littleton.

5

TABATHA

"Are you sure you are okay, Tabatha? You don't look well." Hunter reaches over and takes my hand in his, lifting it to his mouth to kiss the back. This is the third time he's asked on our short drive home.

"I'm fine. I think I just overdid it in yoga this morning," I tell him. Truth is, I overdid it remembering how good it felt to have my hands on Pax again. I may not be able to stand the man, but he has always had a beautiful body that I love to touch.

Loved.

That I *loved* to touch. Not love, I'm happily engaged to a wonderful man who I also love to touch.

More so than anyone else.

Ever.

Yeah, keep telling yourself that.

I shut my eyes and lean my head against the cool glass of the car window. Marrying Hunter is the right decision. He's handsome, polite, attentive, and he adores me.

He calls you "my queen."

But really, in the grand scheme of things, how horrible is that? Not at all.

He worships the ground you walk on.

Which is a good thing.

Literally. Like he would lick the bottoms of your shoes if you asked him to.

We never argue.

Because he has no passion.

He's very wealthy.

So are you.

Ugh.

Hunter uses an app on his phone to remotely open the gate at the start of the drive before pulling in.

"Wait right there," he says as he parks the car. "I'll come around and help you into the house."

"That's not necessary, I'm fine."

"Nonsense, you barely touched your lunch." He shuts his car door and comes around to open mine and help me out, then walks me to the front door with one arm around my waist and the other at my elbow.

I allow him to lead me into the living room where he pushes me gently to the couch, then kneels and pulls off my shoes. As he lifts my feet to turn me from sitting to lying down, I peek to make sure the edge of my control top shorts aren't showing beneath my skirt before he covers me with a blanket and kisses my forehead.

"Do you need me to stay with you?" he asks.

"No, I'll be fine."

"I can send the doctor over to check on you. Nothing is too good for my queen."

"Really, Hunter, I'm fine. I promise."

"Okay, I'm heading into my office, but I'll see you later. Call me if you need anything."

I nod and smile, then close my eyes and try to banish from my memory the feeling of Pax's hands around my waist. His fingers curving toward my ass. He used to hold me like that when he'd fuck me on the table. Or the counter. Or the vanity in the bathroom. My core clenches thinking about it.

I pull my phone out of my purse and flip through my old pictures until I find the one I'm looking for. It's Pax, in bed, first thing in the morning. His hair is mussed and he has a slight scowl on his face, but his eyes are shining with so much love.

For me.

He wouldn't often let me take pictures of him, always more comfortable on the other side of the lens. But I'd straddled his waist, waking him with the movement, and capturing the moment before he had a chance to stop me. It was shortly after we'd moved to Los Angeles. We were so young. It hurts to see how innocent we were.

God, what I wouldn't give sometimes to have that innocence back.

Even though I was grown up far beyond my years in a lot of ways, thanks to Hollywood, I'd experienced very little sexually. Pax was my first everything. First boyfriend, first real kiss, first orgasm, first person I had sex with, first person I lived with aside from my mother, and of course, my first marriage and subsequent divorce.

I wasn't even planning to get married again. My first one was too public, too painful, too eviscerating. Until I met Hunter. He's good, calm, and kindhearted. The opposite of Pax in so many ways, that I can't help but be convinced it's right. That it will work between us for that very reason.

A message pops on the screen, from Liza, our wedding coordinator.

LIZA: Just to keep you updated, I'm setting appointments with photographers. Will have samples of their work for you to review once I narrow it down. Have one in particular am hoping to get, if so will just hire. Otherwise, getting quotes to capture the planning, rehearsals, and wedding day per Mr. Simpcox's request.

ME: That's fine. Thank you, Liza.

At first, I felt funny doing a big thing for my second marriage, but it's Hunter's first and it's important to him. Plus, I didn't have a big event the first time around. Pax and I eloped and then holed up in a cheesy love-themed hotel for the weekend. It was pretty damn perfect. We couldn't take off work much longer than that. I was filming a made-for-TV movie at the time and Pax was about to take his first trip overseas for a small tour with a group of Marines in Afghanistan.

For our honeymoon, Hunter and I plan to take a three-week tour of Italy to visit as many vineyards and wineries as possible. Hunter dreams of one day owning a winery, and he really wants to experience the differences between the right and left banks of the Rhone River; in layman's terms, the difference between Cabernet Sauvignon versus Merlot.

I'd originally cleared my schedule for this afternoon thinking that Hunter and I were meeting with a couple wedding planners and deciding together who to hire. Since that didn't happen, I find myself with an unusually free afternoon. Not that I would have had *that* many demands on my time, but I still would have filled it with something, like usual.

Feeling better, I busy myself looking through a few bridal magazines and earmarking pictures I'd like to show Liza. Dresses, bouquets, flower arrangements, monogram styles, and place settings. It's important to Hunter that everything be super upscale and classy. His words, not mine. Because, *image is everything*. Also his words.

I look at the clock, surprised to see that only took a little over forty minutes. I don't do well with idle time. I need to stay active or my brain gets too busy and kind of wraps around itself, so to speak. My stomach rumbles, acid bubbling up my esophagus. I drank too much champagne and didn't eat enough lunch when we were out, so I pop an antacid pill and sit still for a moment until it starts to work. I know it's not healthy to take them as often as I do, but I'd rather take too many pills than have my insides roiling around.

I don't do well with stress.

Which is why this is a good step that I'm taking toward my future. It is the right step. Because Hunter adores me; he has me up on a pedestal.

You hate the pedestal.

Maybe. But that doesn't mean it's bad.

It means he doesn't know you. *Not the real you anyway.*

He knows enough.

He knows the you that you've pretended to be with him.

It doesn't matter. Whatever he knows, it's enough that he wants to marry me and take care of me. Plus, we never argue. He caters to my every need. He's the opposite of Pax, and that's what I need.

Pax.

Stop thinking about Pax. He doesn't matter.

The acid rolls in my stomach. I pop a few more antacids, then look around for something else to occupy my time. My mother's tell-all book waves to me from where I'd tossed it on the coffee table. It's bound to be filled with half-truths and exaggerated tales, begging me to let it fill my idle time. I'm not going to read it. To prove my point, I grab it and put it under the mattress in the guest room. Then I take it back out, put it in a brown paper bag, wrap it with packing tape, and shove it back between the mattress and box spring. I don't need for it to be easily available when I'm feeling weak.

Like now.

It's funny, I always thought my relationship with my mom was great. Until I went to public high school and realized what other mothers did. And high school girls didn't even like their mothers most of the time. Thus began the divide and we've never been able to bridge the gap since.

It's not until I begin to pace that I realize I really need to take my mind off everything for a while. I'm too wired to meditate. So, I succumb to weakness, which I hate about myself, and do the other thing I hate about myself. I make and then eat an entire box of sugar-free JELL-O. Then lock myself in my office and watch reruns of my talk show from when I was younger. From a time before I was jaded. Back when I was happy. Because what they say is correct: innocence *is* bliss.

An email from my ghostwriter arrives an hour and a half into my pity party, saving me from further self-condemnation. When I spend too much time revisiting the past, I have a tendency to spiral down. And by past, I mean everything from my pre-Hunter days.

I send the file to the printer, noticing the chapters from the ghostwriter are about the move from Los Angeles to Seattle, navigating the sudden departure from the glitz and glam in the public eye to public school and life in suburbia. In some ways, I think it was my mother's way of *punishing* me for wanting to take a leave of absence from acting. A decision she did not support. So, she found the furthest thing from it and forced me along for the ride.

Of course, it didn't impact her life so much as that she just didn't have access to the social circles of the industry. Otherwise, her days barely changed, still consisting of managing me; making sure I was where I should be when I should be. Which, after moving, was much more easily achieved than before, until people figured out who I really was.

We should have known it wouldn't be easy. There's only so far that hair dye and fake glasses can get you before your mannerisms or something else indicative of your personal character calls you out. For the first time in my life, I wasn't playing a role or another person or a caricature of myself. I was having to be me, and at that point I wasn't sure who that person was. Which made it easy to slip into various personas until one or two eventually stuck.

I'm certain that I still have a crisis of identity to this day. It shouldn't surprise me, or anyone for that matter, that I re-invented myself with Hunter. It's why I'm so bothered by him calling me *my queen*. It's not me. It's his idea of me.

My fault.

I'm the one who has perpetuated the myth, allowing him to believe he knows who I am, when really he only knows the small piece of me I've allowed to break free and be shown. Crystal is the only person in my life who truly knows me. And she isn't afraid to call me on my shit, in her own passive way.

I'm an enigma to everyone else. Purposefully.

Except Pax.

Well, sure, but Pax isn't in my life, so it doesn't matter.

Oh, pashaw.

The pages from the ghostwriter finish printing and I settle down on the couch with my favorite red pen to rip it to shreds. While a small part of me enjoys recounting stories from my past and allowing another person to turn that into something worthy of audience amusement, a larger part of me wants to make sure the portrayals are accurate without so much of the embellishment that is favored in the entertainment industry.

My publicist loves to remind me: *The smallest detail to you, about you, may be fascinating to a fan.*

However, the details that I don't need fed to the public are my feelings toward Pax as we journeyed from my high school graduation to living together, moving back to LA, marriage, reality show, and divorce. Against my better judgment, I allowed the ghostwriter to make copies of select journal entries of mine from that time period. A time when I was known to be melodramatic and wordy. This ghostwriter loves to play up the *tumultuous* love affair aspect that ended so public and tragic on the front lawn of our coastal Los Angeles townhome.

As such, I "X" out more than a third of what she has sent because it's too vivid. Too accurate. Too telling. I don't need people knowing my innermost thoughts. What's the point of reinventing yourself and becoming someone new if you are just going to send out written invitations to the inner workings of the person you were before?

6

PAX

Liza Littleton is not what I was expecting. The movies always show wedding coordinators as organized, slightly controlling, attractive women, looking for love, which they supplement by helping others with theirs. Funny enough, that's typically what they are in reality.

Just not Liza.

Liza is big: big speaker, big thinker, big spender, and tall. At least six feet tall if my estimation is correct.

"Matthew Hanhauser?" she calls to me from her office when I enter the reception area.

"That's me," I reply, sauntering in, my Matthew disguise in place, dressed in jeans, white t-shirt, and cowboy boots. An ensemble that is surprisingly effective in masking my true identity. Especially since it's similar to my typical attire as Pax: jeans, random t-shirt, biker boots, and mirrored aviators. Except Pax has no 'stache and keeps his hair cut close to his head.

"Well, you are not at all what I was expecting." She looks me up and down and back up again, pausing briefly at my groin. "You look like you could be in front of the camera not behind it." She purses her lips and taps her index finger against them. "I'm undecided on the mustache, though. Tell me, does it tickle?"

"Uh, no. I'm used to it."

"I meant with the ladies. Does it tickle the ladies?" She winks.

I don't quite know what to say.

She doesn't seem to care. "Well, never mind then." She waves a hand in the air. "I've heard a lot about you. I have to say that your reputation definitely precedes you."

"Thank you."

"Yes, well, come, come, sit, sit. Let's get started." She repeats certain words as she speaks. "Have you got your portfolio?"

I nod and hand it to her as I take a seat across the desk from her.

"Good. Good," she says, thumbing through it. "I'll be honest, you're my top pick. I mean, what's not to like? Talented, handsome, in demand, tall, mmm-mmm." She licks her lips. "But I'm supposed to run a few choices by my clients and let them make the final decision. That said, I already know that you are the right man for the job."

"Remind me again who the client is?" I play dumb.

"Hunter Simpcox, the tech millionaire. Lovely man. Just lovely."

"And the bride? Or is it a second groom?"

Because with a name like Simpcox . . .

I snicker to myself.

If Liza notices, she doesn't say anything. "Tabatha Seton, actress, entrepreneur, and creator of *Tab it Together,* the clothing line for women."

I look at her, brows raised, as though I'm not familiar, even though I'm more than. I helped Tabs start the company before we divorced. And I let her have the entire thing when we split. I do okay with what I do and live comfortably, but Tabs makes bank with that fucking clothing line.

"It's the best, absolutely the best. Each article of clothing has a colored tab and as long as you match it with another of the same tab, you know that it goes together. Some tabs are more conservative and others a little crazy with mixed prints. I'm sure I had something similar as a child and loved it. She's clever, that woman. So clever. I'm wearing one of her outfits now, from the plus-size collection." She stands and turns, stopping in a pose. I have to admit the outfit works on her. Some kind of tight legging type pant tucked into boots, with a billowy top.

"It's very nice," I say.

"I know, right?" she replies. "Anyway, enough of that. Let's talk price. How much are you going to charge for this. I need a quote for the planning, the rehearsals, and the big day."

"My hourly rate is three hundred dollars," I say.

She doesn't bat an eye. "You understand there could be events happening every day that require your attention? Every day?"

"Yes, I do," I say.

"And that there is a special in development regarding the courtship and planning, plus parts of the ceremony will be televised. Your pictures will more than likely be used for all of that as well. Will you be charging a licensing fee on top of the hourly fee?"

"No." I shake my head.

She looks surprised.

Shit, I probably should have added a licensing fee. I'd originally planned on taking the next few months off, so anything I make through this job is gravy. Let's be honest, I don't really care what I make from this. I'll be doing it for sport more than anything else.

"Okay then." She picks up some papers from her desk and taps them on the tabletop to straighten them before handing them to me. "Here is the contract we are using for this event. Please review it carefully and return it as soon as possible—"

"Where do I sign?" I ask.

"You don't want to read it?"

I glance at the top page, seeing boilerplate verbiage. I know it's stupid to sign anything without reading it. But I want this gig. Rather, Matthew wants this gig. And I don't care about the rights to the photos of my ex remarrying, which is usually all these contracts talk about anyway. I sign his name in all the correct places and hand it back to her.

"Well, this is great. Just great. Thank you. I'll make sure to get a copy of this emailed over to you today. I am looking forward to working with you, Matthew." She reaches her hand across the desktop and I take it in mine. We shake, but she keeps my hand in her grasp for too long than is customary.

"You have nice hands, Matthew." She lets her fingers trail against my palm as she lets go. "I'm going to let the happy couple know that we've decided on a photographer. We have a cake tasting this week you'll be expected to cover. As soon as I have the exact day, time, and location, I will let you know."

"Sounds good, thanks, Liza."

"The pleasure is all mine, Matthew. Just a pleasure."

Traffic is light on the way back to my house, I catch the ferry at just the right time, and find myself at home with most of the afternoon still free. I remove the ball cap/wig and the porn 'stache then use a special cream to get the remaining adhesive residue from my upper lip.

My house is built into a hill with a small part of it being subterranean. It makes for an exceptional darkroom. I do some work in there as well as some in my studio, then grab a beer and sit out on my back deck to watch the boats in the sound.

I grab one of my cameras and capture a few shots as I sit there. I probably have a million of the sound already, but it never grows old. Neither does Mount Rainier or the Olympic Mountain Range. That's the beauty of nature, it changes by the second and no two shots are ever the same. There is always something new to commit to film or paper.

I go back inside to start dinner, taking a steak from the fridge to grill and throw a potato in the oven to bake. It's a simple meal, but still my favorite. I turn on the sports channel while I wait for the potato. One beer turns into three and I start to feel antsy.

Tabatha's picture taunts me from the wall. She doesn't know I still have it. She may not even remember posing for it. She's sitting on the bed, naked, her head leaning in one direction with her hair covering her face, and her body leaning in the other. Her knees are bent to the side before her with her feet covering any lady parts that might otherwise be exposed to the camera. One arm is crossed in front of her, hiding her breasts, the other crossed over and clasping her side. The shot is incredibly sensual despite not showing any actual nudity.

I've got it enlarged on my wall to near life-like size, and only I know who it is. Even Gregor doesn't know. I'm sure that Tabs would recognize herself if she ever saw it. But she won't ever see it, so it doesn't matter. I took it a few weeks before the final split. During a "good" time in our marriage. You can't tell from the photo, but she's on the bed, waiting for me. A little drunk, a little tired, a little turned on. She was in motion when I grabbed the shot, but it's a perfect moment in time.

She's just too fucking beautiful for her own good.

Time to eat, you sap.

I turn on my grill to let it heat, then prep a quick salad, thinking all the while about Tabs and just how different life may have been if we were able to keep it together and get along. After I finish my dinner, I clean up, grab a book, and settle down to read before bed. I like my solitude for the most part. Yeah, sometimes it's lonely, but I'd rather be lonely than with the wrong person.

That's my favorite sentiment to come out of a year plus of therapy. I was a bit of a wreck after Tabatha and I split, spiraling from girl to girl, job to job, drink to drink. It was Gregor who finally pushed me to reach out to talk to someone. Someone professional. Which is how I found Doctor Cal and grew the fuck up. He helped me both in ways that I didn't expect and in ways I didn't even know I needed help with.

It's one thing to get a divorce, but it's a whole other thing to realize the divorce was probably caused by the interference and manipulation of outside forces with the sole purpose of increasing viewership. And to then acknowledge I was too young and stupid to realize it or stop it. So, I went along with everything happening, not quite believing my marriage was ending until it was too late to turn back. Because Tabby and I had both said too much in the heat of the moment and stayed too proud to be rational about it.

Only sometimes do I believe Tabatha was the wrong person. More often than not, I think she's the right person, but we were together at the wrong time. That we needed to grow more as individuals before being able to handle a relationship as potentially volatile as ours.

As I'm settling down and turning in for the night, I get an email from Liza Littleton asking me to attend a cake tasting two days from now in downtown Seattle. Both Wimplecox and Tabatha will be there. I don't have a full plan in place yet for what I want to do, I just know there won't be a single decent photo of either one of them to be found by the time they are through with all the planning. Maybe Gregor was right, and I can substitute a dildo for the groom's nose in all the photos. I fall asleep with a smile on my face.

7

TABATHA

I find parking near the bakery shortly before noon, having made good time from my hair appointment. I had my hair extensions swapped out today. My hair is long and thick anyway, these just make it more so. And my hairdresser is a genius at matching my natural red, not an easy task. Between fake lashes, control top undergarments, push-up bras, acrylic nail polish, and hair extensions, I'm not sure which parts of me are even real anymore. At least I don't need Botox yet.

Do I?

I take a peek in the visor mirror, turning my face to and fro. Deciding I'm good for now, I move to exit the car, then quickly glance in the mirror, thinking back to my conversation with Hunter this morning about my breasts and wondering if maybe they do need to be larger. I'd just exited the shower and was drying off with a towel.

"You've lost weight," he'd said.

I'd nodded and smiled. "You noticed."

"You look good, my queen. Really good."

"Thank you."

"But are your breasts getting smaller?" He squinted at my chest, then put his glasses on and looked closer. "I think they are. Should we have them enlarged?"

I'd cough-laughed. "Excuse me?"

"While I love you thinner, my queen, I do prefer a more ample bosom."

"And my C-cup is not ample enough?"

"You know what they say, bigger is better." He'd smiled.

I'd changed the subject before I lost my temper. There's a lot I will do to enhance my appearance, it's a must in the entertainment industry. And even though I'm not sure if I plan to return to it, turns out Hunter is a fan of the same alterations. But I'm not there yet, mentally, at a boob-job. I mean, I prefer a larger dick, but I didn't offer to get him an enlargement.

I pull open the door to the bakery, peeking at the exterior before going in. It's a cute little shop, very unassuming from the street front. There's a large display case near the cash register when you first walk in. Then, off to the side is another room with table and couch seating, a fireplace, bookshelves filled with books, and an even smaller room off that one where it appears the tasting will be taking place. Enlarged photos of cakes cover the walls, and the air is filled with the scent of sugar and vanilla.

I'm surprised I'm even on time, considering lunch hour in downtown Seattle is often crazy busy and crowded. Liza is already in the small room, talking to a man with scraggly hair and a camera around his neck, and another in his hand. It stops me. The only person I've ever known to do that is Pax.

Of course, Pax is the only photographer I really know in my adult life. Still, it isn't something I've seen often with the paparazzi or on movie sets. Liza had all but insisted we hire this man. She swears he is the *best of the best, just the best* and that we are *lucky, so very lucky* to have caught him when he's free. I've started to notice she uses the same words in repetition, over and over, and it's annoying.

Pfft. You just did the same thing, Tabby.

"Tabatha, I'm so happy you are here. It is lovely to see you again, just lovely. This is your photographer, Matthew Hanhauser. Matthew, this is Tabatha Seton, soon to be Simpcox."

"I'll be keeping my name," I say, unnecessarily.

"Oh," Liza says. "Okay. Okay, well."

"Nice to meet you, Matthew." I hold my hand out to shake his, and a jolt passes through me when we touch. His hands are rough and warm. They feel good against mine. I look at our joined hands, then up at him. It's hard to see his eyes behind his thick glasses, but I'd swear they are laughing at me.

"It is nice to meet you as well, Tabatha. Or would you rather I call you Ms. Seton?" His voice reminds me of Pax, but I couldn't identify why. They don't sound similar.

Jesus, Tabs, quit thinking about Pax, you are being ridiculous.

I know I'm not thinking of Pax for any reason other than this is a wedding and he's someone I've married before. It's the correlation of circumstance that keeps him at the forefront of my mind.

"Tabatha is fine, thank you for asking," I tell him.

He nods in response and fiddles with one of his cameras. I take a moment to get a good look at him. There is something about him that is appealing, but I couldn't tell you what. He's not particularly attractive. He might be if it weren't for the hair. On his head and on his face. I didn't think anyone had a mustache any longer except for Tom Selleck and Sam Elliott. Oh, and Burt Reynolds. But it dies with those three. It has to, they aren't a good look on anyone else, especially not on my wedding photographer.

Click.

He takes my picture as I study him. I'm fairly certain my eyes were half-closed.

"Whoa, what are you doing? I wasn't ready," I tell him.

"Mr. Simpcox was real clear, ma'am, he wants candid shots. I'm just gettin' warmed up."

"Well, could you warm up on cakes or something?"

"Sure thing, Ms. Seton."

Didn't I just tell him to call me Tabatha?

I look around, noticing everything is ready. We're just waiting on Hunter. Which is odd since he's never late. I turn my back to the others and try his cell. Voicemail. So, I send him a text.

ME: Everyone is waiting. Are you almost here?

"I'm sure he'll be here any second," I say aloud to no one in particular. Liza is busy on her phone. Matthew is in the other room, taking pictures of the cakes, and the baker has vanished. My stomach growls. I skipped breakfast this morning, opting just for coffee. I'm not relishing the idea of the added calories of cake, but I also don't want to serve a cake to our guests that doesn't taste good. So, I need to try it. I inch my hand toward the one that looks like lemon filling and swipe my finger along the frosting.

Mmmm. Oh, that is good.

I shut my eyes for a brief moment and savor the taste of the sweet sugar and tart lemon explosion in my mouth.

Click.

I look up, Matthew is back in the room with his camera pointed at me. "Gotcha." He winks.

My face flushes, part embarrassment, part anger. I'm sure when Hunter asked for candid shots, he didn't intend for them to be me sneaking frosting when no one was looking. Or at least when I *thought* no one was looking.

Hunter rushes in to the room. "Oh goodness, I'm sorry I'm so late. I got stuck on a call and then traffic was terrible. Did you start without me?"

I glance at the time. Ten minutes after the hour.

"No, we waited," I tell him.

"Ah, this is why I absolutely adore you. Tabatha, my queen, you are perfect in every way." Hunter takes my hand and kisses the back of it. "Isn't she just perfect, Liza?"

"She is," Liza says, without looking up from her phone.

"Hello, you must be Matthew," Hunter says holding his hand out to the photographer. "I've heard so many good things about your work. Thank you so much for fitting us into your schedule. May I call you Matthew?"

"Yes," Matthew says, taking Hunter's hand.

"Oh my, that is some grip that you have," Hunter says, trying to pull his hand from Mathew's.

"Sorry, sir," Matthew says. "Sometimes I don't know my own strength." He doesn't sound sorry when he says it.

"Call me Hunter, please." Hunter claps his hands once and looks around. "Well, shall we get started?"

Liza finally puts her phone down. "Yes, sorry about that, just negotiating with the venues you asked me to look into, Hunter."

"I thought we were going to discuss venues later?" I turn to Hunter.

"We were," he says. "But then I decided that nothing was too good for my queen. So I asked Liza to get quotes from the top three places in the Seattle area and figured we could choose from there."

"Oh," I say, not quite sure if I feel relief over not having to make a larger decision than one of the three, or anger over not being consulted. "Okay." But then I realize Hunter had hired Matthew without consulting me as well.

So: venues, Matthew, *and* Liza.

Again, not quite sure on my feelings about it. Do I really care about the details? No, probably not. The important thing is that I'm marrying Hunter. And that he's happy. A big splashy wedding is important to him, so I'm going to let him have that. Which means he can plan it too.

I look down, lost in thought.

Click.

"Kindly stop that," I tell Matthew.

"My apologies, ma'am. You sure are a photogenic little thing, though." He tips his hat at me.

"She models," Hunter boasts.

I roll my eyes. "I don't *model.*"

"Sure you do, honey, for your clothing line."

"I've posed for some marketing shots for a clothing line," I tell him, not sure why I'm downplaying.

"*Your* clothing line," Hunter adds.

"I'll bet that sells like hotcakes," Matthew says, smiling big.

"It does okay." I nod.

"Okay, shall we get started?" Liza asks.

The baker appears and sets the first cake in front of us. "Per Mr. Simpcox's request, the first is the pink champagne with raspberry mousse and vanilla buttercream."

Both Hunter and Liza dig in.

I pick up my fork and poke at my piece.

Click.

I glare at Matthew. He shrugs.

The cake is pink.

I don't know why, but I have a real issue with a pink-colored cake. It just doesn't look right. It reminds me of those godawful strawberry cakes in the box, where the flavor is some kind of rehydrated fruit and the color is *red #59.*

Just add water.

I turn to the baker. "May I get a cup of coffee, please?"

"Make that two," Matthew says.

I look at him. He thinks he gets to partake?

"That looks real good, Ms. Seton," he says to me. "May I?"

He grabs a fork from the table and before I can say anything, he takes a large bite from my piece.

"Excuse me?" I say, my voice shrill.

"Real good cake, chef," Matthew says to the baker.

"It is, isn't it?" Hunter agrees. He turns to me. "What do you think, honey? I think it might be my favorite."

"It's great," I lie. "I'm not sure about the pink color though."

"Okay, number two." The baker sets a cup of coffee before me, then a plate with the next cake option. "Tropical guava with fresh guava buttercream and guava jam."

Hunter loves guava.

I hate it and do nothing to prevent the grimace from taking over my face.

Click.

Click.

Matthew continues taking shots of the cakes and all of us trying them. I don't touch mine. One, because of my issue with guava. Two, the cake is pink. Again.

"Oh, Tabatha is not a fan of guava," Hunter says. "But I think this is divine."

"Hates it," Matthew says, moving his fork in again. I slap at his arm. I don't mean to. It's just reflex. He reminds me of Pax when he does it. Pax has—had—no appreciation for food boundaries. Nor which plate is actually his.

"What?" Matthew asks me. "It's not like you're going to eat it."

I push my plate at him.

"Not the cake for you, my queen?" Hunter asks.

I shake my head.

"Wait, how would you know I hate guava?" I ask Matthew.

"'Cause you said so," he replies.

The baker places another cake-filled plate in front of me, taking my attention away from whatever weirdness I may have felt about what Matthew said. I wait until everyone else has gotten the same. I feel bad that I have yet to really taste any of them, with the exception of the lemon frosting.

"Salted caramel cake topped with roasted almonds and Amaretto glaze, filled with caramel-infused buttercream and thin layers of salted caramel."

This cake is more a beige color, which I can tolerate. I take a bite and moan. Loud.

Click.

I'm certain he got me with my mouth open. I don't even care. I'm so into this cake that nothing else matters.

Literally.

Which means we can't have this cake. I would eat way too much of it. This cake is way too good to be at our wedding. I take another tiny bite, then push it toward Matthew before he has a chance to move in and take some for himself.

A move that also reminds me of Pax. Since it's what I would end up doing when I wanted him to stop reaching over and eating off my plate.

"This one is too sweet for me, I think. Or maybe not sweet enough," Hunter says. Relief fills me. Now I won't have to worry about eating too much of it. Maybe I should just let Hunter have the guava cake, then I don't have to worry about eating any.

"How many are we tasting today?" I ask Liza.

"Six," she says.

Six cakes. And I've only had two bites of one so far that was the third cake. If I can manage tiny bites of the remaining three, I can probably get out of here with less than one hundred and fifty calories.

The baker presents another plate. "Lemon summer berry, a vanilla cake topped with lemon mousse, filled with fresh strawberry and raspberry compote."

Click.

It's the one I snuck a taste of earlier. No one seems to notice the swipe from my finger. I like this one too. It's light, and the contrast of the tart lemon mousse with the sweet of the cake and the compote is wonderful. Before I can say anything, Hunter says, "Oh, way too tart. Nope, not the cake for me."

At the same time, Matthew says, "That's a damn good cake."

"Liza? What do you think?" Hunter asks.

"I'm not sure a cake such as this fits the theme of the day."

We have a theme?

"What is the theme?" I ask.

"Splendor in elegance," Hunter says.

I don't even know what that means.

"Okay, so do we need a fancier cake?" I ask.

"Something more luxurious for sure," Liza says. "Like that one." She points to the cake that I believe is up next in the lineup. It looks like a lot of chocolate.

The baker sets this one before us. "Chocolate brownie cappuccino torte: brownie and rich chocolate layers separated by a cappuccino mouse and chocolate ganache swirl and brushed with Chambord, then topped with fresh raspberries."

Good lord, that cake has a lot going on.

"I haven't even tasted it and I'm pretty sure that's the cake," Liza says.

"Well, okay then. It looks like we've got a cake," Hunter agrees, not having yet tried it either. Apparently what Liza says goes.

Click.

"Do you want to try it first?" I ask Hunter.

"Of course, my queen."

I push mine directly to Matthew, who immediately digs in, taking over half the piece in his first bite alone.

He moans the minute it's in his mouth. Something stirs in my nether regions; I shift slightly in my chair and clench my thighs. My reaction is ridiculous. Especially considering the man is not remotely attractive and I'm marrying Hunter soon.

Just 'cause you're married don't mean you're dead.

Crystal's voice rolls through my conscience. She'd make an excuse for about anything I did or do. Besides, it has yet to be determined whether being married again will be like being dead.

8

PAX

I've said it before and I'll say it again: wedding photographers have it made. Cake tastings are the best. And we always get fed the day of the wedding too. I'm perfectly capable, financially and otherwise, of feeding myself. But there is something about this wedding, knowing that Tabs and the Simpleton are unknowingly footing the bill, that is darkly satisfying.

I take a moment to scroll through the pics I've taken thus far. The cakes look amazing. Tabby, not so much. In most photos, her eyes are half-shut or her mouth is half-open. It takes real skill to consistently capture a person at the worst possible time. I have to make sure to get a couple that are flattering, otherwise I'm sure I'll find myself without a job soon.

"May I see?" Tabatha leans close to me, trying to see the digital screen on the back of my camera.

"Uh. Uh. Uh." I waggle my finger at her. "No peeking."

"But they're my pictures," she protests.

"Actually, they're *my* pictures until I sell them to you."

She waves her hand dismissively. "Well, I know there are some that caught me off guard and I want to make sure they are deleted."

"Oh, they will be," I assure her. "It would do me no good to have undesirable pictures of my clients."

She sits back in her chair, seemingly relieved. I grab a few shots of Hunter and Liza deep in discussion. They seem to have left Tabatha completely out of the discussion and planning. But as near as I can tell, she doesn't care.

"I will tell you this." I turn to face Tabatha, a reluctant grimace on my face. "There could definitely be *better* pictures of you."

Her lips press together, and she breathes in and out through her nose, nodding slowly. "That is why I asked you to wait until I was ready before taking the picture."

"But then they wouldn't be candid."

"A posed shot can still look candid," she hisses.

"Maybe," I say. "But it wouldn't be very professional of me to fake it."

She seethes.

I snap a photo. It is most unbecoming.

"Delete that immediately." Her voice is low and hard.

"No can do." I shrug. "I never edit during the shoot."

"Okay, my queen." Hunter claps his hands, facing us. "Liza and I have got it figured out."

"Okay," Tabatha says, drawing the word out.

"We are going to do a different flavor for each layer. And have extra sheet cake in the kitchen for the flavors we think will be the most popular. My groom's cake will be—"

"I hate to interrupt," I say, not really hating to. "But shouldn't the bride and the groom be deciding the flavors? Not the groom and the wedding planner."

"It's fine," Tabatha says at the same time Hunter responds, "Tabatha doesn't do cake."

"No offense, Mr. Simpcox." I feign shock. "But I've got pictures of her eating cake."

"I'm so sorry, my queen." Hunters takes Tabatha's hands, his eyes searching hers from across the small table. "What would you like to do about the cake?"

"I don't really care," she says.

"Are you sure? Because I only want for you to be happy. And if there is anything—"

"It's fine, darling." She gives him a small smile. "Do you really think the photographer's opinion matters in this?" Skimpycock raises his brows at me and he sits back in his chair, satisfied with what she's told him.

The Tabatha that I know would never stand for not getting a say on any kind of event with her name on it. Why is she so muted with this? When we eloped, she wouldn't even let me pick out my own jeans.

I take a good look at her. She's aged a bit since we were together. Not in a bad way, mind you. Tabatha will be one of those women who ages gracefully, growing more beautiful as she goes. But she's much thinner. She's always been lean, but a voluptuous lean at the risk of sounding oxymoronic. Gone are her beautiful curves and luscious ass, and in their place the thin and more skeletal physique that women think men find so appealing.

I'm not afraid to say it—there is nothing attractive about pounding into hipbones or tailbones when you are fucking a woman. Tabby has never been this thin. I hope it's not Simplecock's influence that has her starving herself to skin and bones. I may be straddling a thin line between love and hate where Tabs is concerned, but that doesn't mean I want her jeopardizing her health or getting involved with anyone who encourages such a behavior.

The cake tasting begins to wind down. Decisions having been made. Next up apparently is catering and venues. I get a few shots of the happy couple shaking the hand of the baker, walking through the bakery, and out the front door. Then I follow Tabatha to her car.

I have to jog a couple feet to get in line with her pace. "You must be the most low-maintenance woman in the world to just let a guy keep making all the decisions for you. Either that or you don't have any original thoughts in that pretty little head of yours."

She looks at me, eyes narrowed. "Excuse me?" Then stops. "Did you just imply that I'm not thinking for myself?"

"Well, no offense, but yeah, that's kinda how it's looking from here."

"Because I don't care about the cake?"

"Sure, that and the wedding planner and photographer too."

"What makes you think I don't care about those things?" she asks.

"Well, for one, your name never came up when I was dealing with Liza, which tells me you don't care about the photographer, and two, each time that I've talked to her since about anything else, it's been Mister Simplecock this, and Mister Simpcox that."

"Did you just call him Mister Simplecock?"

It's all I can do to hold in the laughter. I tried to say it fast so she wouldn't hear it. But I should have known Tabby wouldn't miss a thing.

"No, ma'am. I believe I said Simpcox."

"Hmmm." She narrows her eyes, obviously not believing what I'm saying. "Are you going to let me see the pictures now?"

"No, ma'am."

"Then kindly leave me be. And stop calling me ma'am. It makes me feel old."

"Yes, ma'am," I mumble and continue to follow her for another half a block. She stops suddenly, so I do too.

"Why are you still here?"

"Here?"

"Here, as in following me?"

"My car is over there," I say gesturing vaguely to somewhere up the road.

She waves me forward. I stay where I'm standing.

"Go on," she says.

"After you," I say waving her forward.

She crosses her arms over the chest. "Look, I'm trying to be nice here, but I don't like you following me or walking so close to me, it makes me uncomfortable. Would you please just go?"

Deciding to give her a break, I tip my hat at her and walk by, not stopping until I see her drive past. Only then do I turn and jog back in the direction we came to collect the car she may have recognized—a '79 Bronco that I've had for years. It was passed down from my dad when I was younger; second only to the cameras and some original prints, it's my most treasured possession. I also have a pimped-out Jeep that she doesn't know about that I got in exchange for the rights to an extremely favorable action shot of a Wrangler cresting a mountain-top. I trade off between driving the two, depending on my mood or the weather.

Back home, I spend some time downloading the photos from today onto my hard drive. I have to laugh when I see that roughly ninety percent of those taken of Tabatha are downright terrible. The bulk of which will never be passed along to her or Pimplecock. I will reserve them for my amusement only.

While I don't do much direct image manipulation during my edits, I do like to crop, enlarge, and blur a bit. Never will you find a photo of mine that has been deceptively altered in

Photoshop or some other such program. But I absolutely believe in cropping out unnecessary background objects as well as empty space. And if I find that a photo will be enhanced by blurring some spots to make others more pronounced, I'm not opposed to that either.

I throw one hundred or so shots into a shared folder that I have given Liza access to. She has requested she be the go-between for me and Wimpycock. Of which I have zero complaints over. The less time I have to spend interacting with him the better, as far as I'm concerned. Tabatha is another story entirely. I like seeing how far I can push her before she blows up at me. She came close today, I think. But the line is thin between pushing her buttons and getting fired, so I need to be careful.

Once I've put the "good" pictures into the shared folder for Liza to peruse, I go back to the bad ones of Tabatha. I've decided my favorite is one where her eyes are half closed, mouth wide open, and fork mid-delivery with cake. There is literally no way to make that shot appealing unless you chop her head completely out of the shot and replace it with someone else. Or even another of her.

I save it as my desktop screensaver then head to the bathroom to take off my fake facial hair. Like before, an angry red stripe forms along my upper lip after peeling it away. Even though I use a cream remover, it's still sensitive. It'll fade in a couple hours though. If I'm to be doing this on a more frequent basis, maybe I should look into a slightly better product to use than this cheap one I have now.

I shut down my system, grab a beer from the fridge, and order in a pizza. Then I sit out on my back deck and watch the views of the sound until my food arrives, thinking again that maybe I should get a dog. Or at least something that would help to cancel out the constant silence that I'm immersed in when I'm home. At least with a dog, I could talk to it, and if I didn't want conversation it wouldn't talk back.

9

TABATHA

Liza has us scouting locations for the ceremony and reception later today. Apparently, we also have to decide if we want them to be in the same place or if we care to travel and have our guests do the same. We've had a five-day reprieve from any sort of wedding activities due to Liza's schedule. I find I haven't missed the planning activities at all.

While Hunter hired her to be at our exclusive beck-and-call, she had a small number of events to wrap up prior to giving us all her focus. Not that dealing solely with us will leave her much free time, since Hunter wants to be married so quickly and with all the planning needed to keep to the "splendor in elegance" theme—whatever that means.

On paper, I'm a busy, career-minded, well-diversified, modern woman. In reality, I don't have a lot to do since I'm not acting and spend much of my time being busy looking busy. Which is work. Real work. If you've ever tried to look busy when you aren't, you know exactly what I mean. I know to some it looks like a life of luxury, but in reality, it's hell. I have no discernible skills, nothing to offer the marketplace, my brand is in constant risk of running its course and becoming a thing of the past, and it's not like this book that's coming out is going to set me up for life. Plus, let's face it, how long can a clothing line or syndication of decade plus old TV shows really pay the bills?

I know what you're thinking, this is where Hunter comes in. With his ability to make money, I won't have to worry about a thing. And you'd be right. Don't get me wrong, I adore Hunter. I think we make a good team. We work, travel, and entertain well together. I enjoy his company and he loves me. There isn't much else a woman can ask for.

Because, believe you me, that crap you see in books and movies, the happily ever after? The fairy tale? It doesn't exist. Because, stories are just that. Fiction is . . . well, it's fiction. Any romance you see in the movies is scripted, rehearsed, shot, and re-shot until it appears seamless. And passion? It's fleeting. And infantile.

The real testament of a relationship is in compatibility and staying power. You can't have one without the other. Which is how I know that Hunter and I are in it for the long haul. We are compatible to a fault, which in turn gives us staying power. That's all it takes.

Crystal and her husband are a different story. They are an anomaly. Normal relationships aren't like theirs. They are the one in a million couple that all the myths are fabricated from: they laugh and flirt, enjoy date night, have regular sex, seek counsel from the other, are the best of friends, and share a dynamic chemistry.

When I was young, I thought I had that one in a million with Pax. Instead, being with Pax convinced me of the dubious existence of such a coupling for the remaining nine hundred, ninety-nine thousand of us. After which I decided the only answer for me was to take on life alone. But being alone can be lonely.

Enter Hunter.

And with him, the end of my alone and the answer to my future.

My phone alarm sounds. It's time for me to leave to meet Liza and Hunter to view locations. I double-check my makeup and outfit in the mirror. It's important to Hunter that we exude a good impression at all times, by which he means one that meets his approval. So, I have my hair in the chignon he liked so much the other day.

I sincerely hope that photographer won't be there. Liza assured me his pictures from the cake tasting were lovely. But I know for a fact he predominantly took pictures of me with my mouth open or eyes closed. The fact that he was even allowed a camera near me when I was eating is out of the ordinary. But Hunter, via Liza, had already okayed the shoot. Far be it for me to take that away from my groom. It doesn't mean I have to let any unflattering pictures of me make it beyond the darkroom floor, so to speak.

I back my car from the garage and circle the drive to leave the property. GPS shows it taking about fifteen minutes for me to get to there. I use my hands-free to call Crystal.

"Hey, fancy pants," she answers.

"Baby mama, how's it going?"

"Oh, you know, at the same time I'm weaning from the boob, I thought it would be fun to potty train. So, I've got Armageddon happening."

To reinforce her point, I hear the twins yelling in the background. They don't sound happy.

"Does that mean you don't have time for drinks later?"

"If by drinks, you mean you come over here and we lock the kids in the play-yard and have martinis in the backyard, then yes, I have time."

"It's a deal," I tell her, laughing. I could use some Crystal time. Sometimes an hour every few days in the morning just isn't enough.

"What are you doing this afternoon?" she asks.

"Venues."

"Fun! Did you decide?"

"No, we're looking at one today and then one or two more later this week. Hunter and Liza decided on three. They've negotiated pricing and everything, we just have to decide which one we like the feel of best."

"Wow, he's really getting into this, isn't he?"

"You have no idea."

"What's the first stop?"

"Doso Park."

"I've heard it's amazing. Can't wait to hear all about it—"

Something crashes in the background and I hear one of the babies begin to cry. The other joins in soon after.

"Shit," she says.

"I'll let you go and see you later," I tell her.

"Thanks."

We hang up and I refocus on my driving. Even after living here so many years before, I still tend to get lost in downtown Seattle, with GPS. In theory, the street layout is disjointed rectangles. But in reality, it can be confusing as hell. Especially with all the road construction that is constantly going on.

I arrive at the venue a minute or so late. They've arranged for valet parking for us, so I turn my car over to the attendant and step up to the entrance. The door opens for me from the inside.

A familiar mustached face smiles at me.

Great.

"Matthew," I say.

"Ms. Seton, ma'am, you are looking lovely as always."

"Tabatha." I sigh.

"Right, right. Tabatha. Sorry about that."

I wave a hand dismissively. I don't want to continue the conversation, but I also don't want him thinking it's that big an issue.

"Where are the others?" I ask, looking around.

He shrugs. "Don't know."

"How long have you been here?"

"I came in just before you."

"Did you ask at the front desk?"

"There isn't one."

We stand there for an awkward moment.

Click.

Goddamn him.

"I'm going to go see if I can find them," I say, turning my back to him and his stupid camera.

"I'll go with you," he says.

As I enter a hallway, I hear voices in the distance.

"I don't know what's keeping her, she's always on time."

I recognize Hunter's voice. I look at my watch. I'm barely seven minutes late at this point.

We find them in the main room.

"Oh, there you are. I was so worried, you're never late." Hunter comes to me, putting his hands on my upper arms and looking me over as if trying to see if I'm harmed.

"I'm only a few minutes late."

"I was about to call. You know how I get. It's just not like you, is all."

"I'm here now," I say. Even I can hear the impatience in my voice. Has he forgotten he was ten minutes late to the cake tasting?

I take a deep breath to calm myself. I don't know why I'm losing my temper with Hunter, since that rarely happens. Plus, he's right, I am late.

Matthew busies himself taking pictures of the venue. It is incredible. Old world rustic meets modern industrial.

I walk around the room and try to imagine myself in a wedding gown here—mingling amongst our friends, dancing with Hunter to our song, cutting cake, toasting with champagne.

I have a hard time with it.

A hard time with the venue or the groom?

I shake my head to clear it. My thoughts are obviously veering in a ridiculous direction.

"I love it, Liza. This is exactly what I had in mind." Hunter's voice carries in the empty hall.

This is not the place I want to be married. It's just not the right venue.

"Are you thinking what I'm thinking?" Matthew asks, sidling up to me.

"What's that?"

"That this isn't the place for you."

"What makes you think this isn't the place for me?" I protest. "It's gorgeous."

Plus, how would he know?

"I just can't picture you here," he says, ignoring my question.

"Well, I think it's perfect," I lie.

Matthew's nod agrees with me, but the look on his face says he thinks I'm lying.

Fuck him.

"Excuse me," I tell him as I move to join Hunter and Liza as she is saying, "I don't know how we missed this before, but you'll have to cap it at three hundred for a sit-down dinner."

"Oh." Hunter's disappointment is clear.

"That's okay, isn't it?" I ask.

"No," Liza says. "We've got an initial list of over five hundred now."

"Five hundred?" I turn to Hunter. "How did that happen? We haven't even put together a guest list yet."

Hunter scratches his jaw and begins to pace. "It's just a rough estimate that Liza and I put together."

"For some reason, I assumed you and I would select the guests for our wedding, how silly of me," I mumble, frustrated.

Hunter continues to pace. Liza returns to typing on her phone. How can she always have *that* much to say?

"Did you have anyone who you *really* wanted to attend anyway?" Matthew asks me. "I mean, second marriage and all."

I look at him sharply. "Who the hell—"

"How many do you think you'll have, my queen?" Hunter interrupts.

I have to think about it.

Crap. In a way, Matthew is right. I don't have a lot of people that I feel close enough to that I want them attending my second wedding. On the other hand, why do I care? People get married again all the time. But this wedding is not as important to me as it is to Hunter. The marriage is. Just not the wedding.

"Well, how many can I have?" I know I sound petulant, but I don't stop myself.

Click.

I turn to give Matthew a dirty look, then decide against it in case he takes a picture of *that* as well. I've got to not let his comments influence me. Hunter wants him as the photographer and his work speaks for itself. He seems to have this uncanny ability to get inside my head and I don't like it. At all.

Click.

Matthew snaps one of Hunter in thought.

At least he's not solely focused on shots of me.

Hunter ignores Matthew and the camera. "Obviously as many as you'd like, of course."

"I'm sure I can keep it at one hundred if I do mostly close associates," I say.

Hunter nods at Liza, who in turn begins to type furiously on her phone.

"Maybe we should sit down later and devise a list together," I suggest to my fiancé.

"I just didn't want to bother you with such things," Hunter says.

"Things like the guest list?" I clarify.

"It sounds kind of silly when you say it out loud," he says.

"Yes, I'm sure it does."

"You tell 'em, Tabs." Matthew bumps my shoulder with his.

Tabs?

How ironic. The only other person in the world to call me that annoys me just as much as Matthew does. If not more. What are the chances?

I scoff.

Wait.

What *are* the chances?

Of the thousands of people I've met in my life, only one person before this has ever called me Tabs. And they both happen to be photographers.

I look at him closely.

There's no way.

The profile is similar if not the same. The hair is all wrong. But he's the same height, weight, and build. Pax would never have that mustache. Unless it's fake.

Oh.

My.

God.

I'm going to be sick.

"Hunter, I'll be right back," I call. "I need Matthew to grab a photo of something outside."

I grab Pax-Matthew's sleeve and drag him toward the exit.

10

PAX

"What in the hell do you think you're doing?" Tabatha's face reddens to an unnatural shade I've not seen before. Her tiny fingers pinch at my arm as she tugs me in the direction of the exit.

Ouch!

"Well, this here is a camera." I stop, holding it up to show her, pissed about her pinching my arm. "And I use it to take pictures. I know you don't like the candids, but Mr. Simpcox was real specific—"

"Oh, cut the shit, I know who you are," she fumes.

"I don't know what you mean," I hedge.

Her gaze cuts through me. We make it outside and she turns once the doors close.

"I know it's you, Pax." She stomps her foot, making her breasts bounce. It takes every modicum of strength I possess not to look. I may hate the woman, but that doesn't mean I hate her breasts.

"I'm not sure about this whole Pax person, but my name is—"

She reaches up and grabs the corner edge of my fake mustache, pulling down sharply and taking skin along with the piece.

"Ouch, what the fuck, Tabs?" I touch my fingers to my upper lip and pull them away seeing blood on the tips.

"I knew it!" she yells. "Oh my god. You are unbelievable. What are you doing here?"

"That fucking hurt!" I grab a lens cloth from my pocket and hold it against the stinging skin.

"I knew you were low, Pax. But this is beyond. How could you do this? I can't believe it." Her voice grows increasingly shrill.

"If you could keep your voice down below dog whistle decibels, that'd be great." I stick a finger in my ear for emphasis.

"I will not keep my voice down. In fact, I'm going to get Hunter out here right now."

"Do you really think that's the best idea, Tabs?"

"Quit calling me that!"

"Think about it, babe. How's it going to look that you hired your ex to be your *wedding* photographer without telling the new sucker?"

She pauses and takes a deep breath through her nose, letting it out slowly through her mouth. "*I* didn't hire you, Liza did. And I'm sure once I explain the situation, she'll understand."

"Uh-huh. Yeah. I'm sure she will." I keep my tone purposefully skeptical. I'm stalling. I haven't quite come up with why she should keep me on, and not tell the others, but I'm hoping to soon. I don't want to get fired. That much I know. The reasons why are what I'm not willing to examine too closely.

"You did this on purpose, you deliberately tricked us into hiring you." She jabs me in the chest with her finger, the nail biting into my skin through my t-shirt.

Fuck, that hurts too.

Stop being a fucking pussy, Pax.

And it occurs to me.

"Come on, Tabs. You don't really think they're going to believe you didn't know I had an alias?"

"Of course I do."

"Matthew Hanhauser has been around for quite a while."

"That doesn't mean I knew about him."

"Are you sure about that? We've known one another for how long now? I'm pretty sure I told you early on in our marriage that I had a false name that I worked under. I mean, you had to have recognized it when you heard it."

"Why would I?" She narrows her eyes.

"It's my middle name and my mother's maiden name. Pretty easy. And, of course my wife would have known both of those things."

Her face pales. "I didn't—"

"I'm sure you didn't." My voice drips sarcasm. "And I'm sure they'll believe you too."

I see it on her face, the moment she realizes she's going to have to go through with this. She closes her eyes and drops her head.

I win!

"What do you get out of this, Pax?" she asks after a moment, looking up at me.

"What do I get? Are you kidding? This is the best. For one, your next Mr. Sucker over there is going to pay me a fuck-ton of money."

She rolls her eyes.

"Two, I've always enjoyed wedding photography."

"You've never liked it," she says.

She's right. I decide to give her that one.

"True," I say. "It pays great but it's boring as fuck and a little beneath me, to be honest—"

"Good to see your ego is still intact," she interrupts. "Unjust though it may be."

"Which leads me to the biggest reason why I'm doing this." I pause for effect. "Revenge, baby. It would behoove you to be nicer to me. I'm in total control of how you're going to look on your big day. Memories are fleeting, but pictures are forever."

"You wouldn't," she gasps.

"I would, I am, and I will."

"Pax, please don't do this. Just let it go. Walk away."

"You begging me, Tabs?"

"Would it work?" She looks up from under her lashes, her eyes pleading and her face soft. A long-practiced look I've seen her use many a time before. She's playing me. Problem is, it's damn effective.

Must stay strong.

I shake my head in response, not trusting myself to speak.

She looks down at her shoes and shuffles her feet.

I watch her, waiting to see what she'll pull out of her magic hat next. I need to be prepared. She knows all the ways to get to me.

"I just . . ." She pauses and wipes at her nose with her finger, while sniffling.

Oh, she's good.

Rarely can I handle crying. Fake or otherwise.

"You know, you and I never had a wedding. I always felt like I missed out on something big. Something important. And this is my chance. I know it's silly, with it being a second marriage and all. But I'm excited about wearing a dress and going through all the pomp and circumstance. And I want beautiful pictures to capture the day, you know?"

She keeps her gaze down.

I tilt her chin up with my fingers, half-expecting to see tears in her eyes, even knowing all the while this is a ploy. The look she gives me confirms my theory.

She's faking it.

"That was almost convincing, Tabs."

"Fuck off, Pax." She turns to head back into the venue.

I grab her hand and pull her back to me. She stumbles into my chest.

"Must you?" she asks.

"Must I what? Be so irresistible? Used to be a time you liked your body pressed up against mine."

"Hardly." She scoffs.

"You aren't that good an actress, babe."

"Don't call me babe."

"Got it."

"And don't call me Tabs."

"Yup."

She pushes at me, I let her go. "I hate you," she seethes.

"Feeling's mutual, darlin'."

"Don't call me that either!"

"That?"

"Yes!"

"Or darlin'? I'm making a list but it's hard to keep track."

"Seriously?"

"Hey, I'm just trying to be clear on what I can and can't say."

If she were a cartoon character, this would be the time when steam blew out her ears and her face turned bright red. "You know my name, use that." She turns and walks away.

"Tabatha?"

Her feet stop moving, but she keeps her back to me.

"Can I have my mustache back so I can return to work?"

She holds her hand out to the side and drops the mustache on the ground, then smashes it with her shoe, her sole rotating back and forth on it until it starts to come apart beneath her foot.

"Aw, come on, Tabs. That's my only mustache," I call after her.

She walks into the building, flipping me off as she goes.

Gregor laughs for a good thirty seconds before slapping his knee and pausing to drink his beer. "Oh god, that's a good one, Pax. Holy shit." He wipes at his watering eyes. "Really, she did you a favor. That mustache was not a good look on you, man."

"It was a disguise. It's not supposed to be a good look." I finish my beer and signal the bartender for another. I met Gregor at one of his pubs for a beer after I left Tabatha at the venue. I sent Liza a text expressing my sincerest apologies, but I had an emergency that would take me away for the remainder of the afternoon. I don't see where getting pictures of Tabs and Pimplecock at the place they aren't going to be married at really matters anyway.

"If there is one thing I ever liked about that girl, it was her temper. And she could keep you in line. Never a boring moment with that one."

"Okay, but have you seen my upper lip? It hurts, man." After leaving the venue, and before joining Gregor, I stopped at a drugstore for some ointment to treat the now tender skin under my nose.

"Don't be a pussy," he scolds.

I reach over and pull hard on his beard.

"Ow, man. What the fuck?"

"Hurts, doesn't it?"

"Yes, but that's because it's a real beard growing out of my actual face. Not just something glued on temporarily."

"I have sensitive skin," I mumble.

"You've got a sensitive something." He scoffs.

I flip him off. He blows me a kiss.

"What happens now?" Gregor asks. "Since Tabatha knows it's you."

"I don't know. I don't think she'll tell the coordinator or the fiancé since it will reflect badly on her. I think we just continue to pretend I'm someone else. And I keep taking terrible pictures of her."

"Show me that one again." Gregor laughs. "Where she's got her eyes half-shut and her mouth wide open, shoveling in cake."

I pull up the proof on my phone and we cackle like old ladies over how bad she looks in that one as well as a few others.

"So, what do you got going on tonight?" I ask him once our mirth dies down.

"I have a date." He puffs his chest out and smiles big.

"Really?"

"Yep. New rep for one of my beverage suppliers. And she asked me out."

"Impressive."

"Hey, you want to go with us? I can see if she's got a friend." He pulls out his phone and starts typing.

"Last time you did that, I ended up with a stage five clinger who wouldn't leave the next morning."

"You must just be *that* irresistible, my friend." He smirks.

"Doubtful."

"I told you not to sleep with her."

"I'm not the romantic that you are, G. I don't want to wait until I have feelings for someone to sleep with them. I like my one and done."

He shrugs. "Suit yourself."

I roll my eyes.

"Look here, she's got a friend. And she wants a picture of you for the friend." Gregor points his phone at me as though to take a photo.

"Don't take one with your phone!" I hold my hand out in front of the lens, blocking his shot. "Just send her something of the two of us. What about the one from the Seabirds mixer last month?" I purposely suggest a photo where I already know I look good.

Because, yes, I can be that vain. What of it?

Gregor finds the photo and sends it, then waits for a response. I don't know why I'm agreeing to this. Although, technically I haven't agreed yet. But I also haven't disagreed, so there's that.

"Is she sending a photo of her friend?"

"I don't know, I didn't ask."

"Well, tit for tat, brother. Get that pic." Ordinarily, I would never even entertain the idea of a last-minute, blind double-date. But for some reason, I don't want to go home tonight. At least not yet. I don't know if it's the weirdness I'm feeling after dealing with Tabatha today—because I've definitely got shit swirling in my head, I just don't want to decipher it all yet—or if I'm just bored.

I'm not ignorant, I know that I will always love Tabatha. She's my first love, first wife, first a lot of things, really. And there are bound to be emotional issues that creep up over her remarrying when I'm still single. Especially when I've chosen to entangle myself so directly in her wedding planning process; and now with her knowing that it's me. Maybe it's time for me to get serious about dating. Perhaps I'll find someone else I want to marry. No reason why I can't begin that process tonight.

Gregor shows me a picture with two women. One hot, one not.

"Is mine the one on the left?" I ask hopefully.

"Nope. That's Becky. She's my date. You get the other one."

"Oh."

"Becky said that she's really nice."

"Of course she did."

"Dude, don't be a dick."

"You're right. I'm sorry, man. I'm just feeling weird is all."

"Do you need a hug?"

I laugh when Gregor asks that. But he's serious. For such a big, almost menacing looking guy, he's a sensitive teddy bear who is totally in touch with his emotions. Including that he's a big hugger and he wants to have feelings for a woman before he sleeps with her. Both boggle my mind.

"No, I'm good." I'm not opposed to hugs; I just don't need them as often as Gregor likes to offer them. "So, where are we going?"

"Bowling." Gregor smiles at that and pats me on the back. Hard. He's happy about it because he's in a league and a great bowler.

I suck at it. In a really big way. Like, no way am I impressing this girl tonight. I should really find these things out before I agree to tag along.

"Fine." I sigh. "What time and where?"

11

TABATHA

I'm still pissed about Pax and his little ruse hours later. I haven't told Hunter, and I'm not planning to. Pax is right, it would be weird if people knew we hired him. And there's no way I'll be able to prove I didn't know about his alias. *And* I just don't see the need to make Hunter feel uncomfortable unnecessarily.

I pour myself a large glass of chardonnay, pop an antacid pill, grab my cell phone, and head out to the balcony to call Crystal. She had to cancel drinks in person, the kids were acting up too much. Instead, we are drinking virtually over the phone.

The balcony is my favorite place in the house to go when I want to think or be alone. It's covered, so I'm shielded from the elements, and there's heating and cooling. Regardless of the time of year, I can keep the temperature comfortable. In the morning, it's perfect for sitting and drinking my coffee, the sun is usually shining, and I can listen to the birds. In the evening, I can enjoy a glass of wine with an uninterrupted view of the city lights, and the heaters take the chill out of the brisk night air.

The phone barely rings before Crystal answers. "Hey, fancy pants."

"Hey, is it a good time? Babies asleep?"

"Yes and yes." She sighs. "It's perfect. I just poured a glass of wine and am lounging on the couch like a sloth. You on your balcony?"

"You know me too well." I smile.

"Sorry about having to cancel. Just be happy you weren't subjected to the wrath of my children. Hey, how did venue viewing go today?"

"Oh, Crystal. You aren't going to believe it." I sigh.

"I sense a story coming, do tell."

"You know the photographer that Hunter just had to have?"

"Matthew Hanhauser, right? The celebrity photographer guy? He's supposed to be amaz—"

"That's the one," I interrupt. "It's Pax."

"Wait. What?" She laughs. "How can that be?"

"I mean, there is no Matthew Hanhauser," I hiss. "It's Pax in a disguise pretending to be someone else. It's an alias."

"No!" she gasps.

"Yes!"

"Ohmigod!"

"I know!"

"What are you going to do?"

"What can I do?" I ask.

"You have to fire him, of course."

"Okay, I know. But how? Why?"

"What do you mean how, why? Because it's Pax and not Matthew Hanhauser, that's why."

"That's because there *is no* Matthew Hanhauser."

"Unbelievable."

"I know."

"Okay," she says. "What are you thinking?"

"Well, let's say that I do fire him, what do I tell Hunter or Liza? I've been thinking on this all day and I have yet to come up with anything remotely suitable." I look back toward the house to make sure I'm still alone and Hunter can't over-hear me.

"You don't need suitable. Stop being so formal about it. Just tell them you don't like him."

"But they love him."

"Well, sucks to be them."

I laugh at her. "I can't do that. Hunter is so excited to have this guy, because *he's the best*. And I already feel—"

"This guy, meaning Matthew?"

I sigh and take a large sip of my wine. "Yes."

"You already feel what?" she asks.

"Like the decision has been taken away from me anyway. Not that it matters, Liza hired him, Hunter agreed, and Pax knew exactly what he was doing."

"So, obviously it's been him the entire time, right?"

"Yep." I make a popping sound with the "p." I'd told her about how annoying Matthew was at our cake tasting. Which is way more believable now that I know that it was Pax. "You want to know the weird thing?"

"There's more?" Crystal giggles.

"Before I knew he was really Pax, we had this moment where I felt like this Matthew guy really got me and was on my side, for lack of a better explanation."

"What happened?"

"I just, I knew that it wasn't the place I wanted to get married. But I hadn't said anything yet. And he knew. He came up to me and basically told me it wasn't the right place. That it didn't *fit* me."

"Well, that's not so weird. Pax knows you."

"I know. But I felt this connection with Matthew over it. And to know that it's really Pax doesn't change that, does it? I mean, let's face it, does Pax really know me?"

"Almost as well as I do, I'd say."

"I guess." I tip an empty glass to my lips, surprised to discover I've finished the entire glass already. "Hang on, I'm going inside to get more wine." I refill my glass and wait until I'm back situated on the balcony before continuing, "Is it weird that I felt . . . I don't really know how to describe it . . . I felt accepted or justified when he knew it wasn't the right place for me. I mean, Hunter and Liza tend to just bulldoze along, making plans without really consulting me—"

"I thought you didn't really care though," Crystal interrupts.

"I don't. Not really."

"Then what's the problem?"

I have a love/hate relationship with "drinking Crystal" because she's not afraid to call me on my shit. Which I need, but it's not a part of our normal daily discourse. Which I would hate.

"Well," I start. "I feel left out."

"Ah, there it is." She sounds triumphant, as though she figured something out instead of me telling her something. Hence the love/hate.

I roll my eyes. "There what is?"

"The whole point is that you feel left out, and you don't like it when you aren't the center of attention."

"That's not true!"

"It's not a bad thing. I'm not criticizing you. It's just a facet of your personality. And, let's face it, even though you kind of hate that Hunter literally worships the ground you walk on. I mean, he calls you 'my queen,' for god's sake, and you count on it at the same time. You expect it. It's a comfort for you."

"It's not a comfort for me," I scoff.

"That's not a bad thing either. None of this is negative, sweetie. I'm just trying to help you understand how you feel."

"When did you become Dr. Phil?"

"Earlier today." She giggles. I do too.

"Okay, in all seriousness," she says. "If you aren't going to fire him, how is this going to work? It's Pax. You guys don't exactly get along. Won't Hunter or Liza wonder what's going on if you're being mean to each other?"

"I don't know. I hadn't really thought it through that far." I refill my wine glass for a third time, glad I'd just brought the bottle out here with me. I'll have to work out an extra hour tomorrow to rid myself of these extra empty calories.

"Clearly you just need to avoid him at all costs."

"Not exactly easy to do when he's constantly taking my picture," I grumble.

"At least it explains some of those bad ones from the cake tasting. He probably did it on purpose."

"Oh, he did. He all but admitted it. He said, and I quote, 'You'd better be nice to me, I'm in control of how you'll look on your big day.' What a dick, right?"

"Wow," Crystal says. "Do you think he's doing this just to get back at you for something?"

"He said it's revenge. But I can't imagine over what."

"Uh, the divorce?"

"That was ten years ago."

"Yeah, but things got pretty ugly."

"Not just on my part though. He did terrible things too."

"Yeah, but . . . the camera," she says.

Oh god, the camera. Not my finest moment.

"The camera," I repeat, nodding.

"And the print," she says.

I always forget about the print.

"I mean, no offense, but I can't blame him if he's still trying to get back at you for that, you know?"

"I paid him a lot of money for breaking that camera."

"Yeah, but it was kind of irreplaceable, right? It being his grandpa's and all. And then you never gave him back the print once you had it restored. He doesn't even know it still exists."

I think of where I have the print hanging in my office. How I've kept it close to me after all these years. How I had it painstakingly restored, but then never returned it.

"You aren't helping. And quit taking his side."

"I'm on your side. Always. I'm just trying to come up with rational explanations for why he might be doing this."

"Well, good luck with *that*. There isn't anything that is rational about him." The door opens behind me and Hunter steps out on the balcony.

"Hey, Crystal, Hunter just got home, so I'm going to go. I'll talk to you tomorrow, okay?"

"'Kay. Good luck. Love you."

"Love you." I disconnect the call and stand to greet Hunter.

He pulls me into his arms. "Mmm, you feel good after a long day."

"I'm sorry you had a long day. Did you have a lot going on after we met?" I ask.

"I did." He sits in the lounger and tries to pull me into his lap. My wine spills in the process.

"Oh dear, what a klutz I am," he says. "Here, sit up and I'll get a towel and some club soda." He pushes me off him, and I stand unsteadily. It's amazing what two plus glasses of wine will do to your equilibrium when all you've barely eaten all day.

"It's fine, Hunter," I tell him, my words slurring a bit. "It's white wine and not much spilled. Sit with me. Let's talk about your day."

He leaves anyway to get a towel and some club soda, coming back and dabbing at my skirt until he's satisfied. He takes my wine from me and sets it on the side table, then sits and pulls me back into his lap again. We stay like this for a few minutes.

It's nice.

"How was your day, my queen?" he asks, still not having told me about his. He nuzzles my neck and breathes in deeply, his lips connecting with a sensitive spot behind my ear that never fails to excite me. I feel a stirring down in my belly. One of the best things about Hunter is the routine and dependability. When he's in the mood, he starts by kissing the spot behind my ear. If I respond in kind, he keeps going. He's a conscientious lover, always making sure I'm taken care of. And I'm attracted to him. Sex with us is good. It's just not the fire and brimstone that I had with Pax. And I'm convinced that's okay.

Not everything has to be so passionate that it's chaotic and unpredictable. With Hunter, I know the position he favors: missionary so he can kiss me; and I know that if I don't orgasm during, he will usually make sure I do after. There's always enough foreplay to make sure I'm ready for him and the actual intercourse will last a solid two minutes, if not longer. He will bring me a washcloth to clean myself with after, and we'll cuddle until one of us falls asleep.

It's solid, reliable, good, and exactly what I need in my life. When all I've ever known is the roller coaster of uncertainty, Hunter takes me on a ride where I can see the twists and turns in plenty of time to prepare for them.

He reaches his hand around to cup my breast through my blouse, massaging my nipple with his thumb. I turn my head to the side to kiss him. He pecks my lips softly in return, then goes back to kissing my neck and shoulder blades. I reach behind me to fondle him through his slacks.

"Oh god, my queen, that feels so good. Let's go inside?"

I run my palm down his length and back up again. "We could stay here," I whisper.

"No, someone might see. I'd rather that not happen."

I stand and take his hand to lead him to our room. He brings mine to his mouth and kisses each of my fingers as we go. When we step into our room, he removes my clothing, almost reverently, and lies me on the bed before disrobing himself and crawling between my legs. He's inside me within seconds and groans his appreciation.

"You feel so good," he moans.

I grasp his face and bring his lips to mine, kissing him hard.

Hunter lets me lead for a moment, then pulls his head away, his lips leaving mine somewhat reluctantly. "You okay?" He stops his thrusting while he asks.

"Yes. Why?"

"You seem a little different tonight is all."

"How so?"

"That kiss. It was different. Harsh and angry."

"I thought it was passionate," I defend.

"That's not how it came across," he says. "We aren't animals."

He leans down and kisses me gently. Softly. His lips barely whispering across mine. And when he slips his tongue in to meet mine, it's a gentle greeting that I receive. Tenuous in its exploration even after more than a year together.

Don't get me wrong, I enjoy how tender Hunter is with me. But every so often, I wish he'd just push me against the wall and slam in balls deep. Like he can't control himself, like his attraction for me, his need to possess, is so overpowering he loses all control.

But he doesn't.

And that needs to be okay.

12

PAX

I know better than to trust Gregor with setting me up on a blind date. And it's not that he would pick someone so wrong for me, he wouldn't if he knew them. But since I pretty much know everyone that Gregor does, they're all ruled out. If he's setting me up, it's because his own date has a friend who needs one. Which is what has happened tonight.

Becky, Gregor's date, is amazing. A single mom who works for an international marketing firm. She's beautiful, funny, smart, outgoing. Gregor is smitten, I can tell. Not that it would take much. Hell, I'm practically smitten. And she's a hell of a bowler.

My date, on the other hand, is one of those girls who is *so* opposite of her friend you wonder how they ever get along with one another. Her name is Tricia but says everyone calls her Trix. However, when I do the same, she says I have to earn the right. Okay. No problem. I'm all for female empowerment in any way you need or want. You are woman, I hear you roar. And I'll call you Tricia while you do it.

We get to the bowling alley at the respective time, deciding to order food from the concession stand as opposed to hitting a restaurant beforehand. Becky's idea. And I'm a fan. Chips with melted faux-cheese never taste so good as from a concession stand. Whether movie theater, ball game, or bowling alley, there is something about that oddly orange liquid goodness drowning round, salty chips and covered in soggy jalapeños, that just hits the fucking spot. Especially when accompanied by a beer.

Becky and Gregor share a hotdog, popcorn, and nachos. Which is funny because I know for a fact Gregor could eat all three as just his appetizer. But it's cute to see him split it with his date, even giving her the bigger half of the hotdog. I guarantee we'll be stopping somewhere on the way home for food.

We've split into teams, Becky and Gregor against Trix and me. Sorry, *Tricia* and me. She sucks at this game just as much as I do. It's pretty much a shutout. Becky and Gregor score strike after strike while Tricia and I are lucky to knock out the middle five on any given first try. Our (lack of) skill ensuring neither of us will never get the spare/split on the second go-round.

Which means it's time to make this game interesting. So, I propose to Tricia that we do a shot every time we don't get the spare. Which has us pretty much doing a shot with every turn in the lane. Tricia chases her shots with water. I, on the other hand, chase mine with beer. It doesn't take long before I'm sloppy and she's fired the fuck up. Not a good combination. I take to slapping her on the ass after she collects her ball, but before she lines up her shot. Because I adhere to bowling protocol and don't bother the bowler in wait. She, in turn, starts to sit on my lap during Gregor and Becky's turns.

Before long we're making out and shortly after that, she's going down on me in the men's restroom. She deep throats so well my eyes cross.

"Oh, yeah, baby," I moan.

"Call me Trix," she mumbles around my cock.

Apparently, having my cock in her mouth gives me the right to call her Trix. She takes me to the brink of coming and lets me slip from her lips with a "pop" sound.

"Oh, don't stop," I complain.

"I want you to come inside me," she whines.

My brow furrows. "Inside you?"

"Fuck me." She draws the words out as she unbuttons her jeans and starts to push them down her thighs.

"Uh. Okay." I mean, it's one thing to get a blow job in the handicapped stall at the bowling alley. But it's a whole other to have sex. It's a family establishment. Kids could come in, for god's sake.

Still, I comply.

I grab a condom from my wallet and rush to put it on before I think too hard on the wisdom of this latest life choice and go soft. She turns her back to me and leans forward, resting her hands on the toilet seat, turning my stomach slightly. Who knows what's been on that seat? And those same hands were just on my cock.

Ugh.

It doesn't stop me.

I still slide my cock in, grab her by the hips, and start to pound away.

"Oh god, yes!" she screams.

Screams.

Like a porn star on an audition.

"Shhh." I reach a hand around to cover her mouth.

She licks my fingers. Ambitiously. Making a loud moaning noise as she goes.

"Shhh," I say again.

She ignores me, laving away at my fingers and palm.

"Oh, so good, unh, yeah, baby." In between licks, she speaks, and starts to rock back into me as I thrust forward. I appreciate her enthusiasm. I do. And the assist is helpful as I'm close to coming. I don't think she's come yet, and I almost feel bad about that. But I've had enough to drink at this point that I don't want to care. Still, I lower my hand from her mouth to diddle her clit.

"Unh, unh, unh, unh." She grunts in time with my thrusts as her muscles clamp down. She's coming. Thank god. Now I can focus on me with a clear conscience.

"Oh, cowboy, ride 'em. Yeah. Ride 'em, cowboy. Get on that horse. Oh yeah, god yeah. Fuck yeah." She keeps talking.

Even after her climax.

I can't focus.

Am I the cowboy here or the horse?

"Go cowboy," she moans. "Get 'em. Ride 'em. Fuck yes."

I think she's the horse and I'm the cowboy.

I can't think about this and finish.

Focus, Pax. For fuck's sake.

Tabatha's face creeps in and I imagine it's her I'm slamming into from behind.

"Get it, cowboy. Get it," Trix cries.

But, in my mind, it's Tabs calling me a cowboy. And it's not creepy. She's wearing boots, a fringe vest, and a hat. Nothing else. Her pert ass thrusts toward me. She's not touching the toilet seat though. Because we're fucking in a fancy unisex restroom. Against the vanity. Like civilized people.

I sigh with relief as I finally come. It's not even a good orgasm. More a release from pressure than anything. As I still against Trix's ass, she straightens and brings her toilet seat hands behind her head to grab my face and force my lips to hers. "You sure fucked that horse, cowboy," she mumbles appreciatively.

Confirming, without a doubt, the role we each played in her fantasy.

"All I'm saying is, it's never happening again," I tell Gregor. He laughs, as though he doesn't believe me. I don't blame him. I've said the same thing before after we've left a double date he's set me up on.

"Believe it when I see it, brother."

I scowl at him, but his eyes are on the road and not me.

"Dude, I washed my face with antibacterial gel after she touched me with her toilet hands."

"I love how the only thing that bothered you about this is that she touched the toilet seat."

"What else should bother me?" Because if I'm missing something, I'd like to know.

He shakes his head and laughs to himself.

The girls had met us at the bowling alley in a separate car and left the same way. So now Gregor is driving my slightly drunk ass home. I yawn and lean my warm head against the cool glass of the passenger window. "Tell me how Becky was?"

"How she was? Not all of us had sex in the bowling alley bathroom, man."

"No, I mean, as a person. As a date. How was your night?"

"It was good. Real good. I like Becky a lot, but she's real skittish about getting into anything."

"I thought she asked you out?"

"She did. I have a feeling that the idea of dating was more appealing than actually dating. We're going to keep in touch and when she's ready, I told her to give me a call."

"You're a good guy, Gregor. You know that?" My words slur.

"That I do, my friend. That I do." He sighs.

"I'd date you," I tell him impulsively. "Hell, I'd marry you even."

"I'm touched, Pax. That means a lot. Especially coming from you," he says drily.

"Thanks, man." My voice is sincere even though I know he's not serious. "Hey." I change the subject, just not necessarily for the better. "Do you think it's odd that I had to picture fucking Tabatha in order to finish tonight?"

He laugh/coughs. "Do I think it's odd?"

"Yeah, like that I'm still hung up on her or something?"

"We both know you're still hung up on her," he says.

"No, I'm not!"

He looks at me. I do my best to hold his gaze.

"She was my first love," I whine. "That shit sticks with you forever."

He shrugs.

"G, you aren't helping."

"What would you like me to say, man? I'll be honest. It sucks that you thought of her, absolutely. But not just for you. You were inside one woman and thinking of another. How do you think that makes Trix feel?"

"She doesn't know."

He glances over, one eyebrow raised.

I roll my eyes. "There is no way in hell she knew. And even if she did, in her mind I was fucking a horse, so really, who's in the wrong here?"

Gregor chuckles. "I already forgot about that."

"Yeah, well." I gesture aimlessly, thinking that somehow proves my point.

He turns onto the main road leading toward my house. "You going to call her?"

"No." I scoff. "Actually, I didn't get her number. Come to think of it, she didn't even offer it . . . why the fuck didn't she offer me her number?"

"Maybe she just doesn't like you?"

"That's impossible. I'm a catch."

Gregor makes a sound reflecting disbelief.

"Fuck off, man," I tell him.

"It's a good thing she didn't, brother. This way, there are no false hopes or expectations on either part."

"But how does she not realize that I'm a step up?"

"I do love your humility, P. It's awe-inspiring." He slows the car in front of my house.

"Appreciate the ride home, G. Talk to you later?"

"Yup." He pulls away before the passenger door is all the way closed. I stumble to my front door, suddenly exhausted. I manage to get it unlocked on the third try, kick off my shoes and fall onto my couch, clothes and all. I'm passed out within minutes.

13

TABATHA

Hunter falls asleep shortly after we make love, as is his habit. I don't even know if he ate dinner. But instead of worrying about it, I throw on some yoga pants and a sweatshirt and head out to the living room. As much as I hate to admit it, this is a routine that we've fallen into of late, where I'm wide awake after sex and he's conked out. I enjoy sex with him, very much, but it isn't typically an activity that will exhaust me.

I grab my favorite throw blanket and spread out on the couch, grabbing the remote to turn on the TV and flip the channel to infomercials. Between them and any sort of home shopping channel, I can occupy my mind for hours on end. The key is to not think too hard on any one thing. I suppose, in that respect, it's almost like meditation. If I start to concentrate too much, I just switch the channel. If there's one thing that late night television is never short of, it's mindless marketing.

Right now, my thoughts tend to breed discontent. Which is not to say that I'm unhappy. Or maybe it is, I'm not sure. I'd be lying if I said that seeing Pax, knowing that he is lying about who he is just to participate in my wedding, doesn't do strange things to me. And by strange, I mean those thoughts that lead to discontent.

My life with Pax was not what I would have called *healthy*. But there was a passion that is hard to ignore when looking back. When you're young, or at least when I was young, it was easy to confuse passion with love. Still, I know in those deep moments when I'm honest with myself, that Pax is the great love of my life. Regardless, it doesn't make him right for me.

Which is just one of the many gems I've learned in therapy. Along with just because she's my mother doesn't make her a good one. All it takes to become a mom is compatible eggs and sperm, along with a nice place to hang out for forty weeks or so. Which, in no way qualifies a person to take responsibility for the molding and sculpting of another human being.

According to my therapist, my mother and I have the classic representation of a co-dependent relationship. As long as you understand that I'm the co-dependent one.

I hate that *diagnosis,* by the way. Hate the way it sounds, hate the way it makes me feel. My therapist says that much like most things we are trying to change, acceptance is the first step. So, here I am accepting that I am co-dependent on my mother.

All of which makes my mom sound like a horrible person, and she's not. She's just not a good mom. She was a great business manager and motivator in my career though. If she was careful with the money I made her, she'd never have to work again. I can't say the same for myself. With "my" money, we were more reckless. Since Hunter doesn't really want me acting, the clothing line is a much-needed lifeline. As is the autobiography. It's near impossible to stay relevant when you aren't thrusting yourself into the public eye.

Since social media has become more and more prevalent, and with the upsurge of citizen journalism, you have to be one of the lucky few who are in demand just because you exist, or you work your ass off to remain interesting. And the only way to do that is to put your life on display. Your very fractured and imperfect—as is everyone's—life.

It makes me think of a very well-known actor. He was huge up until about five years ago. He's still a box office success with everything he touches, but his personal life has gotten in the way. Mostly because of his wife, a B-list actress at best, who comes out with something near-headline worthy every couple of months to get her name back in the press. She's addicted to porn, she's a sex-addict, she was abused as a child, she hasn't cried in twenty years. All of it is sad, but the near compulsion to reveal it so publicly, that's what I can't take anymore.

My talk show was so popular due to the stories I would share with my guests. In reality, I was a kid no matter how mature I may have acted. Because it was acting. As such, the shit that would come out of my mouth was usually honest and brutal. Whether about myself and my life or someone who I'd worked with before. It was pretty much no holds barred, all speculation and gossip to get the laughs.

So, it stands to reason that I no longer want to be on display. Hunter, however, craves it. He craves it like his next breath of air. The irony of who I picked to share my life with is not lost on me. Hence the big wedding, the media announcements, the photographic proof of the entire process, and he's entertaining the idea of broadcasting the ceremony on the internet. Like we are royalty or reality TV stars.

Shit, I kind of am a reality TV star. Or at least I was.

I grab the remote to change the channel again. I need something a little more engaging if I'm ever to turn my brain off and fall asleep. I have sleeping pills that I use in an emergency, but I don't like to rely on them all the time.

I find an old black-and-white movie with Cary Grant and Katharine Hepburn, two of my all-time favorites, and settle back into the couch to watch it. Cary Grant plays a scientist who gets caught up in one of Hepburn's many schemes. If I were to go back to acting, this is the type of movie I'd want to star in. Unfortunately, there isn't a market for slapstick comedy that relies solely on dialogue any longer. Even with comedies now, special effects are key. Unless it's raunchy. Which I don't care to do. And it's not like Seattle is the hub of the entertainment industry.

Sigh.

I wake with a start just as the sun starts to rise. I fold my blanket and place it back over the arm of the couch then make my way back to our bedroom. I'm not sure if Hunter realizes I sleep on the couch most nights. It's nothing to do with him, I just can't relax with the silence and I don't want to disturb him.

I crawl into bed next to his prone form. It amazes me how he can fall asleep on his back and stay that way until he wakes the next morning. I will wake up thirty-seven times a night and in a different position each time. I curl on my side, tuck my pillow between my arms, with my cheek resting on the back of my left hand and somehow fall back asleep.

"Good morning, my queen." Hunter sets a cup of coffee on my nightstand and wakes me with a kiss to the forehead. He's dressed for his day already.

"What time is it?" I ask groggily.

"Just after eight," he says. "I didn't see anything pressing on your calendar and didn't want to wake you."

"Oh, thank you." I smile, pleased with his thoughtfulness. I sit up and take a small sip of my coffee and sigh with happiness. Hunter makes perfect coffee.

He checks his watch and before he turns to leave, he says, "I have to go, but I will be at the Cascadian House at four-thirty."

"I'll see you then," I call after him. He's already clicking away on his phone. Today, we are viewing a venue that is large enough to accommodate seven hundred people. A number that makes me shudder. Because I'm sure if he put his mind to it, Hunter could justify inviting that many people.

It's an older venue set atop a cliff overlooking the sound. I know from the photos that the views are absolutely breathtaking. And it's one of the few properties with its own lighthouse. But it has some flaws. Many of the features are outdated as they are original to the time when the home was built. It tends to get a little too cool inside the buildings and the ancient elevator has been known to spontaneously stop working.

Some say it's the ghost of the original builder, William Cascadian, and his wife trying to get people to leave so they can spend eternity in peace, relaxing in his masterpiece. As legend has it, it took Cascadian ten years to finish the property, and he went bankrupt doing so. Shortly before it was completed, he traveled to Chicago to meet with potential investors for funding to finish the project and open as a luxury hotel. On his return flight, the plane had mechanical difficulties and crash landed. It was reported there were no survivors.

Upon hearing the news, his wife was so distraught she took her own life. Days later, William appeared, having survived the crash along with a few other passengers. When he learned of his wife's passing, he locked himself inside the main ballroom and drank himself to death. Literally. Hence the reason the ghosts yearn for peace and the chance to enjoy the fruits of their labors. Who knows if it's true, but I like the story anyway.

So, this venue excites me just because of the history involved. That, and a number of fantastic movies have been filmed there. I would love to immerse myself in the vibe and soak up the ambiance. It's my first pick for a venue, but I don't want Hunter to feel as though that gives him free reign to invite twice as many people.

I finish my coffee and head to our home gym for a workout before getting ready for my day. I think about calling Crystal to see if she can come work out with me, but I know it is more hassle than it's worth. For her, not me. I'm more than happy to section off an area for the twins to go crazy in. But it means she has to get them all packed up and ready to go, get toys and changes of clothes, snacks and drinks, diapers and wipes, and any other number of things that I'm forgetting in order for her to come over here for an hour.

She gets her workout in getting them ready to go before she even comes over for the workout. But she loves it. And I'm happy for her in the same vein that I'm jealous of her. Her life is complete, she has everything she wants. Meanwhile, I feel like I'm over here flailing to keep my head above water, plan a wedding, and convince myself it's okay to spend my life with a really good guy.

I hit the elliptical machine and force myself up to level seven for thirty minutes. Then I sprint on the treadmill for another thirty before moving on to free weights. Yes, I know I obsess about my weight. See how you would feel if you grew up in the public eye during puberty, playing a role that required you to stay cute and small. Next, imagine adulthood when you might finally relax about it, only Hollywood prefers hipbones to show and your fiancé likes you to be rail thin. *Then* he decides he wants pictures and videos of the planning and wedding to be plastered everywhere.

Weight would be your primary focus as well.

14

PAX

Today's wedding adventure has us touring the Cascadian House located on a neighboring island. The only way to get there from Seattle is by ferry. At least with some of the islands, like the one I live on, I can take Tacoma Narrows Bridge through a few neighboring towns and over to Port Orchard. It's not super convenient, but it lets me avoid the mess that is the commuter ferries when I want to. And trying to be anywhere at four-thirty in the afternoon using the ferry, puts us at commuter times. So, it's crazy busy.

Like right now, I'm in line to drive onto the ferry. It's like waiting in line to get on an airplane. Everyone lines up and waits. Then sits and waits. Then travels and waits. I'm not even on the ferry yet and I already feel like this outing has taken too long. There's still a twenty-minute ferry ride to get there after this. Good news is, I'm charging Nipplecock by the hour and that includes travel time.

Today is my first foray into the photography world as Matthew Hanhauser *without* my mustache. I'm fairly confident I won't be recognized. I haven't really been in the press since the breakup with Tabatha. And you'd have to be a hard-core photography fan to have seen a picture of me or know what I look like anyway. But I'm still using the remainder of my disguise—the hat/wig and the glasses.

Tabatha is the only one who will know it's me, making me wonder if she said anything to the fiancé about Matthew being me and vice versa. I can't imagine I'd still have this job if she did, so I'm going to guess the answer to that is no. I drove my Jeep today so I can enjoy satellite music. "She's So Cold" by the Rolling Stones is playing. I drum my hands against the steering wheel in time to the music, take a peek at the surrounding cars, then drum my hands some more. I seem to be the only person this agitated. The person behind me is just staring off to the side. I wonder if she's asleep.

Wait a minute.

I'd know that red hair anywhere. Tabby is in line behind me.

I suppose, given the appointment time versus the ferry schedule, the chances are good that we'd be on the same one. But one in front of the other in the same lane is a surprise. I watch her for a while, but she doesn't move or do much. She looks good. Sad, but good.

A car horn sounds from somewhere behind us, Tabatha jumps and accelerates. Her car bumps into mine, which flusters her. There can't possibly be any damage, she wasn't driving more than five miles per hour. I watch her put it into park and move to exit the car. The lot attendant knocks on her window, gesturing her forward. I laugh when she tries to argue with him. More honking occurs. And I notice I'm actually the problem in our line, not her. The cars in front of me have moved, and I'm still sitting here. I proceed onto the ferry and park my car, waiting for her to pull up behind me.

She gets out of her car and peers first at her front bumper, then at my back one.

"Any damage?" I ask, ignoring Tabs and looking only at the bumpers.

"I don't think so, I'm so sorry—" She looks up. "Oh god, of course it's you. How did you manage this one? I mean, I'm actually impressed that you somehow engineered me running into you." She makes a *pfft* noise and throws her arms up. "There couldn't possibly be any bigger pain in my ass for me to run into anywhere in the greater Pacific Northwest."

I pretend to see her for the first time. "Tabatha? Is that you?" I narrow my eyes at her. "Are you stalking me? Or do you hate me so much you just want to wreck my car?"

"You wish. This was an accident and you know it," she says. "I didn't even realize it was you in front of me. Someone behind me honked and I was looking in the rearview mirror at them when I accelerated. I just assumed that whoever was before me had moved on along with the line of cars like they were supposed to."

"Tsk, tsk, Tabs." I shake my head. "You know you should always be looking in the direction you are driving."

"Yes, well—"

"And you should never assume anything when behind the wheel. I thought I'd taught you better than that. Always be driving defensively."

She rolls her eyes. The ferry horn sounds off, echoing through the parking level, as it pulls smoothly away from the terminal.

"There's no damage, as you can clearly see." She gestures to the bumpers.

I knew there wouldn't be.

"So, I should call my insurance company back and tell them never mind?"

"You already called your insurance company? What the hell, Pax? When did you even have time? Plus, I was barely even moving and—"

"Relax, Tabs. I'm kidding. I was just trying to get a rise out of you."

She sighs heavily, running her hand over her brow. "You know, today's just not the day for that, Pax. Any other day and I'm happy to fight you. But today, I'm just too tired."

In her defense, she does look tired. Beautiful, but tired.

I feel guilty for trying to rile her up.

Kind of.

"Hey, I was going to get a cup of coffee," I say. "Would you like one? My treat, as an apology for getting in your way."

She raises an eyebrow.

"And for trying to get a rise of you."

She looks at me, her face a blank stare.

"And for not telling you sooner that I'm Matthew Hanhauser."

She dips her chin in a gesture I take to mean acceptance. I wave my arm for her to walk ahead of me to the stairwell that will take us to the enclosed upper level seating area and coffee bar. We get our coffee and take a seat across from one another in a window-facing booth.

"I'm guessing you didn't tell Simple—err, Hunter who I am since I still have the job?"

She shakes her head, then looks off toward the fading shoreline.

"You okay?" I ask.

She shakes her head again, tears pooling in her eyes. I'm tempted to move to her side of the booth and put my arm around her shoulders and comfort her. But I refrain, instead reaching a hand across the table.

"Hey, Tabs. Everything okay? What's going on?" I don't touch her, but I do leave my hand there as a nice guy gesture.

She pulls a tissue from her purse and dabs at her eyes. "Nothing. I'm fine. Just emotional."

"Pregnant?"

"Pfft. No."

"No sex before the wedding, huh?"

"What? No. I mean, yes. Of course we have sex. Actually, what business is it of yours?" She blows her nose delicately. "None, that's what."

"Hey, no judgment here. I'm all for sampling the goods before final purchase. You need to know what you're getting. After all, you and I sampled—"

"I know what I'm getting and I'm perfectly happy with it."

"Perfectly happy, huh? That doesn't sound too convincing."

"It's great, okay. And if you must know, you're the reason why I'm upset."

"Me? What did I do?"

"You're here, for one."

I look around dumbly. She laughs despite herself. I'll admit it, that's the reaction I wanted.

"Don't be a dork," she says, pulling out a compact and fixing her still perfect makeup.

"You look beautiful," I tell her, my voice low.

"You don't have to say that," she says.

"I know." I smile. "You're too thin though, Tabs. Your curves are gone."

"Oh god, now I know you're laying it on thick."

"I'm not. I swear. One friend to another."

"Pax, I've got mere weeks before I get married. Which means I either need to find a designer who is willing to make me a dress, like, yesterday, or I have to be able to buy something off the rack. You have to be thin for those."

"You were already thin."

She rolls her eyes at me for what seems like the millionth time.

"Is Wipplecock making you lose weight?"

She giggles, then covers her mouth and gasps, looking around to make sure no one saw her laugh. Not that anyone would care.

"You know that's not his name," she says. "And no, he's not. He thinks I'm perfect just the way I am."

"Well then." I sit back in the bench seat and cross my arms over my chest. "My job here is done."

She glances at my biceps, then back up at my face. If I'm not mistaken, her face reddens. It's hard to tell sometimes with all the makeup. She wears a lot more of it these days.

"I like your hair better down," I tell her. "And when you aren't wearing so much makeup. You don't need all that stuff. It just takes away from your natural beauty."

Her eyes meet mine, but it's hard to tell what she's thinking. So, I purposely blank the expression on my face. Because right now I'm thinking too much. And the too much that I'm thinking is comprised of thoughts I should not be having. Thoughts about a woman who is about to marry another man. I had my shot and I blew it.

She blinks after a moment, collecting her thoughts. "It doesn't matter what you think anymore, does it?" And with that, she shuts the moment down for both of us. I'm grateful, because I don't know that I would have been strong enough to do the same. It was a huge mistake agreeing to be her photographer. Having to spend this much time with her. Too many memories get dredged up, which just confuses emotions and creates feelings that aren't really there.

The horn blows, signaling the time to return to our cars as we'll be disembarking soon. I take her coffee cup and toss it with mine into the recycle bin, then we make our way back downstairs, along with most of the other passengers.

Neither of us say another word. I'm sure it's better that way.

15

TABATHA

It doesn't take long to make it from the ferry terminal to the Cascadian House. Even though I'm using my GPS, I'm still pretty much following Pax since I'm still the car behind him. We pull into the lot at the same time and I park next to him in the front row. I see Hunter is already here and I'm assuming one of the other cars is Liza's.

The front grounds are breathtaking. The perfect blend of indigenous plants and trees interspersed with green grass, annuals, and perennials. To one side is the coast and to the other is rolling hills. It's hard to tell what is behind the property, but my guess is more of the same. I'm out of my car before Pax and I head toward the front door, not bothering to wait for him. He catches up to me anyway and we walk in together.

The building itself is only nine stories tall with maybe twenty-five rooms per floor in addition to varying sizes of ballrooms and meeting rooms. The first floor hosts the lobby and staff areas, a restaurant, cafe, gift shop, and lounge. According to the brochure, there are 180 rooms and another fifteen suites. With the guest list that Hunter has planned, we could end up filling the entire hotel.

The hostess points us to the elevator and lets us know Liza and Hunter are upstairs on the eighth floor in one of the larger ballrooms.

"The elevator attendant is on break, but it's easy to use," she tells us. "One lever for pretty much everything, one way to go up, and the other way to go down. And you can only go up from this floor." She smiles big and her voice sounds overly cheery. If I had to listen to her all day, I'd slap her and throw her in the sound.

The entire inside of the elevator car is copper. It's gorgeous. We get in and Pax moves the lever to the door close position. A gate closes first, then the doors, and we start to move slowly. Very slowly.

"It may have been faster to take the stairs," I say, knowing full well it wouldn't have. I'm in heels and a pencil skirt, the last thing I want to do is walk eight flights of stairs.

I watch as the floor indicator moves from one to two.

Two to three.

Three to four.

Four to five.

Five to six.

Six to . . .

The arrow stops between the numbers six and seven. And I realize the car has stopped too.

Pax moves the lever back to open; the doors don't budge. He moves it back to up. Nothing.

"You broke it!" I tell him.

"I didn't break it," he says. "It's an old elevator, it's probably just tired and needs a little break. I'll just call—"

"There's no phone."

He looks at the elevator panel. "There's no phone," he repeats. "But there is an emergency button." He pushes it. Nothing happens.

I reach over and push it.

"What? You think somehow when you push it, it's better than when I do?"

"You might have pushed it wrong," I say.

"Really? I might have pushed the button wrong? You don't think that's a skill I learned, oh I don't know, when I was two?" He pulls off his hat/wig and runs his hands over his head. The glasses come off next and he pinches the bridge of his nose. He holds it so tight I can see the skin turning white under his fingertips.

I remain silent, then remember, a bit belatedly, that Pax gets a little panicky in small enclosed spaces.

He pulls his cell phone out of his pocket and holds it up. "I don't have a signal. Do you?"

I shake my head. It was the first thing I checked, but I don't tell him that.

He bangs on the gate. "Hello! Hello, can anyone hear us?" With his other fist, he bangs on the wall. He continues banging for at least a solid minute.

"I don't think they can hear us," I say when he finally pauses.

"Well, someone has to hear something. This is crazy. We can't just be stuck in here. I can't be stuck in here. I don't like this. I don't like elevators. Why didn't I take the stairs? Stupid. So stupid."

I put my hand on his shoulder. "Deep breaths. Calm down and take deep breaths."

He does as I suggest.

"There you go," I say calmly. "Smell the flowers in and blow the candles out." I use the same saying I know his dad taught him as a kid when he would get upset.

He laughs. I do too.

Pax leans back against the elevator car wall and slides down until he's sitting on the floor, legs bent, and lowers his head between his knees.

"You're supposed to put your head between your knees while you're still standing if you're going to hyperventilate," I tell him.

"I know, but I feel better sitting. And I'm not going to hyperventilate." He takes off his jacket and spreads it on the floor. "Join me?"

I move to sit but realize I can't with how tight my skirt is. I squat a bit and push my butt to the right but can't make it all the way down to his level. Repeat to the left results in the same outcome. Pax stands, laughing.

"Here, take my hands and I'll lower you down," he says.

I do and he helps me lower to the floor, bottom first. I tuck my legs to the side and pull my heels off.

"Oh god, that feels good," I moan, rubbing my insoles with one hand.

We sit there a moment, each lost in our own thoughts.

I'm the first to speak. "I'm sure that Pax will realize that I'm late and come looking, see my car and realize we're stuck in here."

"Hunter," Pax says.

"Hunter, what?"

"Hunter. You're sure Hunter will realize you're late."

"That's what I said."

"No, you said Pax."

I scoff. "No, I didn't. Why would I say Pax? Especially when you are sitting right here and I'm talking to you."

He shrugs. "Just telling you what I heard."

Did I say Pax?

Good lord, get it together, Tabatha.

He laughs after a moment. "Hey, remember that time we snuck into the photo lab supply closet to make out and got stuck?"

"Ohmigod, yes!" I giggle. "I thought for sure Mr. Henderson was going to suspend us when he finally unlocked the door."

"I thought we were going to die in there and never get out." Pax chuckles.

"You were very brave," I tell him.

"Eh. I'm pretty sure I wet my pants in fear and just hid it from you." He ducks his head as he laughs some more, then looks up at me with a sidelong glance. Big bright eyes, long dark lashes, wide smile. He's just as handsome as ever. It makes me almost proud to have once been his.

I look away to cover the sudden discomfort I feel. I know that seeing him like this brings up past emotions and memories. But that's just it—past. Because I definitely do not have feelings for him now. That ship sailed long ago. I clear my throat and collect my hands in my lap, back straight. Thinking about the past does nothing to help our circumstances right now.

I pull up a word game on my phone. I like to play against the computer.

"What are you playing?" Pax asks.

"Scrabble."

"Let's play together. Start a new game and we'll pass it back and forth."

"Okay, but you know the rules, no more than sixty seconds per turn," I remind him. That was my rule when we were together and it's still my rule now. Though now, it's just self-imposed. I had to institute the rule back then, otherwise Pax would take five minutes per turn and it would take days to finish one game.

"Fine," he agrees with a sigh.

I start a new game and play my word—*unfold*. I pass it to him.

He plays and hands it back. His word: *hug*.

"Is that really the only word you could play?" I ask.

"It's too much pressure when you put a time limit on it."

"Okay, but if I don't put a time limit on it, then you take forever. Besides, it's more fun with the added pressure. Keeps you on your toes."

"Speak for yourself."

I play my word: *triaged*.

We keep going back and forth, until I realize it's been over thirty minutes.

"Why haven't they come for us yet?" I ask and immediately regret it. Pax was calm and playing the game with me. The minute I remind him we're stuck, he stands and begins banging on the doors again.

I look up at him. which is when I notice the roof hatch.

"Oh, Pax, we're dumb."

"We are?"

I point up to the hatch. He closes his eyes for a minute, I know he's chastising himself for not seeing it or thinking of it first. He reaches up, but is short by at least half a foot

"Let me boost you up," he says.

"I'd rather wait, thank you."

"Come on, Tabs. Let me just boost you up to get the panel open and then I'll jump up and grab the edges and haul myself out."

"How do you even know there's a way out?"

"You're the one who pointed out the hatch. Why'd you do that if you didn't think it was a way out?"

"Because it's always a way out in the movies."

"Well . . ."

He has a point.

I let him pull me to my feet. "Okay," I start. "How are we doing this?"

He goes down to one knee. "Stand on my thigh to boost yourself up to my shoulder. You sit on my shoulder and I'll stand, then you'll be able to reach the hatch."

I do as he says, and perch myself on his shoulder, hoping I'm not too heavy for this.

He stands with ease, holding my calves to his chest to keep me balanced. I'm not wearing stockings, and the feel of his arm hair against my bare skin tickles, making me squirm.

"Hold still or I'll drop you," he growls straightening to his full height. I have to duck to avoid hitting the ceiling. I push at the hatch using one hand, but it doesn't budge.

I try again using both hands. Nothing.

"I don't think I'm strong enough."

"Okay, I'm going to crouch a little. Straighten your arms against the top, then when I start to push up, lock your elbows. That way the strength is coming from my legs and not your arms."

He's pretty good with this stuff.

We try it his way. It still won't budge.

He makes me try it three more times, but there is no way that hatch is moving.

"Do you think it's locked?" I ask.

"I guess it could be," he says, sighing. He takes a step toward the wall just as the car jolts and begins to ascend. Pax loses his footing. I grasp at the ceiling for balance. It's no use. Before I realize what's happened, we are tumbling down.

"Aaahh!" The sound is too high-pitched to have been Pax, so it must be me screaming. To his credit, Pax somehow catches me as we go down. I land firmly in his lap, one of my arms around his neck, one of his arms around my waist. It reminds me of how the hero catches the heroine in the old-time movies when she escapes out the window.

Pax throws back his head and laughs, so I do the same.

Which is how Hunter finds us when the door opens.

16

PAX

"What on earth? Tabatha, what is going on here? Who is this man?" Hunter asks her.

I realize I don't have my hat or glasses on, so he would have no real way of knowing I'm actually the photographer.

Tabby scrambles to get off my lap, turning and contorting until she's in a pose akin to yoga's downward dog before straightening with superhuman core strength.

"Hunter," she starts, pushing her feet back into her heels. "Thank god, we've been stuck in this elevator for over half an hour."

She moves forward and gives him a hug. Hunter does not return the gesture. Instead, he looks over Tabby's shoulder at me. I collect my jacket from the floor and hold it in one hand, my camera bags in the other. He looks annoyed, not worried. Just saying, if my girl was half an hour late, I'd be happy to find her okay when all was said and done.

"You had your shoes off," he says to Tabby.

That's what he's going with?

"Uh, yeah," Tabatha says. "I had to climb on Pa—Matthew's shoulder to try and open the roof hatch. But we couldn't get it open, I think it's locked—"

"Why didn't you call someone?"

"We didn't have service," Tabatha explains.

"I have service," Hunter says, narrowing his eyes.

"Well, I didn't." Tabatha takes a step back from him. "What? Do you think I'm lying?"

Hunter remains silent.

Wow. Okay.

"Uh, I didn't have service either," I add, putting my hat back on and tossing the glasses in my camera bag.

"I don't need to hear from you," Hunter says to me. "Who are you anyway? Clearly the hat and hair are fake, so you can take that ridiculous thing off. And what happened to the mustache? Did you shave or was that fake too? Are you even a photographer?"

"I assure you, I'm—"

"It's Pax, Hunter." Tabby looks down at her feet for a minute, then squares her shoulders and looks back up at him.

"Pax?" His mouth drops open. "Pax, as in your ex-husband, Pax?"

"Yes. I didn't know it was him when you hired him," she says.

"You mean when *we* hired him," Hunter says.

"Well, it was mostly you and Liza. I mean, I wasn't really—" Tabatha starts.

"Oh, come on, Tabatha. Give me a break." Hunter sneers. "You expect me to believe that you didn't know it was him. That you didn't push for him to take our pictures?"

"No! I didn't. In fact, I didn't even get a say in the matter, Liza is the one—"

"You're going to blame Liza for this?" Hunter asks, his expression cold and impassive.

"I hired Matthew Hanhauser," Liza pipes in. "I don't know who this guy is."

"Tabatha didn't know," I tell Hunter. "I use an alias and a disguise when I work as Matthew Hanhauser. I never told her about it."

"You expect me to believe that?" Hunter's tone is haughty. "That this isn't some kind of ploy to get—"

"Yes, I do expect you to believe it," I interrupt. I don't know what he was going to say, but I have a feeling it would not have been kind to Tabatha if he continued. And she doesn't deserve that.

"Why?" he asks me.

"Why would I lie about it?"

He makes a sound, like he doesn't believe me.

"Revenge. Okay? My plan was to get the worst pictures possible of her through this whole process," I admit, being as honest as I possibly can.

He rears, pulling his arm back.

He's going to try and hit me.

I sidestep and grab his wrist as he throws his punch, wrapping his arm behind his back and yanking it up. "There's no need for violence, man. No reason why we can't talk about this like civilized folk. I swear to you, Tabatha is one hundred percent innocent in this. No one knew about the alias except my best friend, Gregor."

"Gregor?" he parrots.

"Yeah, Gregor Stravinsky. He's the only person who knew I used an alias."

"You're friends with Gregor Stravinsky?" Hunter confirms.

I just said that, didn't I?

"Yes."

"Can you get him to come to the wedding?" His voice is excited, the complete opposite of his tone a minute ago.

"Your wedding? I don't know. Sure, I guess." I let his arm go and he turns to face me.

"Okay, you do that. Find me another photographer today, and I'll forgive this transgression."

Forgive?

Anger surges through me. Who the fuck is this guy to say *he'll* forgive *me*? Then I see Tabby's face, she looks distraught. If I'm honest with myself, I don't want her to suffer because I was a dick. I hold my hand out to him. "Deal."

We shake on it.

"Good," Hunter says. He turns to Liza. "You make sure to get the contact information from him for the new photographer. I expect them to start immediately. Same terms as before." She nods in response.

He turns back to me. "I presume getting the rights to the photos you've taken thus far will not be an issue."

I wave a hand at him. "You got it, man. No problem."

And finally, he turns to Tabatha. "We will discuss this later. I'll see you at home."

"Hunter," Tabatha starts.

"I need some time to myself, Tabatha. Please."

She nods and gives him a small smile. He turns to leave, and Liza follows after him, prattling off questions.

"Apparently, he only needs time from me, not anyone else," Tabby says sourly.

"Sorry, Tabs."

"It's fine." She sighs. "It's not your fault. It's just one of those weird things."

"Actually, part of it is my fault," I say.

She looks up at me. "Ohmigod, you're right. You lied, you jerk!" She pokes me in the chest with her fingernail. I back up as she moves forward. "An alias? Seriously? Who does that? I can't believe you!" She continues to poke at me with each sentence, until finally I grab her finger to stop her.

"Okay, I get it. No need to continue bruising me. I'm a delicate flower."

"Delicate flower, my ass," she mutters.

"Hey," I say, really wanting to know. "You going to be okay with all this? Him and stuff?"

"Oh yeah," she says with a wave of her hand. "It will be fine. He's upset. I get it. But nothing happened, other than us getting stuck in an elevator."

"And me lying about my identity," I add.

"Yeah, but that's really something more for me to be upset about, not him."

I nod. "Did you still want to take a look around before leaving?" I don't know why I'm asking, it's not like I own the joint or have any control over her schedule.

She shakes her head. "I don't think so. I'm probably just going to go." She sounds subdued. I hope she's being honest with me when she says it will all be okay.

We make our way back to the parking lot in comfortable silence.

She turns when she reaches her car. "Thanks for standing up for me back there."

"Of course," I say. "I didn't want him to get the wrong idea, that wouldn't be fair."

"True."

I nod in agreement. She opens her car door and tosses her purse in.

I don't want her to leave.

"Yeah. Um, hey, you wanna go grab a drink or something?" I ask.

Her lips curve slightly. "I don't think that would be a good idea. Do you?"

"Eh, probably not. Never hurts to ask." I throw a half-smile in her direction.

"See you around, Pax." She gets in her car and shuts the door. I stand there next to my Jeep and watch her until she's out of the parking lot completely. Then I give it another two minutes before I get in my car to leave. The last thing I need is for the two of us to be next to each other again, whether in traffic, in line, or on the ferry. I'll wait hours for the next one if I have to.

"So you told him I would go to the wedding?" Gregor confirms.

"Yeah, G. I had to, man."

I met Gregor at one of his pubs after leaving the Cascadian House. One, because I had to tell him he's going to the wedding. And two, because I had to tell him Matthew Hanhauser had been found out. Lucky for me all this shit in my life is going down in the offseason and he's more available than he would be ordinarily.

"You couldn't just offer a custom jersey or a signed ball? Something easy?"

"Nah. Offering up you was the only thing that was going to save Tabby at that point. Dimplecock was pissed. And, to be honest, I'm still not real sure why."

"To save Tabby, huh?" He grins. "Not to save you from a jealous fiancé?"

"Pfftt. No. That guy has no upper arm strength whatsoever. He came in for a punch, and I grabbed him by the wrist and had him twisted with his arm up behind his back before he could even follow through on the hit."

Gregor chuckles. "I love that he was going to hit you. That shit is funny."

"Glad I could entertain," I mumble.

"When is it?"

"The wedding?"

"Yeah, man. When is the wedding?"

"In, like, seven weeks."

"Seven weeks exactly? From today? Or . . . ?"

"I don't know, maybe seven weeks from Saturday then. They just kept saying two months and that was, like, a week ago."

"Well, how were you going to know when to show to take the pictures?"

"Someone was sure to tell me at some point. I don't have much else going on."

"Some of us do have other shit going on, man. I need a date and a time."

"Okay, okay, I'll get it for you. But once I do, you can't say that you're busy or some shit like that."

"Hmmph." Gregor grunts, then switches topics. "So, you're not the photographer anymore?"

"Nah. I passed it off to Toby Benson. He's a local, and totally pumped to get the referral."

"Great, so now you can be my plus-one," Gregor says, a villainous smile on his face.

"Oh no. No way. I am not going to that wedding. Besides, Wimpycock would have a fit, and Tabby would be the one who would suffer."

"He won't even know you're there. Didn't you say they've got, like, seven hundred people coming?"

"I said that venue could hold up to that many. I don't know how many they'll invite. I think it's going to depend on where they have it."

"So, what do I have to do when I'm there?"

"None of that came up. I think he just wants to know you're going to be there. He idolizes you or some shit. You should have seen his face light up when I said your name. Go figure."

"Shut up, man. I'm important to people. I'm like a fucking figurehead."

We both laugh at that.

"Leslie," Gregor calls out to his bartender. "Aren't I important?"

"Yes, sir," she replies. "The *most* important. Mr. VIP is what you are."

Gregor looks at me as if to say, *see?*

"You sign her paychecks; her opinion doesn't count."

I finish off my beer and hold my empty pint glass up toward him. "Another round? My treat?"

He waves his hand dismissively in my direction and picks up his beer to finish it off. "Your treat? That's funny. Like you ever pay for anything here."

"It's the thought that counts, man."

"Okay." He motions to Leslie for another round. "One more, then I gotta get back to work," he says. "I've got a ton of paperwork back there to finish up."

Leslie sets fresh pints in front of us. "Thanks, Les," Gregor says.

"No sweat, boss man," she says before, heading to the other end of the bar to help other patrons.

"Maybe you should date Leslie," Gregor suggests.

"I'm not going to date Leslie," I reply.

"Why not?"

"Well, for one, I'm pretty sure she has a girlfriend. Two, I'm not attracted to her. And three, if she does have a girlfriend, then she's definitely not attracted to me. Be fighting a losing battle."

"You forgot reason number four," he says.

"What's number four?"

"You're still hung up on Tabby."

"I'm not still hung up on her."

"You are, man. It's the only reason why you, as Matthew, agreed to be the photographer."

"We've been over this, G. I agreed to be the photographer so I could ruin the wedding photos, not because I'm still in love with her."

"Which means you still care."

"How does that figure?"

"Otherwise, ruining the wedding would be a non-issue in your life."

"So, you're saying because I wanted revenge, I still care about her?"

"Care, love, hung up on, yeah. That's exactly what I'm saying."

"No. No way, man. I moved on long ago."

"Really? With who?"

"Lots of chicks."

"You jumped to her defense today with Nipplecock, according to you."

"So?"

"So, you also sacrificed me in the process."

"And?"

"And it means you still want her."

"It does not."

"Okay, riddle me this: how'd you and Tabby leave things earlier?"

"What do you mean? We said goodbye and we both left."

"Were you okay with that? Or did you want to keep hanging out with her?"

I think back to how I felt when we said goodbye in the parking lot. I can either be honest with Gregor and own up to how he thinks I feel, or I can save face and deny everything.

"I'm not answering that, G. It's a stupid question."

"Twenty bucks says you asked her to go for dinner or drinks and she said no."

"I'm not taking that bet either."

"Oh, man. You did, didn't you?"

He's such an asshole.

"Yeah." I hang my head and make condensation circles on the bar top with my glass.

"So, the question is, what are you gonna do about it?"

"Do about it? Nothing, man. She's getting married."

"Uh-huh," he says.

"Subject change," I say. It's like our personal conversation safe word. If one of us can no longer handle a particular topic, we can say *subject change* and the other person has to honor it. Which Gregor does.

Leaving us to talk about nonsense for the rest of our beer. Or at least the rest of Gregor's beer, since he finishes his way before I finish mine.

"You gonna be okay if I leave you to yourself?"

"Of course. Why wouldn't I be?" I ask.

"No reason," Gregor say, a little mysteriously.

"Okay, then. I'm just going to finish my beer, hang out with my pal Leslie, and I'll be out."

"Les, keep an eye on him, will ya?" Gregor calls to her.

"Sure thing, boss man," she says to Gregor and then turns to me and says, "How goes it, Paximus?" She likes to make word play with my name, same as I do with Skimpycock.

"It's going, Les. How about you?"

"Can't complain. I hear you're still hung up on your ex?"

"What? Where'd you hear that?"

"Boss man said you're stalking her and messing up her wedding photos."

"That's a bit of a stretch. I'm doing no such thing. Don't believe anything he says. I turned it over to another photographer today. And even if I hadn't, it doesn't mean I'm still hung up on her."

"Whatever you say, Paxidermy."

Pfft. Whatever.

I can't be still hung up on Tabby. That would be about the worst idea ever. No way in hell that's the case.

Right?

17

TABATHA

My phone ringing wakes me at eight o'clock in the morning. I grope around on the nightstand until I feel it, then bring it close to my face to see who it is.

Angela. My agent.

"Hey, Ang," I answer.

"Tabatha, are you sitting down?"

"Technically, I'm lying down, why?"

"I've got you a part. It's the part to beat all parts."

"Oh, I don't know, Ang—"

"Well, I do. And this is not one to pass up."

"What is it?"

I barely get the question out before Angela jumps in excitedly and starts describing the project and the role. And she's right. It's not one I want to pass on. Even though acting isn't a top priority any longer, it's the kind of role that could bring me back into the fold if I wanted it to. And, since my name is in the news due to the engagement, it's the perfect time to capitalize on the free publicity I'm already getting.

The role is in a three-part, mini-series based on the first book in a (so far) seventeen book series. So, the potential to continue the role in future projects is good. I'd be playing a Seattle cop-turned-private investigator after she botches a high-profile kidnapping case and is asked to leave the force. In her free time she continues to look into the kidnapping, trying to solve it, and is convinced she's been set up.

Angela's already emailed me the script and sent me a link to the e-book that it's based on, and says that hard copies of both will be delivered by messenger later this morning. She then informs me that I have to let her know by this afternoon if I'm interested, and disconnects the call. It seems like a stupid question—whether I'm interested—since I already know I am. Why wouldn't I be? It's a six-week shooting schedule— wrapped just in time for the wedding—and since Hunter and Liza are taking care of the bulk of the details anyway, it should be fine if I'm not available all the time.

I almost email her immediately and tell her I'll take it, but then decide to get some coffee, wake up a bit, and peruse the script before deciding for certain.

Hunter's side of the bed is cold, so I know he's been up for a while. And if my guess is correct, he's long gone to his office downtown. I'd thought when we got home last night that we would discuss the whole Pax thing, but he didn't bring it up. When I tried to, he told me it was over and done with, to leave the past in the past. So, I am. But I still worry I've hurt him somehow and that is definitely not my intention.

I dress in yoga pants, tank top, and a hoodie, pad to the kitchen for coffee and then sit in my favorite chair on the balcony to take a look at the script.

Two hours later, I've read the entire thing and it's brilliant. I want this role. It's perfect for me. I call Angela instead of messaging to let her know. She confirms the logistics. The mini-series is shooting on one of the islands off Seattle, so I don't even have to travel far for the role. We get the contract and everything else out of the way and I settle in to read the book that it's based on.

Morning turns to afternoon and it isn't until early evening that I've finished most of the book. I'd silenced my phone while I was reading so I wouldn't be interrupted and could get through it as fast as possible. In the meantime, I missed one call from Crystal, two calls from Liza, and six calls from Hunter. I call Hunter back first.

"Tabatha, where in the hell have you been?" he answers.

"Here. Home. I sent you a text to tell you I was silencing my phone while I worked."

"Well, I didn't get it. And what could you have been working on that required you to silence your phone?"

"I was reading a script that Angela sent over. Well, not just the script, but the book that it was based on as well."

"Why would Angela send you a script? You aren't acting any longer."

"She thought I would want to reconsider once I saw this role."

"You're not taking the role though, right?"

Why wouldn't he want me taking the role?

"Actually, I am. Why?"

"Need I remind you we are getting married in a few weeks."

"I know that, it's not going to interfere. It's only a six-week shoot, so I'll be finished a week before the wedding, just in time for everything."

He sighs heavily.

"Tabatha, I need your help with the planning."

"Well, you haven't really so far. No offense, Hunter, but you and Liza have taken care of everything on your own without needing much from me at all."

"How can you say that? Of course I've needed you. You're my bride, not Liza."

"Okay, I'm sorry."

"So, you'll drop the role?"

"No, I can't do that, I've already committed."

"Surely you can't be that tied to it if you just agreed to it today. Unless you're lying about when you accepted."

"Why would you say that? Why would I lie about something like this?"

"Never mind."

"I promise the role will not interfere with planning the wedding."

"I don't see how you can promise that."

"I'll make certain the director knows before filming begins. I'm sure it won't be a problem." I already know I can't promise him that. And the director probably won't do anything about it, but I don't want him to worry further. What's that saying? Ask for forgiveness later, instead of permission now? Plus, I really don't think he and Liza will need me for anything anyway.

"Fine. I won't be home for dinner, I'm working late."

"That's . . . fine. I don't want you to be angry. Are you?"

"No. I'm not angry."

"Okay, if you're sure. I'll see you later then. I love you."

"See you later."

He doesn't say he loves me back. He doesn't call me "my queen." He's definitely upset and just not willing to admit it. This is our first fight. I mean, it's not really a fight. More like a disagreement, but still, it makes me uncomfortable. My stomach rolls, acid burning as it flares up. I take an antacid pill and drink a large glass of water, then make a salad for dinner and settle in with a glass of wine to finish the book. To say that I'm excited about this role would be an understatement. It's a game changer for me and my career. I text Angela once I'm through with the book reiterating how thrilled I am with the opportunity.

My phone dings a short time later with a text.

But instead of Angela, it's from Pax.

PAX: Hey, sorry if it's inappropriate for me to text you. I just wanted to make sure everything was okay from yesterday. With you and your guy.

My heart warms at that. It's easy to forget sometimes just how kind and caring Pax can be. Because we are divorced, my thoughts of him aren't always fond. There's something about the act of divorce that makes you automatically remember only bad times. Or at least it's that way with me.

ME: I think he's still a little upset . . .

I erase that and start again.

ME: No problems at all . . .

I delete that too.

ME: Thank you. He was caught off guard is all. But it's fine now.

That one I send. Along with:

ME: Sorry you lost the job.

PAX: Ex's weddings aren't my bag, baby.

I can't tell if he's calling me baby or just quoting Austin Powers. Deciding it's Austin Powers, I say:

ME: That why you pissed in my Prada? :-)

I'm not asking him seriously. He said bag, I thought Prada, and it reminded me of the past, our epic fight just prior to the divorce. And on TV, no less.

PAX: And just when we were getting along. . .

ME: I wasn't being mean. Didn't you see my smiley emoticon?

PAX: With you, Tabs, that could mean about anything.

ME: True. LOL.

PAX: As long as I'm being inappropriate in texting you, I'm going one step further—

ME: I would expect nothing less.

PAX: And say you are going to make a helluva beautiful bride, babe.

ME: Thank you, Pax. That means a lot.

PAX: Also, G expects me to be his plus-one at your wedding, unless he finds someone prettier. Which won't happen. So just a heads-up, I'll be there.

ME: You okay with that?

The three dots appear, then go away. Appear and go away two more times before he responds.

PAX: There's a part of me that will never be okay seeing you with someone else. I'm not going to lie. But all I've ever wanted is for you to be happy. If he makes you happy, I'm good with that.

That stops me. It's the closest he's ever come to admitting he might still have feelings for me. Not that we've spoken much over the years or anything. I know that there's a part of me that will always love Pax, I can't help it. The feelings will always be there. And to know that he just wants me to be happy is huge. Like we've reached that point where we don't just want to hurt one another. Where we actually want there to be good where the other is concerned. That's a big step. Because, of course, I only want what's best for him as well.

PAX: The minute that's not the case, he'll have to answer to me. Deal?

ME: Deal.

PAX: Take care, Tabs.

ME: You too, Pax.

I set my phone aside and reflect on our conversation just now as well as what happened during the filming of *Keeping Tabs*. I'm not stupid, there's a part of me that knows we completely allowed the producers to interfere with and manipulate our reactions to one another. And I'm sure that's a big part of what led to the divorce. Was I really *that* upset about a fictitious zombie fight? Probably not.

But if there is one thing that was always consistent in my relationship with Pax, it was my inability to control my emotions. I couldn't hold anything in. If I felt it, I expressed it. In some ways, that's incredibly freeing. And in other ways, it's self-destructive. That flailing feeling that happens when you aren't able to keep a tight lid on yourself and your emotions. Do I feel more in control of my life and myself with Hunter? Absolutely.

I wonder what it will be like to have Pax in attendance when Hunter and I marry. Will I feel weird? Self-conscious? Will we dance at the reception? If so, will it remind me that he and I never had a reception dance of our own? It's hard when feelings from the past start to mess with your head in the present. Part of you knows that they have no bearing on your life now—that's the intellectual part. But the emotional part gets confused, because feelings are just that.

My phone dings again and I wonder if it's Pax.

But it's Angela, letting me know that everything is set and she's excited too.

And see, there goes the emotional part, getting confused. I have no right or reason to wonder if it's Pax texting me. He has no reason to text me, I have no reason to expect it. No good can come of it. It's destructive, to both myself and my relationship with Hunter. It's just because we are fighting today and I feel insecure about it. There's no other reason to feel comforted by Pax's words.

No other reason at all.

18

PAX

"All I'm saying is, you got me roped into attending this wedding, which is what got me roped into going to this bachelor party tonight. So, you are going with me to both. Unless I find a nice date to the wedding. Then I'll gladly dump your ass for someone prettier."

"Dude, I do not want to go to Nipplecock's bachelor party. Can you imagine how completely dull it's going to be? And then, if it's not dull and he does something disrespectful toward Tabatha, it's going to piss me off. I can't win, man."

Gregor shrugs in response.

We approach the second hole beer table and get our glasses filled, drinking it while we wait for the guys in front of us to finish. I'm doing some sort of charity golf game with him and each hole has a different craft beer with a beautiful girl serving it. It's my kind of golfing because if I play shitty—which I will—I can blame it on the beer. I golf about as well as a I bowl. Unfortunately, so does Gregor. In fact, come to think of it, I don't know of a sport that he's *not* good at.

"Hey." I hit him on his big-ass bicep to get his attention. He turns to me, and I continue, "Is there a sport you can't play?"

"What do you mean?"

"Well, not football, obviously you're great at that. You can bowl, you can golf, I've seen your swing at softball games. So, what can't you play?"

He thinks on it for a minute. "Hoop."

That makes me happy. I'm a decent hoop player, so maybe I could beat him. I make a mental note to have that be our next sport outing.

We drink our beer in silence, still waiting for the guys ahead of us to clear out. There aren't very many golfers taking this game seriously. Most of us are, however, taking the beer drinking seriously. There are a lot of past and present Seabirds Players here as well as muckety-mucks that paid a shit-ton of money to play with them. We are supposed to have two such muckety-mucks with us, but they are late.

"Gregor, my man." I hear from a distance, the voice sounding vaguely familiar. I turn to see who is approaching.

No fucking way.

None other than Wimpycock is climbing out of the golf cart and walking toward us. Awesome, now I get to see him all day today and then again tonight. I can tell the moment he sees it's me.

"Oh." Dimplecock stops suddenly, his friend trailing behind almost bumping into him. "I knew this was a charity event. I just didn't realize the actual charities would be here." He looks at me when he says it.

Is he dissing me?

"That motherfucker is dissing me," I mumble to Gregor.

"Stay calm, brother. This is a nice shindig, can't have you causing trouble," he says.

"*I'm* not the trouble," I say back.

Hunter, as I've decided to refer to him as from here on out today, in hopes of seeing him in a more civilized manner, reaches out to shake Gregor's hand. He does not do the same with me. He then introduces his friend. "This is Andrew Freeman, CEO of . . ." He blabs on about how important his friend is, but I tune him out. I don't care who his friend is or what he does. I'll be doing well if I remember his name and address him appropriately, so disillusioned with my day of fun and sun and beer with Gregor am I.

Andrew turns to shake my hand. His grip is limp and clammy. I repress the urge to shudder.

How does Tabatha put up with this life?

They've already taken their tee shot from the first hole and are now caught up with us. I chug the remainder of my beer —barely registering what it tastes like—and put my commemorative pint glass in my cup holder of the golf cart, then wait my turn. Because this is the first hole that we are playing together, we randomly pick the order. It's a 163-yard par-3, that shouldn't be too bad to start. I think.

Andrew leads off, choosing a 6-iron. His shot is straight and the ball flies about 160 yards onto the green, seeming to land close to the pin since he's smiling and Gregor is patting him on the back. Next up is Gregor, then Hunter, and finally, me.

I do not want to embarrass myself in front of Hunter, but I fear that is exactly what I will do. My pride is at stake. My manhood. Every fiber of my masculinity is on display to be judged and found not worthy.

I step up to the tee box and tee my ball up. I try to do it one-handed like Gregor does, but the first time the ball rolls off, so I'm forced to use two hands to get it to stay on the tee.

My first swing misses the ball entirely. I whiff.

"Practice swing," I call out.

"You were at the tee," Hunter says.

I turn to him. "Does that mean I can't take a practice shot?"

"Yes."

Dick.

I step up to the tee, do a little forward press to release some tension, setup and take another swing. There's a rewarding feeling in my body when the club connects with the ball. My mid-section arcing in just the right way, my feet turning, the club stopping before it hits me in the back. I feel like Tiger-freaking-Woods.

Take that, Hunter!

My ball soars into the air. Victory is mine! I don't even wait for the ball to drop before turning and smirking at Hunter. He chin-bobs toward the green. I swivel back to watch my ball, devastated to see it's traveled about thirty yards over the green. I've completely overshot the hole. In fact, I'll probably have to re-tee my ball, the idea of which is mortifying. Gregor pats me on the shoulder and mutters in my ear, "Don't worry, it happens to the best of us. Next time, try hitting a six iron instead of a driver."

I wait until we are in the cart and heading down the hill before saying anything. "Can you just take the remainder of my turns for me, man?"

"No can do. Don't worry about it. You're doing fine. It's just a charity event, no biggie. We aren't even keeping score."

"Hunter is keeping score."

"Pimplecock? Nah, he's good. Just ignore him."

Easier said than done. In fact, I *know* that Gregor *knows* there's no way I can ignore him. For whatever reason, I view him as my competition. As the man I need to put down. I can't have him be better than me at anything. He's the second choice. The second husband. The backup plan. *Not* the better man.

I sigh and run my hand over my face roughly.

"Look"—Gregor turns to me—"we'll get to the third tee, we'll get another beer from another hot chick, and everything will seem better. Plus, you'll get to go first since your shot was the worst."

I nod in response to Gregor, even though I know he's wrong. I'm not going to feel better until Hunter is eating my golf swing dust.

~

By the time we reach the thirteenth hole, I'm drunk. Legitimately drunk. Most holes since the third, I've had two beers instead of one. The girls are generous pourers and never say no to a refill. I'm borderline sloppy and I don't even care. It's actually good since I no longer give a fuck what Hunter thinks about me. I may whiff the ball more times than I hit it, but now I get to play from the forward tees, so I'm that much closer to the hole and it's not even considered cheating.

Take that too, Hunter.

The other guys definitely have a decent buzz, but they aren't as drunk as me. There's something amplifying about drinking beer in the sun. I know it will hit me hard later and I can't find it in myself to care. I spend most of my time flirting with the beer girls and sitting in the cart. Hunter and Andrew ignore me. As usual, Gregor is my only friend.

"I love you, man." I slap him on the shoulder as I talk. Luckily, he's the one driving the golf cart. I'm going to hate myself in the morning.

"And they say you don't know how to express your emotions," Gregor deadpans back to me.

"How many more times do we have to do this?" I ask.

"Five, including this next one," Gregor says. "Then we can get you all tucked into a Lyft to get you home, where you can pass the fuck out until it's time to go out tonight."

"I gotta tell you, that sounds awesome, man. Not the part about tonight, the part about passing the fuck out."

"I figured it would." Gregor stops the cart and we pile out. "You're up," he says to me, handing me the club he thinks I should use. Because I'm the worst player, I have to go first— every time. Some sort of fucked-up golf etiquette. Shouldn't I be punished for sucking? Really, they should make me go last. Or not let me go at all. The only good thing about having had this much to drink is my eye-hand coordination seems to have gotten better. There are even times where I hit the ball on the first swing and others where it travels far. Hashtag winning!

I place my club back in the bag and grab a bottled water from the cooler, draining it quickly. Andrew moves to take his turn, and Gregor turns to talk to Hunter.

"So, tell me about this bachelor party you've got planned?" he asks.

"Mostly low-key. Golf today, of course, then a nice dinner this evening, followed by scotch and cigars, after which I guess we'll see where the night takes us," Hunter answers. I have to admit, outside of the golf, it sounds like a good celebration.

"And what's the little lady doing for her bachelorette?"

I grab another water bottle and lean a little closer, wanting to hear what Tabatha has planned.

"She's shooting a movie right now—"

She is? That's great!

"Even though I specifically asked her not to. Which has not gone over well. It's already exceeded the expected shooting schedule, she was supposed to be finished this last week, leaving her the week of the wedding free. My thought is, she won't have time for one. Which I told her would happen. But she didn't listen. So typical. I honestly don't know what's come over her lately."

Andrew comes to stand by them. "Tabatha?" he asks. Hunter nods in response.

"You're going to have to get her back in line. Can't be letting her go off doing her own thing."

"I know," Hunter says, giving me a look of superiority as he does. "It will not happen again. She knows better."

She knows better? What the fuck is that supposed to mean?

I ask Gregor about it once we are back in the cart on our way to the next hole. "Yeah, I thought that was a little weird too," he says when I mention Hunter saying Tabatha should know better.

"He better not be thinking he can boss her around or stop her from pursuing her own interests. That shit's not okay."

"I'm sure we just heard it wrong," Gregor says. "I mean, I may not have a lot of love for Tabatha, but even I know she wouldn't put up with that."

"Are you ever going to forgive her?" I ask.

"She broke your heart, man."

"Yeah, but you didn't like her even before that."

"Well, that's 'cause I was young, stupid, and jealous."

"Hey, maybe I broke her heart, not the other way around."

"I don't think so," he says.

"Well, I do."

"Okay."

I hate it when he does that. Stops a discussion by just agreeing. It drives me nuts. We pull up to the next hole.

"Hey, can you just par me out, I've gotta take a leak," I say to Gregor.

"That'll be your best score yet," he says. I flip him off and head out toward the nearest restroom. I hear Hunter ask where I'm going, then clench my fists when he responds with a similar comment to Gregor's about this being my best score yet.

Dick times two.

19

TABATHA

"*Cut!*" the director calls and everyone scrambles to prepare for the next scene. "That was fantastic, Tabby. Your best yet."

I smile in return, grateful for the compliment, and head straight for my trailer. Shooting this mini-series has been the hardest and most rewarding thing I've done. The hours are grueling, the action exhausting, and the lines ever-changing. Aside from that, it's been fantastic. The only letdown is, I've not been able to keep my promise to Hunter about participating with the wedding planning. But I don't regret it. I think he and Liza have done great without me. And I'm not picky about what we are doing or serving. As long as I feel pretty in my dress, that's all I really care about.

Which I already know I will. The designer that I chose to make it for me is one of my favorites. Her name is Si, pronounced *sigh*. She's crafted a dress that is absolutely perfect for me. I had her design dresses for both Crystal and Angela too based on ideas they liked. We are going for the final fittings later today.

Si is making a concession for me due to my crazy hours lately, which I know is due in part to the buzz about this miniseries. The online streaming service is hyping the crap out of it. They've been working to do a lot of the editing and post-production as we shoot, which saves them time, but also requires more adaptability from the cast than would ordinarily be expected.

The other good thing is I've lost that last ten pounds I hated. More than that even. They are having me do many of my own action shots, which is just as fun as it is tiring. It's got me used to working with a trainer again though and my body is toning in places I'd forgotten I have. It's also altering my outlook on life a bit, in that my character is way more gritty and raw than I've ever been. I'm a firm believer in method acting and can easily lose myself in a role to the point where I almost get confused as to who is the real me. It makes for great screen presence but isn't always so great on my personal life.

Hunter does not approve of this "new" Tabatha. Not at all. But I find her to be refreshing. At worst, I'm transitioning into a combination of the two. The real me tempering the character and that character roughing up the real me. Needless to say, it's been cause for more than one disagreement between Hunter and me. I'm hoping to make it up to him once we wrap, which should be in two days.

As long as we are on time, then I'll have Tuesday through Friday free before the wedding on Saturday. And I still feel like that's plenty of time. I mean, Liza has got all the little things under control, that's what we pay her a boatload of money for. But what has been put on hold is the documentation of the planning process that Hunter wanted. Because I haven't been around much, there hasn't been a need for the new photographer to take pictures of us.

Which he hasn't been super happy about, since I'm sure he was counting on a big payday. But he'll still be capturing the week just prior as well as the rehearsal dinner before the wedding. And from what I've been able to gather, the rehearsal dinner is almost as elaborate as the actual wedding, just with one-tenth of the attendees.

Hunter is at a charity golf tournament today, and then is having his bachelor gathering this evening. I'm not really having a bachelorette party, but Crystal, Angela, and I are getting together for dinner and the fitting. After which, we'll all kick back, have some drinks, and cut a little loose. Crystal has a babysitter all night, and Michael is on call, so she has no responsibilities. We haven't had a night like this in probably three years or more.

I work for a couple more hours before the director calls it a wrap for the day. On a whim, I invite one of the makeup girls, Maisey, to go out with us. She and I have gotten along really well during the entire shoot and it seems like she doesn't get out much either.

She's a single mom and she and her daughter live with her mother, who was also a single mom before she remarried when Maisey was in high school. Sadly, her mom was widowed a few years back, which is when Maisey and her daughter moved in with her. Most of Maisey's makeup work experience is proms and weddings or special events as the chance of a movie or show being shot on location in Seattle is slim. Sometimes she fills in for the news stations, but according to her, that's as elaborate as it gets. She's grateful for any job she's given.

I already hired her to do both mine and Crystal's makeup for the wedding, as well as Angela's, my other bridesmaid. And she's offered to do my makeup tonight, so we are going to get ready in my trailer before having the limo take us to pick up Angela and Crystal. We'll all go to the fitting, and then go out from there.

Maisey is a statuesque blonde and naturally crazy beautiful. The only way I can believe she is still single is because she's got a kid and most guys are stupid. We decide to borrow clothes and shoes from wardrobe. There are a few scenes where my character attends either a formal party, or has to scout out a nightclub for suspects, and she dresses to the nines when she does. There's a slew of options as a result. We both pick items that are out of character from what we would normally wear.

She goes with a khaki-colored, knit, long-sleeve crop top with a deep V in the front, and a matching knit, wrap-style skirt with the slit in the middle. Even though it's seemingly conservative with its long sleeves and skirt, it actually shows a lot of skin and is sexy as hell. She pairs it with metallic gold, strappy stilettos, and the khaki green color makes her green eyes totally pop. She straightens her long blonde hair, then curls just the ends to give it a tousled look. Her makeup is light and natural. She's stunning.

I let her make my hair big—like Julia Roberts in *Pretty Woman* big—and then give me a smoky eye with a shiny lip. My outfit is a one-piece romper-goes-to-the-disco. The top is a cold-shoulder style with a three-quarter length sleeve. It's a cowl neck, loose and billowy. The bottom is short shorts—tight short shorts that show a lot of leg. It's a black base with purple and silver slashes and sequins. I pair it with black, strappy stilettos. I feel fierce in it. Like I can kick ass. More like my character, than myself.

We start with champagne while we are getting ready and finish it in the limo after picking up Angela. By the time we get to Crystal's, we are well on to the second bottle. It's safe to say we will all be just a little tipsy by the time we reach the fitting.

The dresses Si designed—the only requirement being that they're black—look amazing. Crystal's is a tea-length, A-line silhouette with a sweetheart neckline and cap sleeves. It showcases everything about her body that is beautiful, and it makes her look tall, which she loves. Angela's choice is a short, body-con, bandage style with long sleeves. Both look stunning in their dresses.

Of course, this dress disparity goes against Hunter's big idea of total coordination at the altar, but I don't care. The worst possible thing a woman can do to her friends is make them buy a bridesmaid dress. Everyone says you can wear it again, but you can't. Unless it's to another wedding where you're a bridesmaid *again* and they've picked the same dress.

"Your turn, Tab!" Crystal claps her hands and bounces in place. I've only tried the dress on once before and it was more a mock-up and not the actual dress. When I finally see it in the dressing room, I'm overwhelmed with emotion and gratitude. The dress is breathtaking on the hanger, looking almost see-through by design. I'm taking a huge risk with it since Hunter does not like to see me in revealing clothing.

Tight, yes. Just not revealing. I hadn't realized there was a difference before I met him.

I want my dress to wow him. To the point where immediately after our vows, he pulls me into a closet somewhere and fucks me up against a wall because he can't help himself. Because he is so overcome with desire and so possessive that he wants to know that his seed is dripping down my thighs all night long.

The gown is very delicate looking and made almost entirely of sheer tulle. It's a blend of ivory and gold threading, with tiny spaghetti straps, plunging neckline, and almost no back. With a wide waistband in the middle and then a flowing A-line skirt. At first glance it might appear as though it's transparent, but it's not. And it's exquisite.

I put my big hair up in a smallish bun and take off all my jewelry. Si helps me get it on, taking care with the delicate straps and skirt. She will be there the day of the wedding to help me put it on. I keep my eyes shut as she buttons the back and then situates the dress better on my body to analyze the fit.

"Ees peerfect," she says in her thick accent that I can't quite place. "You look now, Tabeetha."

I open my eyes.

She's right.

It's perfect.

Tears form in my eyes. I grab a tissue to dab at them before I ruin my makeup.

"Are you guys ready for this?" I call out to the girls.

"More than," Angela yells back.

Si opens the privacy curtain and I turn from the mirror to face the girls.

All three faces look back at me with similar awestruck expressions.

"It's beautiful, isn't it?" I ask, looking down at my gown.

"No, Tab, *you're* beautiful. Wait until Hunter sees you, he's going to lose his techy little brain," Crystal says, tears streaking down her face.

"I have never seen a more gorgeous bride," Angela says.

"You are breathtaking, girl," Maisey adds.

I admire my gown some more in the mirror, as well as me in my gown. Si has outdone herself with this. After a few minutes of wedding talk, the girls and I change back into our clothes to go out. We make the final arrangements for delivery on the wedding day and discuss the time schedule. Si also says she will try to stay for the wedding.

"It would mean a lot to me if you could," I tell her as I give her a big hug. She kisses me on both cheeks and walks us to the door.

"I don't know about you, but I'm freakin' hungry, and now that I know I can fit in my dress, mama wants to eat," Crystal tells us.

Maisey fixes my hair in the limo, returning it from the messy bun to the original loud red mess it was before. I almost feel like my hair gets there faster than I do, it's that big.

Instead of stopping somewhere for dinner, we hit a drive-thru burger joint and picnic on the trunk of the limo, watching the sunset and drinking a third bottle of champagne. The food helps, because I was feeling a little drunk. And even though Crystal and Angela drink the bulk of the third bottle, I still feel those first and second bottles. I'm a lightweight, which I hate.

I switch to water for a bit as we make our way to the first club, not wanting to be too drunk to enjoy myself. This is my night and I want to make the most of it, stretching it out to last forever. The driver pulls up in front of the club, and I notice where we are and what's across the street.

"Ladies, I have an idea . . ."

20

PAX

I take my time hitting the restroom and returning to the guys. By the time I catch up to them, they are just finishing the seventeenth hole.

Thank god!

The sooner this miserable game is over the better. I'm sobered up a little bit, the walk having done me some good. As have the five bottled waters I've forced myself to drink. They aren't huge bottles, mind you. Maybe twelve ounces apiece, but it still helps.

One thing remains certain, I do not want to go to Hunter's soiree this evening. Not even one little bit.

"I was wondering what happened to you," Gregor calls to me as I approach.

"Yeah, I just took a little walk, no big deal."

"Your score has gotten considerably better since you actually stopped playing," Hunter says. I fight the urge to flip him off.

No matter how hard I try, I can't figure out what Tabby sees in him.

I step up to the forward tees to take my final turn. Visions of grandeur race through my mind as I prepare my stance and attempt to channel anyone who is better at this sport than me. I look down the fairway, picturing my ball flying through the air and landing just short of a hole-in-one, resulting in a putt so easy, that even I will be able to sink it.

Tee in the ground, ball balanced atop. Legs widened, knees relaxed, the head of the club at the base of the ball, take it back, curve my body, and swing. That solid feeling of ball connecting with metal head travels up the club, through my arms, and into my soul. I watch as it soars through the air, clearing one hundred, then one fifty, and what must be two hundred yards before dropping on the green.

It's like a fucking modern-day miracle.

Or the power of positive thinking.

Either way, I'm a fucking golf-god right now. I turn to the guys, trying my best not to gloat, probably not succeeding. Gregor gives me a well-deserved high-five. Andrew gives me a chin nod with a "nice shot." And Hunter pretends he didn't see it.

Asshole.

The other guys take their turns and we head down to the green.

I hit Gregor in the biceps. "Did you *see* that shot, man?"

"It was a helluva lucky shot, brother."

"Pfft. Lucky, my ass. I mastered the game of golf today."

"Don't get ahead of yourself. The fifteen holes before your little break say something else."

"That was practice," I tell him, even I know I'm full of shit. But for some reason, I'm going with this.

He rolls his eyes. "Whatever you say."

We pull up to the green. My ball is a good thirty feet from the pin. Practically a hole-in-one as far as I'm concerned. Until I realize I'm the furthest from the hole and I still have to go first.

I eye the pin from where my ball sits. It seems much further when you're standing at the ball looking at the pin, and not the pin looking at the ball. I know, from my earlier experiences today, the chances of overshooting the hole are good, so I give my ball a light tap. It rolls about ten feet before coming to a stop.

Shit!

I replace my ball with the marker and wait for the other guys. Gregor sinks his, Andrew and Hunter do not. I'm up again.

Tap.

It goes straight for the hole. I hold my breath, waiting for my redemption of the day.

"You overshot," Hunter says.

"I did not," I reply, as the ball does that half-circle thing around the rim of the hole and keeps going. He smirks. I refrain from punching him as a combination of embarrassment and rage courses through me.

I hate this fucking game.

Both Hunter and Andrew sink it on their next shots, leaving me up again.

I take a deep breath and focus.

See the ball go in the hole.

I almost have to giggle, because ball and hole. Except that I'm a grown man despite the fact I've had way too much beer today and I'm perpetually immature. Today, I'm a golf-god.

Deep breath in.

Deep breath out.

And . . . tap.

My ball rolls nowhere near the hole.

Fuck!

This bullshit fucking sport is fucking bullshit.

I one-hand it.

And it's a miss.

Kick it with my toe.

Sink the motherfucker like a boss.

That's what I'm talking about.

Yes!

Except the guys have moved on. The par was three. I'm way over that. No one cares. Not even Gregor.

Why am I here again?

～

Gregor convinces me to go back to his place before we meet Hunter for dinner, not trusting that I'll show up for the bachelor shindig after drinking all day. I've done my absolute best to sober up, and I think I'm pretty much there. I shower and change into the clothes we stopped for at my place. Gregor makes us both an espresso from his fancy machine, reminding me of when we were younger and would pound energy drinks before going out.

"Okay," I say, feeling fired up. "So, is tonight gonna be like the Gregor and Pax show, or are we respectful and shit?"

"We're respectful and shit. My agent said that I have to lay low before the season starts."

"Why? It's not like you ever get into trouble?"

He shrugs, like that's an answer.

I order a Lyft to bring us to the restaurant Hunter has chosen for dinner. I'm still dying to know where we are supposed to enjoy cigars and scotch afterward because Washington is notorious for its lack of cigar lounges. Want a smoke shop? Done. Dispensary? No problem. Cigars? Oh, now there's the brake screech. Supposedly, this place we're meeting Hunter at has a backroom for rent, and smoking is allowed.

I love a good cigar as much as the next guy. I mean, a glass of Macallan neat, and a Padron Anniversario—I'm in fucking heaven. And before cigars and scotch, we get a big cowboy steak, medium rare? Fuck, yes. Bring on the night.

We arrive at the steakhouse. Hunter and the rest of his friends are already seated. It's clear that Gregor is his guest of honor, since the seat directly to his right is open. Me? I have to ask the hostess for another chair and then squeeze in between two other computer guys at the opposite end of the table. Gregor is used to this. He has his Gregor persona that he puts on and he charms the fuck out of everyone around him. It's a gift.

I don't have that same gift. So, I introduce myself to Geek Number One on my left, and Geek Number Two on my right, then I order an entire bottle of pinot noir, just for me. And when she brings it, I tell her to make sure my glass is never empty, but do not afford the same courtesy to my neighbors.

Drinks flow heavily, and we all get a little loose-lipped. Before long, Geek Number Two is asking me how I know Hunter.

Because I am the epitome of grace and class, I answer with, "I used to fuck Tabatha."

Geeks One and Two look at me, then each other, then start to laugh. "Of course you did," Geek One says.

"I did," I say.

"Yup," Geek Number Two chimes in.

"I took her virginity, mother fuckers," I add, immediately regretting it, but caring more about my pride than Tabatha's feelings at this point.

Because, first and foremost, apparently, I'm an asshole.

"Yeah, right," Geek Number One comes back with. Then he elbows the other geek next to him. "This guy says he took the queen's virginity."

The other geek gives me a onceover and responds with, "Yeah, right."

Bunch of articulate motherfuckers.

"I'm Pax Baldwin, her high school sweetheart, first husband, star of *Keeping Tabs*. Ring a bell?" I ask.

Both shake their heads.

I pour myself some more wine and drink it.

"Why would Hunter want her ex to be here?"

"Uh, because Gregor is my best friend and that was the only way to get him here."

"Yeah, right." Geek Number Two rolls his eyes.

Fuck these guys.

"Gregor," I call down the table. Conversation stops. Gregor looks at me, eyebrow raised. "Who am I?" I ask him.

"Pax," he says.

"Right," I say. "But who am I to you?"

Gregor smiles, pushes back his chair, and stands. Then he starts to sing, in true Gregor style, a little ditty by Joe Cocker made famous by a TV show called *The Wonder Years*. Asking about what we'd do if he sang out of tune. And I know he's singing to me. I think the rest of these blowhards might think he's including them as well. But no way, mo-fos, this here is *my* best friend. And he's singing to me. So, what do I do? I get up and sing with him.

Now, we've never made this a duet before. Really, we've never made anything Gregor does a group effort, so it's not just this song. I'm not entirely sure, once I get up there, that he's okay sharing the spotlight. Mostly because I don't quite have the rhythm he does, nor can I really carry a tune. And public venues don't typically give me the same leeway they do G. I know this all makes it seem like I can't do shit. But I can.

First, I take pictures in the middle of fucking wars. Like, with gunfire and bombs and shit. I mean, yeah, I can't golf or bowl, I can't carry a tune, and I'm not the best solo dancer. But I jump out of planes, rappel buildings, run from explosions, and dodge rapid gunfire, all in the name of realistic photojournalism. And I'm a total badass when I want to be. So, the fact that these douchebags don't believe me when I tell them who I am, is on them. Not me.

But with this song, I have to admit, it probably would have been better had I just let Gregor do his thing. Now it's too late. I'm up here with him, the song is coming to an end, and I'm not real sure what to do.

"We're taking requests," I yell out, belatedly realizing all eyes in the main dining room are on us. Gregor can get away with this stuff. One, he's a really big guy so no one ever has the balls to stop him. And two, even more importantly, people expect it from him. He dances on the sidelines during games, he breaks into song whenever he wants, and he's a celebrity. Sports celebrities always get to do what they want.

"No, we're not taking requests," Gregor responds as he sits back down.

I take my seat. Geek's One and Two are suitably impressed with my status in Gregor's life so I feel as though I've redeemed myself in their eyes, even if they don't still believe that I slept with Tabby first.

We move into the back room for scotch and cigars about an hour later. Hunter and his friends take forever to finish a meal. I finally get to sit next to Gregor again and only have to deal with a geek on my other side. Hunter has brought in a number of leather couches and chairs for us to sit in. The lighting is dim, but not so much that it's hard to see, and ceiling fans spin on low. Enough to circulate the air around the smoke, but not so much that you can't light a cigar properly.

Hunter has girls that wander around with trays filled with cigars, different brands of scotch, and expensive-looking glasses. Another has whiskey ice rocks for those who prefer a chill to their heat. The girls are dressed like vintage "bunnies" in nightclubs. Short shorts, heels, fitted jackets, pillbox hats, and trays more like low-side boxes with straps around their necks to help them hold it.

"Won't Tabatha mind about the girls?" one of the geeks asks Hunter.

"No," he says. "She's not the type to get jealous. Very even-keeled, that one."

Even-keeled? Tabatha? Is he thinking of the right girl?

"Besides," Hunter continues, "what's to mind? It's not like they are strippers or prostitutes. This is my bachelor evening, so I'm sure even if I had a stripper, she would be fine with it."

"And are you?" I ask him.

His gaze hits me. "Am I what?"

"Are you having a stripper?"

"Of course not. Are we not civilized enough to be able to enjoy an evening of conversation and wit without having breasts and buttocks shaken in our faces?"

I look around the room at the guys assembled here. "No, I don't think we are." I'm only halfway kidding. And it's meant to be a joke. Hunter doesn't seem to take it that way.

"You're welcome to leave anytime. You weren't even on the guest list."

I hear a noise of suppressed laughter. I'm sure it was Geek One or Geek Two if not both. I catch Hunter's eye and hold his stare, not looking away until Gregor interrupts.

"So, how 'bout those Seabirds?"

We laugh, which was his intent.

I get up to grab a bottled water from a chilled bin on a side table. A body appears beside me. I know it's Hunter without even looking.

"Don't push me, Pax. I could bury you so fast it would make your head spin."

"I don't think so, bud."

"You're a photographer." He says it like it's a dirty word. "It's nothing in my world. I could buy and sell you one hundred times over. I know the deal. If I want Gregor, I have to take you as well. But mark my words, it won't always be this way. At some point, he will realize the trash that you are. Then who will you tag along with to the big boy parties?"

I could hit him. I really could. I won't. But I could. My fist tightens at my side. He's just such a—

The door to the room crashes open.

"Surprise!" In walks Tabatha, with her little entourage behind her.

21

TABATHA

I'm kind of nervous walking into the steakhouse where I know Hunter and his friends are. Though, I can't really tell you why. The girls follow closely behind me as the hostess shows us to the private back room. We get to the closed door, whereI smell the faint aroma of cigars and hear male laughter. It makes me smile knowing that Hunter is in there with his friends, doing what he enjoys.

Maybe we shouldn't interrupt.

"This was a dumb idea," I whisper. "We should just leave them alone and let them have their guy night."

"I think it's cute," Crystal whispers back. She would. Michael would be happy to spend his bachelor evening with her. Hell, he'd probably rather. But I'm not sure Hunter and I are the same way.

"Just go," Angela urges.

"Okay, fine." I push open the door and waltz in. "Surprise!" I cough a bit from all the cigar smoke in the air and look around for Hunter.

Instead, the first person I see is Pax.

What in the actual fuck is he doing here?

He catches my eye, then purposefully looks me down and back up again slowly. Appreciation and desire are written all over his face, and a hunger in his eyes.

That's it right there!

That's how I want Hunter to look at me on our wedding day.

Speaking of, *there* he is. Right next to Pax.

"Tabatha? What are you doing here?" Hunter calls out, walking toward us.

I laugh uncomfortably. "We were heading to the club across the street and I thought I'd pop in and surprise you. Surprise!"

"It's lovely to see you, of course," he says as he gets closer. Then he grabs my upper arm and pulls me into the corner. I'm expecting him to kiss me, just with a little privacy. Which is so like him—

"What are you wearing? And what did you do to your hair? Is it going to stay like that? You look so . . . common. Where did you get that outfit?"

Hold up.

"Did you just say I looked common? What's wrong with my outfit? And this *is* my hair. I just always straighten it for you."

"I much prefer it straight. Straight and up."

"If it's up, how would you know if it's straight? Look, forget it. This was a bad idea. We're just going to head across the street."

"You're going to a club?"

"Yes."

"Have you already been drinking?"

"Of course. We've been having champagne in the limo. Why, all of the sudden, is it a problem if I'm drinking?"

"It's not. I just . . . this outfit, and showing up, it's just unexpected, that's all. I'm sorry. Of course you're dressed for having fun with your girlfriends. You should go a little crazy. Just not too crazy. We don't need any undesirable pictures showing up in the media." He laughs at his comment, but I'm pretty sure he's dead serious. He's always been reserved, but not controlling. Or am I just now noticing?

I look around him for the girls and see that Pax and Gregor are talking to them. Crystal has always loved them both so it's not surprising she would say hello. If I'm not mistaken, Gregor seems to be taken with Maisey. I have to warn her. She does not need an Igor BigJerksy—

"Tabatha, are you even listening to me?" Hunter interrupts my thoughts.

"Of course I am. That's fine," I lie.

He looks at me, eyes narrowed. He knows I'm lying. I know he knows I'm lying.

Exit, stage left.

"Okay, girls, ready to go?" I call out to them. "I'll see you later," I say to Hunter. I don't hug him. I don't kiss him good-bye. I strut to the door, yell out, "Woot! Woot! Party time!" and pump my fist in the air as I disappear through the doorway without once looking at the rest of the room, or to make sure the girls are with me.

Luckily, they were.

"What was that all about?" Crystal asks once we reach the sidewalk again.

"He can be so weird sometimes."

"Oh, honey, I'm sure it's just pre-wedding weirdness. It happens."

"I don't think that's what it is," I tell her.

"Well, I say this calls for some tequila shots and girl talk in a crowded place where we can lose ourselves in a corner and ogle men," Angela says.

We tell the limo driver where we'll be and head across the street to the club. Angela called ahead and got us a private table in the VIP area. We weave through the crowd, centipede style, with me in the front. The music is loud and thumping, reminding me of crazier times.

Hunter prefers classical music, which is what we listen to a lot at home. I'm a closet pop-music addict. "If I Can't Have You" by Shawn Mendes comes on, and I raise my hands above my head and swing my hips as I walk. I'm in the mood to let go with my girls. I haven't had a night like this since I started seeing Hunter.

Angela orders us shots as we head into the VIP section. The club has a few raised areas around the perimeter as interconnected designated VIP areas with private restrooms, servers, and bar. We have one all to ourselves.

"And with our first shot of the night, congrats to Tabatha. May marriage bring you all the happiness you deserve."

"Here! Here!" Crystal cries.

We lick, salt, shoot, and lime.

I shake my head and grimace. Sometimes I forget how potent tequila is. The warmth spreads down my center through my body. It feels good. I don't want to talk about Hunter. I want to dance until I sweat. Dance until I forget all my problems and just feel.

Billie Eilish's "Bad Guy" begins, I start to move my body with the beat, singing along, the girls right along with me. We do a few more shots and a lot more dancing. I'm feeling badass and invincible, and in the perfect mood to go a little crazy when "Like a Girl" by Lizzo blasts through the speakers.

"I am in love with the music at this club," I yell to no one in particular.

Maisey and I sing to each other at the top of our lungs, jumping around in our little circle of women. Shaking our shoulders, wiggling our hips, laughing at everything without a care in the world.

I dance for another three songs or so before I motion to the girls that I'm going to sit down. I need a break. I grab a bottled water and drink most of it.

Crystal joins me a moment later. "Ohmigod, I forgot how much fun this is. How come we never do this anymore?"

"'Cause we're getting old and have to take breaks." I motion to the two of us.

"Truth," she says. "So, what's going on with Hunter?"

Ugh.

"I don't know. He's just being weird lately, like about my taking this part, my clothes and hair tonight. It's like he doesn't know me at all."

Angela and Maisey join us.

"We finally chick-chatting?" Maisey asks.

"Yes," Crystal and I say at the same time. Angela orders another round of shots.

"To happiness and dancing," Angela says. We repeat the sentiment and take our shots. I don't shudder with this one at all. In fact, it goes down easy.

"Oh, that's good, what was that?" I ask Angela.

"Buttery Nipple," Angela says.

"Of course it was," I say, laughing.

"What's up, buttercup?" Maisey asks. "I'm sensing some weirdness tonight."

"I'm just . . . I don't know. You're right, I'm feeling weird. Or I'm feeling like Hunter is being weird. And I don't think it's just wedding jitters. I think he really is being weird."

"About what?" Angela asks.

"About Pax being the wedding photographer—"

"Who's Pax?" Maisey asks.

"Oh, girl. We've got to catch you up," Crystal says. We order drinks, and Crystal and Angela briefly fill in all the missing parts for Maisey. I sit back and listen. It sounds bad to hear someone else tell it. Not bad like evil, more like maybe Pax and I have unresolved feelings. Or bad, like maybe I'm not in love with Hunter. When of course I am.

Aren't I?

I laugh at myself. I wouldn't be marrying him if I wasn't. I wouldn't even be with him. I was fine being single. I mean, I figured I wasn't ever going to get married again, so that I am to him means my feelings are strong. I was happy when he proposed. I was—

"Wow, it kinda sounds like Pax still has feelings for you," Maisey says, interrupting my thoughts.

"Trust me," I say. "He doesn't. We were kids, barely knew what we wanted."

"If you say so," Maisey adds.

"Look, it's ancient history," I tell the girls, mostly to wipe the snarky looks off both Crystal and Angela's faces. They both think Pax and I belong together, well, if the choices are between Hunter and Pax anyway.

"Even if it didn't work out between Hunter and me, that doesn't automatically mean Pax and I would be together. There are a gazillion guys in the world. Not just two," I say.

They don't look convinced.

I give Crystal a look. *The* look, actually. The one that two best friends can share that says everything without a single word leaving anyone's lips.

"Fine, I'll drop the Pax thing," Crystal says. "For now. What else is going on with Hunter?"

"He's just different, maybe more presumptive and controlling about what I should say or do. It's like he thinks he's got me all figured out and tucked away in some category that fits. I don't know, it's little comments, about my weight, my tits, my hair. I mean, even tonight, he told me I looked common!"

"I'm sure he's just stressed between planning the wedding and selling his tech baby. It's like two huge things the guy has to divide his focus on. You know how hard it is for guys to do even one thing, let alone two." Crystal laughs at her own joke.

"I get that," I say. "Like I said, it's just a feeling. And I'm sure it's nerves, no big deal. Another round?" I raise my hand to get the server's attention before waiting to hear if they want one. I order another round of Buttery Nipple shots. I've lost count of how many it's been on top of the champagne, but I know the number is at least five.

"I can't do any more shots," Crystal says. Maisey seconds her sentiment. So, I take both their shots as well. Because, fuck it.

Until my head starts to spin.

"I need to dance more," I say, standing. I move off to the side of our VIP area that we've designated as our dance floor, close my eyes, and start to move my hips to the beat.

I feel someone come up behind me and turn quickly. It's Jonah, one of the guys who's shooting this new mini-series with me. He's a side character but we've had quite a few scenes together and I'm happy to see him.

"Hey!" I cry out as I step in to hug him, albeit a little sloppily.

"Wanna dance?" he asks.

"Yes!" As I answer, the song changes and "Fireball" by Pitbull comes on. We start a sort of modified salsa dance, only a little dirtier and cornier since neither of us know how to truly salsa. Pitbull just inspires it with his music. When it gets to the middle of the song, when they start taking it down, Jonah leads me to the platform and helps me step onto it, where I start to shake my ass and head to the beat. Dance like no one is watching, as the saying goes. I lose myself when they start with bringing it back, and then jump down into his arms when the music starts again, feeling crazy free and inspired. I've never laughed so hard in my life.

I like Jonah.

"How come you don't have a girlfriend?" I ask him.

"Because I have a boyfriend," he says with a wink, and I laugh.

Not having to worry about his intentions makes him all the more fun to be around.

I don't want this night to end.

The song ends way too fast, and the sultry beats of Rihanna pound through the room. It sounds like a mashup of "S&M" and "Only Girl (in the world," both of which I love. I can barely contain my excitement. Not just over the song, but being out with my friends, drinking, dancing, feeling free, laughing with Jonah, the floor vibrating with the bass. It's a rush, all of it. Plus, the power of music on my mood is amazing.

Jonah moves in behind me and we dance with my back to his front. Joking around and dirty dancing like we were before, I move away from him a bit and shake my head to the beat. I make a mental note to see if Hunter would be into tying me up during sex. If whips and chains excite Rihanna, they can't be all bad, right? I throw my head back and laugh, losing myself completely in the music.

Arms up, eyes closed, hips swaying, ass shaking, head bobbing.

Jonah puts his hands on my hips and dances us back further into the corner, then pulls me back against him, which is when shit gets a little serious. His cock hardens as I move my hips against him. And, damn, if Jonah isn't packin' heat in his jeans. Maybe we aren't joking with the dirty dancing.

I thought he had a boyfriend? Is he bi?

Jonah moves his hands up and down my hips lightly. Roaming a little higher and a little lower on my sides each time.

His hands feel good.

Clearly, I've had too much to drink if being touched by a younger gay man is turning me on.

I should go sit down.

When's the last time Hunter touched you like this?

Shit, we're just dancing, for god's sake. I'm pathetic.

Relax and enjoy it, Tabatha.

Another Latin-inspired tune comes on. I expect Jonah to start spinning me and salsa dancing again, but instead he pulls me even closer to him. All of me is touching all of him. My bare legs against his jeans feels naughty and sensual. I lift my arms over my head then reach back to circle them around his neck. He seems taller, which doesn't make a lot of sense. Jonah reaches up and trails his fingers down my arms, making me shiver. He snakes an arm around my waist and spreads his hand across my stomach, holding me firm to him. His hands seem bigger when they are on me. Possessive. Sexy.

Sexy as fuck.

I should go sit down.

It's just dancing.

I deserve to enjoy myself for a night. I'll have to admit to Jonah that he was turning me on, but I'll also have to make a joke of it so it doesn't get weird. For me. Maybe that would make it weird. I mean, Jonah is a good-looking guy, but I'm not attracted to him, and he's not attracted to me. The hard on is probably like morning wood. An inadvertent reaction. Or maybe it's because it's my butt and he's an ass man. I laugh at my stupid joke. This is totally innocent. As long as I ignore the warmth spreading through my belly, that is.

I use the back of his neck to pull his head down toward my mouth, then tilt mine back to tell him I'm going to go sit down.

"One more dance," he says, barely above the music. His voice low and gruff, like he's turned on by me too. The music slows to something haunting and melodic. The shots buzz through my body. I rest my head against his shoulder and shut my eyes. Our bodies sway slowly, moving as one, his hands on my hips and fingers splaying from my stomach to near my bikini line. His touch injects my body with a heat that's not been realized in a long time.

He's young, you feel flattered.

My hips roll, trying to press closer, obviously with a mind of their own. I can't stop the moan that escapes my lips.

He nuzzles my neck, the stubble on his face scratching my skin. "I heard that."

Just go with it.

I smile, reaching behind me to grab his hips.

Different hips. Not as slim as they were a few moments ago.

Wait a minute.

I turn to face him.

My heart stops.

It's not Jonah.

"Pax? What the hell?" I slap him on the chest. "What are you doing here? Where's Jonah?"

"I sent that kid away two songs ago," he says, pulling me tighter against him, his mouth close to my ear. Too close. "Paparazzies were getting way too many incriminating pictures, had to intervene for your own good and pull you over here where you couldn't be seen."

Oh.

I guess that makes sense.

Shit.

"Thanks," I say, still tense. Still thinking I should walk away. Not remotely comfortable with knowing it was Pax turning me on and not Jonah. Somehow, that makes it worse. More dangerous.

Being turned on by Jonah is okay, but turned on by Pax isn't?

"It's just a dance, Tabs. Relax." Again, he knows what I'm thinking. And he's right.

Fuck it.

I mean, why not, right?

Live in the moment, seize the day, and all that crap.

Not to mention, Pax saved me from something potentially embarrassing. Or at least from having pictures taken of me that would be misconstrued into something embarrassing.

The music slows considerably. I rest my cheek against his shoulder and let my body melt into him just a bit. I'm tired from all the dancing. Tired from all thoughts, comforted by the familiarity of his body. If Pax and I did still have feelings for each other, the song would be ironic. The chorus talks about the guy being someone that the woman loved. He let his guard down and she pulled the rug out from under him.

An argument could be made for—

It doesn't matter Tabatha. It's just a song.

I'm getting married in a week.

My face flushes as I admit to myself that Pax still excites me. I'd be lying if I said it wasn't nice to be back in his arms again. I may hate him, but I love him too. As someone I have a past with, as my first love. Nothing more.

I raise my head slightly to look for my friends. Gregor is dancing with Maisey. She looks dreamy. Like happy dreamy. Maybe Igor BigJerksy isn't so bad after all. Angela and Crystal are next to them, swaying back and forth with one another.

All in all, I'm going to say that this has been a really fantastic evening, which makes me smile.

Then my head starts to spin.

22

PAX

It's clear Tabatha and the girls have had way too much to drink. That was evident when I saw Tabby up on the table dancing while that little shit actor egged her on. It was actually a surprise to run into them. Well, for me anyway. Gregor knew they were coming here because Maisey told him. I should have known something was up when he suggested stopping in for a quick drink after we left Hunter's gig. Gregor rarely wants to stop in for a quick drink anywhere that he doesn't already own. And especially not a club.

I look at him dancing with Maisey. He seems pretty fucking happy with himself right now. Not that I'm complaining. I've got Tabby in my arms and it feels good. Right, even. It makes me wonder if we could ever work things out. Maybe Gregor is right and I'm not over her. On the one hand, I find it hard to believe that I found my one true love—if such a thing even exists—when I was so young. On the other hand, I can't imagine ever being with anyone else. And if I had a third hand, that one would be slapping me across the face and reminding me she drives me batshit crazy half the time.

Tabatha's body grows heavy against me. "You okay, Tabs?" I ask, my mouth so close to her ear that my lips brush against her skin.

She shakes her head.

"I don't feel so good," she mumbles.

I steer her into one of the available unisex restrooms, trying to gesture to Crystal at the same time, who is still dancing with Angela. We barely make it into the stall before Tabs is emptying the contents of her stomach, which clearly contained very little food. I hold her hair out of her face and rub her back.

"Oh, Pax, this is not good," she groans, her insides erupting again. And again. I flush the toilet as she lowers to her knees and leans her face against the tile wall. I reach behind us to get a cloth and dampen it for her forehead and the back of her neck.

The door opens and Crystal walks in. "Is she okay?"

I shake my head.

"Oh, honey." Crystal kneels next to her, pushing her hair back from her face.

"I can't do this, Crystal," Tabby moans.

"I know, honey. Nobody likes to throw up. It's awful."

"No, I can't marry Hunter. He won't pound me against the wall."

I try to stop myself from snickering. Not very well if the look Crystal gives me is any indication.

Tabby keeps talking. "We're in our thirties. That's young, right?"

"It is, it's so young. We have our whole lives ahead of us," Crystal murmurs as she brushes the hair back from Tabatha's face again and again.

"Does Michael pound you against the wall?" Tabatha's voice is pitiful.

Crystal looks at me, I shrug. I'm pretty sure I know what Tabatha is talking about, and she's right. Hunter is never going to be that guy to lose control and take her against the wall. Then I think back to the number of times that *I've* taken Tabs against the wall. Including that last day when she threw me out. The hate fuck. Hottest goddamn sex I've ever had, hands down. She was all claws and teeth, it was exceptional.

"You're worrying about nothing," Crystal soothes.

"No." Tabatha tries to push herself up, using the toilet seat as leverage. I'm reminded briefly of my bowling alley restroom tryst with Trix and do my best not to shudder.

"She okay?" I turn and see Angela, Maisey, and Gregor at the door

"I think we just need to get her home."

"I'll call the limo." Angela pulls her phone out and starts the call, putting her finger in the opposite ear to hear better.

"Poor baby," Maisey murmurs. Gregor pats her on the shoulder reassuringly. She reaches up and covers his hand with hers.

Interesting.

Crystal and I help Tabatha stand, but she falls before she's even straightened. I pick her up. "Let's do this quickly before anyone realizes who she is. Where's the limo going to be?"

"Back entrance," Angela says. "I'll go make sure he's there."

Tabatha snuggles against my chest, gripping my shirt in her fist. "Pax?"

"Yeah, baby?"

"Why didn't it work, Pax?"

"Why didn't what work?"

"Us. Why didn't we work?" And then she passes out cold. Even if she hadn't, I didn't have an answer for her. Not a finite one anyway. There are a million reasons why relationships don't work. And probably more than that for why she and I didn't work. Youth. Pride. Reality TV. Stupidity. Immaturity.

I walk us through the club quickly, and out the back door. I'm fairly certain we weren't seen and that no one has realized it's Tabby and she's drunk. The girls clamor in the limo and I move to lie Tabatha down on the seat.

"No." She tightens her grasp on my shirt. "Don't leave."

I try to loosen her fingers. "Tabs, the limo is going to take you home, okay. Crystal and Angela are here, so is Maisey."

"Oh, I love Maisey," she slurs. "She's my new friend."

I smile down at her and attempt to loosen her fingers again.

"Please?" She looks up at me, her green eyes wide. I'm halfway inside the limo anyway. I look back at Gregor, and he shrugs. So, I climb in and he follows me. I sit on the back bench next to Crystal. Angela and Maisey sit on the side seats, while Gregor takes up the other bench seat. Tabatha curls her lithe body onto my lap. Her bare legs go on forever. I have to put my hand on her calf to hold her in place. I don't have a choice.

At least that's what I tell myself.

Her skin burns where I touch her. A sure sign that if hell exists, I'll be banished to it for touching a woman who no longer belongs to me. She was magnificent tonight. Her hair wild, her outfit sexy as hell, dancing like the carefree girl I remember. When I compare the dancing girl with the woman planning a wedding with Wipplecock, it's easy to see how restrained she's become. Whether that's by choice or by his influence, I'm not sure.

It makes the most sense for the limo to drop off Crystal first, then Angela, Maisey, Tabatha, and Gregor. I'll just crash at Gregor's house rather than ask the guy to take me all the way over to Port Orchard. We wait to make sure both Crystal and Angela get into their homes okay. When we get to Maisey's house, Gregor gets out with her and walks her to her door. She kisses him on the cheek before going inside the house. He returns to the limo with a large smile on his face.

"Gregor and Maisey, sittin' in a tree. K-I-S-S-I-N-G," I sing.

"I like her, man."

"You say that with every girl you meet," I tease.

"I know, but this is different."

"How?"

"I don't know. I feel different. Patient, maybe?"

"That would be a new one for you, Casanova." In addition to really wanting a relationship, Gregor also falls for women way too fast. And it usually results in disaster and he gets hurt. Women come on strong because he's handsome, rich, and famous. He falls hard. When it becomes apparent they aren't genuine, he's left dazed and confused.

I feel the limo begin winding up the hills, I assume toward Pimplecock's. The houses in this area are ostentatious. It figures this is where they live, which is also why it's not surprising he has gated access to his home. The driver buzzes for permission to enter, and I hear a scratchy voice answer, then the gate opens slowly.

Hunter is outside waiting when we approach the house. I try to move Tabatha from my lap again, s process I should have started five minutes ago. She protests and wraps her hand in the fabric of my shirt. Before I can do anything else, Hunter has opened the door, his face red and stern.

"Tabatha—" he starts. Then he sees me. And Tabatha. "Well, isn't this becoming quite the habit," he sneers.

"She had too much to drink, we're just making sure she gets home safely," I say.

"We?" Hunter asks. Then he sees Gregor. "Oh, hello, Gregor, I didn't see you there." His tone changes completely to something friendly and inviting. Gregor waves a hand in reply.

I scoot toward the open door prepared to hand off Tabatha.

"Can't she stand?" Hunter asks.

"She was sick earlier," I say by way of explanation, climbing out of the limo and trying not to drop Tabatha at the same time. Not an easy task.

"How convenient that you were there to help her," Hunter says. "What, you had to leave my party early to rush to her side?"

"No," I said. "I didn't even know she was going to be there."

"It was my idea," Gregor interjects, also climbing out of the limo. "Maisey told me where they were going to be, and I wanted to see her again. Pax didn't know."

Hunter does not look convinced.

Tabatha starts to open her eyes. "Oh hey, Pax," she says softly.

"We brought you home, Tabs."

"Home?" She glances around, seeing Gregor first. "Igor BigJerksy," she says, her voice friendly. "I've decided to like you after all these years. But only because Maisey does. So be nice to her. She's my new friend."

"Yes, ma'am," Gregor says, laughing.

"Tabatha, are you well?" Hunter asks.

She looks at him, as if seeing him for the first time. "Hunter! How lovely to see you." Then she looks back at me. "We're getting married."

"I know," I tell her. "In less than a week."

"That soon?" she whispers loudly.

I nod.

"Do you think it's a good idea?" She looks from me to Hunter then back at me again. "For me to marry him."

I watch her expression, trying to decipher what she's getting at. If she's just drunk babbling or actually asking me my opinion.

"That's enough, Tabatha," Hunter says. "Let's go. You need to sleep this off."

She peeks up at me through her lashes. "I need to sleep this off." I nod, suddenly feeling beyond sad suddenly. This is probably the last time I'm going to see her before she marries this idiot. He has no idea what he's getting with her. How lucky he is.

I lean down and kiss her forehead softly. She closes her eyes and sighs. I take a moment to memorize her face one last time and then hand her to Hunter. Where she was easy for me to hold—she can't weigh more than a hundred and twenty pounds—he struggles under her weight.

"I can walk," she slurs.

"It's fine," he snaps.

And with that, they disappear into the house. I watch until I see the lights downstairs turn off, and those upstairs turn on. Then I climb back inside the limo and let the guy drive us to Gregor's. It isn't until we are halfway there that I realize I left my heart with Tabatha.

Where it belongs.

23

TABATHA

"I can't believe you are getting married tomorrow!" Crystal cries.

"I know! It feels like it's happened so fast and so slow at the same time."

"What time do you want me there tonight? Is Maisey doing our hair and makeup tonight too?"

"Yes, so maybe be here around three o'clock if you can swing it, and we can have a relaxing afternoon, just us girls before the rehearsal dinner," I say.

"Perfect," she says. "See you then."

We disconnect the call and I lie back on my bed.

I'm getting married tomorrow.

To Hunter.

A decision I've gone back and forth on all week. His weirdness only got worse after Pax and Gregor brought me home drunk. I don't remember a lot of the night, outside of having a great time dancing, and feeling safe and comforted with Pax. He held my hair back when I puked.

Oh god, I puked.

So embarrassing.

He was fine about it. Supportive even, whereas Hunter was pissed. Which only got worse when some pictures surfaced of me dancing on the table in the VIP area. They are grainy, and obviously taken from far away with a camera phone. But it's still clear that it's me. Big hair, bigger smile, short shorts, high heels, eyes closed, arms raised, hip cocked to the side. I look happy. Slightly possessed. Genuinely happy.

Part of me is tickled to have such a photo of myself. I don't know if I've ever seen me as *me*. Since I was a child, I've always been some version of me based on the situation. But this, this is the pure essence of Tabatha Ann Seton. And she is loving life.

Is it possible to be that happy normally?

Crystal is.

Crystal is the anomaly.

Hunter has only spoken to me this week if it's been directly related to the wedding. And even then, he's been terse and short. I'm interested to see how he acts tonight at our rehearsal dinner, where we are to be the happy couple tying the knot tomorrow. He won't want anyone in attendance to think there is something wrong, so my thought is he will be the doting fiancé.

I'm just not sure how much that bothers me. Oddly, I've not missed him this week. The five days leading to today—

rehearsal day––where we should be in our pre-wedding-honeymoon phase and deliriously happy. Or so I would imagine. I've spent most nights on the couch, and he's spent all his days at the office. I was still on set through Wednesday, longer than I'd originally intended, but it didn't seem to matter since he was upset anyway.

Yesterday—Thursday—would have been the day for us to spend together, discussing last-minute items for tonight or tomorrow, or even just hanging out and having fun. But instead, he was gone all day. So, I spent the day pampering myself. I got a massage, gave myself a facial, deep conditioned my hair, painted my toenails, read gossip magazines about myself, and coveted my picture of *me*.

Today, he was gone before I woke. I'm assuming he's at his office, and I'm fine with it. I'm trying not to dwell too much on the fact I don't miss him and that I'm not bothered by not seeing him all week. What kind of monster am I that I'm not even affected by his absence? Which leads me to the wisdom in my decision to marry him. I remind myself that I love him, he's a good guy.

My go-to phrase for him: good guy. But these last few weeks, he hasn't been. He's been a judgmental and controlling guy. And as far as loving him goes, how do I love someone who wants me to be different? Further, how does he love someone who he wishes were someone else? I take two antacid pills to try and calm my stomach.

Crystal and Maisey will be here in a few hours, that will cheer me up. In the meantime, I check my email, update a social media account, and speak with Liza to make sure she doesn't need help with anything. All of which takes about twenty minutes.

Okay, Tabatha, tomorrow you are going to marry Hunter. Pledge your love in front of six hundred people. Promise to be with this man forever.

Unless we divorce.

You can't think about divorce before you've even gotten married. Though, that's essentially what the prenuptial agreement does, which we signed weeks ago. Even though Hunter assured me it didn't mean he was anticipating the breakup of our marriage. The pragmatic side of me sees the wisdom of a prenup. But the romantic side of me thinks they are evil. A precursor of doom. Admittance of impending failure. How do you go into something, a commitment until death do you part, anticipating it won't last until death. That it will end much sooner than that.

The more emotional side of me began to have my first niggling of doubt that day. Who would I be if I were twice divorced? And if my second marriage lasted as long as my first, I'd be twice divorced before my mid-thirties. Does that put me on the path of Elizabeth Taylor? Or any number of other actors who have married multiple times?

Because, if Hunter can think about the demise of our marriage so easily, then I should be able to as well. Which brings me to today and wondering about whether marrying Hunter is the right decision. Even if it's not, how do I call off such a large production on such short notice? I can't do that to him. I'd rather get married, realize it's a mistake, and be twice divorced than hurt or embarrass Hunter. He doesn't deserve that.

Listen to yourself, Tabatha. Ridiculous on so many levels.

Instead I concentrate on summoning excitement for tomorrow, but instead, all I feel is apathy. Which, in itself, is funny.

Do I love Hunter?

Yes.

Am I in love with Hunter?

I don't know.

Is Hunter in love with me?

I don't know that either.

Hunter is definitely not in love with this version of me. The version that is closer to the real me than I've been in a long time. I think back to the night that Pax and Gregor brought me home, and the longest conversation that Hunter and I have had in almost three weeks. He'd carried me into the house, then set me down and helped me up the stairs to our bedroom.

"You need to take a shower. You smell like vomit and look like hell," he'd said.

So, I did. I took a hot shower first, then blasted myself with cold to help me wake up and sober up. I had a feeling Hunter wanted to talk.

"What is going on with you and Pax?" he'd asked when I exited the bathroom.

"Nothing is going on. They happened to be at the same club we were. I had too much to drink and Pax helped me get home."

"I'm going to be honest, Tabatha. I don't know whether to believe you or not." He'd sounded more like a father scolding a delinquent child than a man speaking with his intended.

"Why would I lie to you, Hunter?" I'd asked.

"You tell me."

"If I wanted to be with Pax, I would be. I wouldn't sneak around behind your back. Especially not when we are about to get married."

"You've changed."

"Changed how?"

"Your attitude, the way you dress, taking the role in the movie, not helping me with the wedding, to name a few."

I'd looked down at my feet, feeling ashamed. Because he was right, I hadn't helped with the wedding, and I did take the role without talking to him about it first. But I'm also a little mad too. It's a mini-series, not a movie. Like he can't even bother to get it right.

"I'm sorry."

"You should be."

"Well, I am," I snapped.

"From here on out, can we just go back to normal?" he'd asked.

I'd answered yes, even though I wasn't quite sure what normal was any longer. Because he was right, I have changed. The problem is, I like the changes. And I don't know what to do if he doesn't feel the same.

~

"Ohmigod, Maisey, you are a miracle worker!" Crystal enthuses. "I can't believe how pretty I am."

"Shut up," I say and backhand her lightly on the arm. "You are always gorgeous and you know it. If Maisey did anything, it was just enhance your natural beauty."

Crystal does look amazing. She has a new dress on for tonight—a sleek, black, long-sleeved mini-dress with a deep V in the front and ruching around the middle—that she's paired with knee-high, stiletto-heeled boots. Maisey has given her very natural-looking makeup with a deep red lip. It's striking.

My dress is a blush colored body-con, with sleeves that fall just off my shoulder, a tiny bit of ruching in the middle, and a ruffled bottom. I've paired it with gold-colored, strappy stilettos. I don't know what I would do without strappy stilettos, to be honest. I must have a million pairs, in different colors and heel heights. They go with almost every outfit, and I love them.

Maisey and Crystal got to my house separately about forty minutes ago, and I opened the champagne right away, wanting the mood to be festive. We'd put on music and so far, the afternoon has been lighthearted and fun. The rehearsal dinner is at one of Gregor's restaurants, the upscale one. I don't remember the name of it. Hunter was quick to change the location and take advantage of his new friendship when Gregor offered to shut down the whole place for him.

At a price.

I don't know if Gregor will be there or not. He has no reason to be, outside of his capacity as venue owner. Unless Hunter invited him, for some reason. If he did, that will certainly make Maisey happy. She said she and Gregor have been texting this week. She was just as busy as I with the wrap of the mini-series, then spending some time with her daughter. And now she's helping me prepare for tonight and tomorrow.

I pour us all some more champagne before I settle in the chair to let Maisey do my hair and makeup. She's got rollers in my hair now, big ones that will temper my natural curls, turning my hair into something a bit more glam than my normal look or when I straighten my hair.

"So, tell me about Gregor," I say, careful not to call him Igor. I haven't told her about my feelings toward him. One, I don't want to sour her opinion since she really seems to like him. Two, Crystal says he's a really great guy and I'm just choosing to remember an immature punk, which is probably true. I googled him—he is quite the humanitarian and philanthropist. And he's not afraid that Maisey is a single mom.

"Ohmigosh." Her face reddens. "He's so funny. And kind. And smart. And, good lord, can that man dance. Holy moly!" She fans her face with her hand, and I laugh. "Do you think he'll be there tonight?"

"I don't know, I was just wondering the same thing myself. Crystal, do you think Gregor will be there tonight?"

"I think if how he was with Maisey last weekend is any indication, then he will be." She steps away from the mirror where she was literally just admiring herself. "I'm sure he'll be there to *supervise*." She air quotes the last word.

Maisey squeals. "I'm so happy I brought a dress," she says.

"You could have borrowed something," I tell her. "We are almost the same size, you're just taller. Still could." I gesture to my closet. "Help yourself."

"I'll peek and see," she says.

I'd invited Maisey to the rehearsal dinner last weekend. We all got along so great, I thought it might be fun for her. Plus, Crystal will have Michael, and I'll be busy with Hunter, so she and Angela can hang out a bit.

But the more I think about it, I hope Gregor is there and that Maisey gets the chance to see him. I like them together. Well, really, I like her reaction to him. It reminds me of how Crystal is with Michael.

And how I wish I was with Hunter.

We arrive at the rehearsal dinner about ten minutes before it's due to start. Hunter sent a town car to bring us, and let me know, via text, that he would meet me there. Crystal and Maisey both stay outside for a bit. Maisey needed to call her daughter and mother and Crystal wanted to check in with Michael to see when he planned to arrive. I notice when I walk in that Hunter is already there and off to the side, talking to Liza. In theory, we are supposed to have a practice run-through of the ceremony at the rehearsal dinner, hence the "rehearsal" part. But Liza says it's not necessary, that we all know how to walk down an aisle, and with such a small wedding party, we'll be fine. She will be there tomorrow to tell us all exactly what to do and when.

She has a number of assistants with her, all wearing those little headsets so they can talk to one another. We have over fifty people here tonight, close associates and friends. Mostly

Hunter's. I'm not sure what she and her assistants do during the dinner. Maybe they eat?

Hunter sees me walk in and excuses himself from Liza. "Tabatha." He takes my hand and leans in to kiss me on the cheek. "You look lovely."

"Thank you." I smile at him, and it feels fake. He smiles back, but it doesn't reach his eyes.

Why are we doing this?

"We will have tray passed champagne and hors d'oeuvres for the first hour, along with the toasts, and then they will begin seating everyone for dinner. The staff has been instructed on the table seating plan." Liza appears from behind Hunter and begins talking.

"Sounds good," I tell her.

She looks to Hunter for affirmation. He nods, and she walks swiftly away.

"Hunter, Tabatha, welcome!" Gregor comes toward us, arms outstretched. "I'm so pleased you chose G's for your event tonight."

"Thank you for having us, Gregor." Hunter gives him a one-armed man hug. "The pleasure is all ours."

"Tabatha"—Gregor turns toward me and pulls me into his massive frame for a hug—"you look stunning. I can see why this guy is so taken with you." I thank him for the compliment and he smiles. He's a charmer, for sure. No wonder he's so popular with fans and patrons.

I elbow him somewhat comically. "I brought Maisey with me," I tell him in a singsong voice.

His face lights up. "You did? Where is she?"

"She's outside. She had to call her daughter."

"Daphne?"

"Yeah." I'm surprised, yet not, that he remembers her daughter's name.

"There she is now, excuse me." Gregor squeezes my arm lightly and goes to greet Maisey.

"Champagne?" The server offers up a tray of filled champagne flutes with our monogram on them.

"Yes, thank you." I take one and look at the monogram. It's nice. Not the font I would have picked, but still nice. I raise it to my lips only to have it pulled out of my hand by Hunter.

"Let's not have a repeat of last week, shall we?" he says, looking at the restaurant and not me.

"Hunter, don't be ridiculous," I say under my breath. "That was a one-time thing. It was my bachelorette party, for god's sake."

"There were pictures of you dancing on a table," he hisses.

"I already apologized for that."

"Well, I'm assuming we can avoid it from happening again as long as you refrain from drinking." He raises the glass to his lips and takes a long drink, then turns and walks away.

"What was that about?" Crystal asks, walking up to me.

"That was a control freak going one step too far," I say, seeking out the server so I can get a replacement glass.

24

PAX

I am fully aware of how pathetic it is that I am spying on Tabatha's rehearsal dinner. I have no business doing so. It's just that I've realized over the last couple weeks that I think I *am* still in love with her. So, what better way to punish myself for letting her go than by watching her move on?

Gregor has an office in the restaurant. It's up a half a flight of stairs, and on the way to the emergency exit and employee entrance. It has one of those secret windows where you can see out, but no one can see in. And there's audio. Don't ask me why. It was already there when G bought the building and he kept it. The secret window blends with the decor so unless you know it's there, you don't know it's there.

When he told me Slippycock had changed the location of their dinner to here, that's when I decided to come watch. So, here I am with a cigar and a bottle of Macallan, ready for the show. It helps tremendously that the space is sweet as hell. He's got a leather couch and chairs, a big screen TV, and a Bose stereo system. There's also an internal ventilation system so the cigar smoke gets sucked outside before it has a chance to sneak around the restaurant. I could practically live in his office.

I see Tabatha enter alone. Wipplecock has been here for a bit already. Toby Benson, the photographer I'd referred to them, was snapping pictures of the decor and monogrammed napkin holders and champagne flutes.

Barf.

Monogrammed shit is lame.

Wimpycock rushes over to where Tabs is and kisses her on the cheek. She smiles at him with, if I'm not mistaken, a smile that is disingenuous.

Trouble in paradise?

One can only hope.

I puff at my cigar and sip my scotch. Gregor greets his guests, he's so good at this crap. No wonder people love him.

There's Maisey. Good. That will keep G happy.

Oh, and what's this? Simplecock has taken Tab's champagne away from her and walked away?

Tsk. Tsk.

Stupid man.

Fury fills Tabatha's face, which is mirrored on Crystal's once she joins her and Tabby explains what's going on.

Oh, that man has no idea what he's in for. Stupid, stupid man.

You never take a woman's champagne away without replacing it with something better.

I'm still watching.

Like the pathetic fucking sap that I am.

I can see they are finally finishing with the speeches and I turn the audio back on. The speeches were boring as fuck to listen to. I'm on my second cigar and my third glass of scotch. Tabatha is on her fourth glass of champagne—yes, I'm counting—and openly flaunting it in front of Sippycup . . .

Nah, that one doesn't work as well as the names with cock in them.

Sippycock? Eh. I think I used that one already.

Dippycock.

That works. I watch as she flaunts her fourth flute of champagne in front of Dippycock, walking around the large room mingling with the guests. And every so often, she catches Hunter's eye and raises her glass to him with a big smile. To the outside observer, it looks sweet. But to the guy who knows her facial expressions and smiles—me—she's on the war path. God love that girl.

The restaurant has been rearranged for the occasion, with a main table for ten in the middle, encircled by six-tops artfully arranged to ensure no one feels as though they have a *bad* table. There are flowers everywhere, along with a banner congratulating the happy couple. Combine that with all the monogrammed shit, and I'm surprised no one has busted out a slide show of how they met.

Liza announces dinner. It's when they are moving to their seats that I see him grab her arm too hard to be nice, then pull her back to the side. He seizes the champagne flute from her hand forcibly, spilling it in the process. She yanks her arm from his grasp. If he hurts her, I will kill him.

I turn the audio up to see if I can hear anything.

Jackpot!

"Don't you dare try to dictate my actions, Hunter. I won't stand for it. I'm a grown woman, capable of making my own decisions. Maybe if you weren't being such an ass, I wouldn't feel the need to drink," Tabby says.

"You don't think you've embarrassed me enough already? Now you want to be known as the town drunk?"

"Drunk?" She laughs. It's forced and fake. "Jesus, Hunter. Are you kidding me? I'm nowhere near drunk. And even if I were, it's a party. Or didn't you notice? It would do you some good to loosen up once in a while."

"I don't even know who you are anymore, Tabatha. It's like you're a different person—"

"It's called growth, Hunter. It's what people do as they move through life. They grow and progress. You should try it sometime."

"You aren't the same person I asked to marry me."

"Actually, I am. I'm just letting you see more of me than I did before," Tabatha says.

"Well, maybe I liked less of you better," Hunter hisses.

Tabatha takes a step back, stunned.

I stand, wondering if I should go down there. Wanting to. Knowing I shouldn't. Before I can decide, the door opens and Gregor steps in.

"You're listening in?" He looks at me eyebrows raised.

"Yeah, but it's not as bad as you think," I say.

His expression remains the same.

"Fine, it is as bad. But they are fighting right now, and Hunter just told Tabatha that he likes less of her better." I sit back down on the sofa with a bit of a flop.

"Less of her? My god, she's so thin already."

"No, like less of her personality. Less of her as a person."

"Oh. Interesting. Okay, scoot over."

Gregor joins me on the sofa I've pulled in front of the window, lights his own cigar, and then pours himself a few fingers of scotch.

"Did you see that Maisey is here?" he asks.

"Yeah, I figured that would make you happy, man."

"It does. She's coming to the wedding with me. I mean, technically she will already be there, but she's going to sit with me at the ceremony and reception, so you're off the hook with being my plus-one."

"No problem at all. It's not like I was going to enjoy watching her do this anyway."

I watch as Tabatha turns to Hunter. "Maybe this isn't such a good idea, Hunter," she says.

"What? You drinking? That would be true, yes."

"No," she scoffs. "Us getting married."

"Don't be daft, Tabatha. We are due to marry tomorrow. There are six hundred people attending. We have over fifty people here tonight. We can't just cancel because you can't control your drinking."

"It was one fucking night, Hunter. I let loose with my girl-friends. It's not like I'm an alcoholic. Jesus Christ, get over yourself."

"One night?" He looks up and to the side, as though thinking. "If that was one night, what's tonight?"

"It's a celebration. Or at least it's supposed to be."

"I don't even know you anymore, Tabatha. This person you are pretending to be. This facade you're portraying. I don't understand why you are doing this."

She laughs, but it's caustic. "You think that's what I'm doing now? Ha! That's what I've been doing up *until* now, Hunter. You've only just begun to see bits of the *real me*." Tabatha's voice rises. People from the restaurant have stopped talking and started watching.

"What are you talking about, the *real you*?" Hunter sneers. "I don't even know what that means."

"I'm an actress, Hunter. All I do is play a part, for every facet of my life—for whatever role I need to play. And that includes with you. I've played the role of myself but only the part that you would find desirable. But it's not the real me."

"So, you're trying to tell me that you're just this elusive crea-ture who plays someone different depending on who she's with?"

"Yes, in a way. Except maybe with my girlfriends, and . . ."

"And what, Tabatha? Pax. Were you going to say, except with your girlfriends and Pax?" The look on his face is ugly and condescending.

"Yes, I was." She juts out her chin.

I fist pump the air.

"I see, so your ex gets *you*, and I get what exactly?"

"You get the Tabatha that you like."

"I can guarantee I'm not liking this Tabatha," he says. "I prefer the other you."

"That's because she's fake!"

Gasps make their way through the crowd that has gathered to watch.

It's too bad popcorn doesn't go with scotch and cigars. This is such a popcorn worthy spectacle.

"Do you realize I get up before you most mornings to fix my face so you don't see me without makeup?" Tabatha asks. "And this"—she reaches up under her dress and pulls something down—"is called a control top undergarment, to make sure I look sleek and thin, just the way you like me." She steps out of the garment and picks it up, tossing it at him.

I chuckle.

She doesn't stop there. "My hair is not naturally this thick, Hunter. No one's is." She fiddles with her curls then pulls a hair extension from it, along with two more, and tosses them toward Hunter. "My nails? Gel polish so they don't chip. My eyelashes? Fake! I have them refilled every two weeks." She blinks exaggeratedly at him.

"I would have sworn her lashes were real," Gregor says. I look at him, not sure if he's joking or not. The sides of his mouth twitch like he wants to smile, but he doesn't. I backhand him on the arm and resume watching.

"Every goddamn thing about me that you find acceptable is fake and has zero to do with the actual me. You even want to enlarge my breasts. I mean, let's face it, Hunter, is there anything real about me that you like?"

Hunter starts looking around, as though finally realizing that they have an audience.

"I won't do this here with you, Tabatha." His voice is low.

"Of course not." She stares him down, her gaze fierce. "Where would you like to do it?"

"I don't even know what it is we are doing. We are to be married tomorrow." His voice rises as he says it and carries across the crowd. "Pre-wedding jitters get the best of everyone, I suppose." He laughs uneasily. "Why don't we all get a drink—I know I could use one—and we can sit down to dinner and try to salvage the remainder of the evening." He walks into the small crowd with open arms, as though he's trying to give them all a hug.

I turn to Gregor. "He's just going to brush the whole thing off? And then what?"

"I'll be damned if I can figure the guy out," Gregor says.

"What a douche." I pour myself another finger of scotch.

Tabatha raises her arms in exasperation and looks at Crystal, mouth agape. Crystal nods, then puts her arm around Tabby's shoulders and leads her over to the main table.

Obviously, she agrees with Gregor and me.

Crystal grabs one of the bottles of wine already on the table and empties the entire bottle by pouring four large glasses. She hands one to Tabatha.

"Crystal didn't get the memo that Tabatha isn't allowed to drink anymore," I say, voicing my thoughts aloud, enjoying the running commentary Gregor and I have going on.

"Well, he did say everyone should get a drink to salvage the evening," Gregor deadpans.

Crystal motions for Angela and Maisey to join them, handing each a glass of wine as well, then starts to say something.

"Hey, turn it up," I tell Gregor. Before we get a chance to hear what she says, Hunter approaches the group.

All four heads turn to look at him expectantly. He clears his throat. "I would like for the two of us to salvage the evening as well. This isn't how I thought the night before our wedding would be. I apologize for voicing such things in front of other people." His voice is loud, I'm sure for the benefit of others in the room who aren't close by.

Tabatha nods at him. "Thank you."

As they all take their seats at the table, I notice that even though Peckercox was feeling all apologetic a second ago, he doesn't sit next to his betrothed during dinner, choosing instead a seat at the opposite end of the table.

25

TABATHA

Hunter and I had already planned to spend tonight apart. The whole, *"don't see the bride before the ceremony"* thing. So, Crystal and I are staying in a suite tonight, where we can get ready together in the morning. I'm assuming Hunter is staying at our house, but I never double-checked with him to see.

"Well, that was an interesting night," Crystal says. It's just her and me in the car Hunter arranged to bring us to the Cascadian House from dinner. Maisey And Angela went home. Maisey, to spend the night with her daughter, and Angela so she can drive herself in tomorrow.

"True. Do you think it's wrong for me to marry him?"

"Wrong? I don't know if that's the right question. No pun intended. I mean, tonight seemed a bit brutal to me. But you're the only one who knows what your relationship with Hunter is like behind closed doors. And what's consistent and long-term."

"Tonight sucked, for sure, but so have the last few weeks, really. Everything has been so up and down."

"Which is your big reason for leaving Pax, and your big reason for being with Hunter, because he isn't up and down. And you never fight. Which, just for the record, I think is weird. All couples fight. That's normal. It's how you make up and proceed that matters. But continue, please."

"Ever since I took the mini-series part, he's been different," I say.

"He knew you were an actress when he first asked you out. Hell, he was a self-proclaimed fan. It's not like he didn't know what he was getting into."

"I know, but I'd said I wasn't going to act anymore."

"And you've been bored to tears."

"I know."

"You're allowed to change your mind."

"I know that too."

"It's his job as your partner to adapt with you."

"It's not his fault though." This I know, when I'm honest with myself.

"What do you mean 'not his fault'?"

"I really did play a part with him, you know. And for so long, our relationship was long distance, it was easy to keep that up. I mean, we've only been living together a few months. Maybe that's just not long enough to get to know someone. I feel like I tricked him. And that I need to follow through with my commitment. If that means that I continue to play the persona that I've built up, so be it." I feel partly mature as I say this, and part like a martyr.

"How is that fair to you?" Crystal asks.

"How is it fair to Hunter any other way?" I return.

"This is your life, Tabby. You can't just coast through it, pretending to be someone you're not and being okay with that."

"Isn't that what being an actress is all about?"

"Sure, when you're actually being paid to play a specific part. Not playing the role of only a small part of the real you, Tabby."

She has a point. But I know I do too.

We arrive at the Cascadian House and the bellhop arranges our luggage while we check in and head up to the room. The attendant is working the elevator this time, and our ride to the seventh floor is smooth and problem-free.

I open the door to our suite, and the first thing I see is an extremely large bouquet of red roses.

"Oh, look at those," Crystal says.

I bury my face in the bouquet, inhaling the decadent scent. She snags the card before I have a chance to.

For my Queen,

I can't wait to make you my wife. Here's to a brilliant future.

All my love, Hunter.

"That was sweet," she says after she reads the sentiment aloud. "Especially after everything else that happened tonight."

"It really was," I agree, my insides warming at the thought of him making such an effort. Maybe this really is pre-wedding jitters, and everything will be fine. He was just thrown off by my taking the mini-series role during the wedding planning, and the short timeline to plan it—even if it was his idea—and tonight was just out of the ordinary oddness. I grab my phone and send him a quick text.

ME: The flowers are exquisite. Thank you. I can't wait for tomorrow!

I add a kissy face emoji at the end and hit send, feeling a renewed sense of optimism and excitement that I haven't felt for a while.

Crystal and I change into our pajamas, open a bottle of champagne from the mini bar, and snuggle into the big bed to watch an old Humphrey Bogart movie. We don't have any plans tonight other than to relax, so this is perfect.

"Thank you for taking time away from your family to be with me." I hug her as I say this, suddenly very grateful that she's here with me.

"You are my family, babe." She kisses my cheek.

"I know. I mean your other family."

"I know what you meant." She smiles. "You're important to me, you're my person. When you need me, I'm here. Michael understands that."

"I love you, C."

"Love you back, T."

I don't remember what time I fell asleep, but I wake up feeling refreshed, despite the amount of champagne we drank last night, both at the dinner and here at the hotel.

Crystal is still sleeping, so I slide from the bed and step into the other room to order room service. The roses from Hunter greet me in the morning light—they truly are stunning—making me smile.

I realize I never heard back from him last night after I thanked him. I check my phone to see if I missed anything.

Nope.

I order coffee and juice, along with some fruit and yogurt. Angela and Maisey will be here soon. When Si arrives in a couple hours with our dresses, it's bound to get chaotic between getting ready and any last-minute details we may need to take care of. So, I indulge in these last few moments of quiet and solitude. By this time tomorrow, I'll be a married woman.

A knock on the door startles me from my ruminations, and when I answer, I'm surprised to see that it's room service already. They set everything up and I pour myself a cup of coffee before I go wake Crystal. She stumbles out of the bedroom before I have a chance. Her hair is a bed-head mess and her eyes barely open.

"Is that coffee I smell?"

I hand her the cup I just poured and point out the cream and sugar.

"You're a goddess. I think I'm hungover."

"I feel fine."

"That's because you're running on adrenaline. It will hit you later. You just wait."

"Maybe." I smile, feeling smug, because today is going to be an amazing day. "You'll be happy to know I've got mimosas coming in an hour or so. Maybe that will help your head."

"Thank god. We aren't as young as we used to be, Tabby. I can't party like that anymore."

"Didn't we fall asleep by eleven o'clock?"

"Exactly," she says and I laugh.

26

PAX

I wake up on Gregor's couch in a panic.

"G!"

He pokes his head around the corner from his kitchen. "Yo." He's wearing an apron over his t-shirt and sweatpants. It's white and black with ruffles around the edges and a big bow at the top.

"Nice apron," I scoff.

"Don't judge. My niece, Taylor, picked it out for me. It's my favorite. And, if I'm wearing the apron, it means I'm cooking."

Breakfast does sound good. And Gregor is a fantastic chef.

Focus, Pax.

"I've made a decision—I can't let Tabs marry Douche Dippycock."

Gregor nods, a serious look on his face. "Pretty sure that's happening today, my man."

"Okay. Okay." I stand and start to pace his living and dining room scratching my head, still in my t-shirt and boxers from the night before. "Well, I need a plan to stop it!"

"Hmmm, okay."

"How can you be so calm?"

"Not sure this will work."

"What will work?"

"Our plan."

"What plan?"

"The one we don't have yet."

"That doesn't even make sense, dude."

"It's not like we've got a lot of options. And all hinge on whether she decides to marry him. You can't force her not to. My thought is you call her and hope she'll talk to you."

"No, that's no good."

"Why is that no good?"

"I don't know. It seems impersonal or something."

"Okay, you could interrupt the wedding right when the guy asks if anyone objects to the union."

"Nah, that's too Mrs. Robinson."

"She's not the one who interrupted the wedding. Dustin Hoffman did. And it was so he could steal Mrs. Robinson's daughter."

"You're just proving my point, man."

"That doesn't prove your—"

"Focus, G. I need a plan that will work."

He shrugs. "Go see her before the wedding then."

"Go see her? In person?"

"How else will you stop her from marrying him?"

"Good point."

"Eat breakfast first, because it's almost ready and it's the most important meal of the day. You don't want to go on an empty stomach and get distracted."

"Good point. Okay, the wedding starts at four o'clock, right?"

He laughs. "Right."

"Are you making fun of me?"

"Yes." He hands me a plate half-filled with some sort of omelet and potatoes.

"Dick." I take a seat and start eating. "This is really good, G," I say, my mouth only partially full.

He thrusts his chin in response and takes a seat across the table from me. His own plate is near overflowing with the largest omelet I've ever seen.

I start talking my thoughts aloud. "Okay, so I go see her in person."

He nods.

"Do I go see her before the wedding, or should I really do one of those interrupting things when the minister asks if anyone objects?"

He shrugs, and takes sip of his coffee, washing down a mouthful of food.

"What if they don't do that part of the wedding? Then I can't object. That's not going to work."

He shakes his head.

I take a few more bites before continuing, "You were right before. The only option is to talk to her before the thing even starts. Fuck, what if she won't talk to me?"

He scrunches his lips as though thinking about it.

"Then I know for certain how she feels."

He smiles, but it's weak at best.

I take the final bite of my breakfast. "Okay, I'm gonna take off. Shower. Get Tabs some flowers . . . wait, no there will already be a million flowers there, that's cheesy."

I take my dishes to the sink and rinse them before putting them in his dishwasher, then order a Lyft. "Maybe I'll get her some chocolate? No, that's even worse."

My pants from the night before are laid out over the back of the couch, which had to have been Gregor's doing because I know I left them crumpled on the floor when I took them off. Just like I do at home. "What do I get her, G? And am I proposing? Or just telling her not to marry him? Do I want to marry her again?"

I finish dressing and tie my shoes, head into the bathroom to finger brush my teeth, then pocket my wallet and cell phone and make a beeline for the front door, stopping before opening it to turn back toward him. "I mean, I guess I do want to marry her if I don't want anyone else to, right? Shit, maybe I'll just get her . . . oh, I know, I'll find her ring from when we were married and give that to her. That's romantic, right? Okay, I'm taking off. Wish me luck. Good talk!"

Traffic getting through downtown is hideous and it takes forever to get to the ferry terminal. By the time I make it home, it's been over two hours.

Eleven forty-eight a.m.

I have four hours to find the ring, shower, dress, figure out what I'm going to say to Tabatha to make sure she doesn't marry this guy, get to the Cascadian House, and stop the wedding. No problem.

Twelve twenty-two p.m.

I thought for fucking sure the ring was in my safe, but it's not. Which makes me wonder if it's in the safe deposit box at the bank. Which is back in downtown Seattle. Although, I have to go back to downtown to catch the ferry to the Cascadian House anyway. So, I need to get dressed, get back to Seattle, get the ring, and get the girl.

One thirty-three p.m.

I missed the one-thirty ferry by three minutes. The next one isn't until two o'clock. Which, at first, caused some panic. But, as I think about it, that should be fine. Then I'm back in Seattle by two-thirty, get to the bank, get back to the ferry terminal and over to the Cascadian House by four o'clock. No sweat.

Five minutes past two o'clock.

Okay, I have thirty uninterrupted minutes to sit and draft a speech worthy of changing Tabby's mind and convince her that we aren't such a bad match after all. Actually, I should be more positive than that. I need to convince her we are a great match.

I make a list.

<u>Reasons Tabs and I are a great match.</u>

1. The sex is fucking fantastic.

2. ~~We get along.~~

2. ~~Compatibility~~

2. Sexual compatibility

Wait, isn't that the same thing as saying the sex is good?

Shit.

This isn't gonna work.

Two fifteen p.m.

<u>Reasons Tabs and I are a great match.</u>

1. The sex is fucking fantastic.

2. ~~We get along.~~

2. ~~Compatibility~~

2. ~~Sexual compatibility~~

2. We know each other (really know deep down, not just stupid shit like favorite song or color).

Two twenty-five p.m.

<u>Reasons Tabs and I are a great match.</u>

1. The sex is fucking fantastic.

2. ~~We get along.~~

2. ~~Compatibility~~

2. ~~Sexual compatibility~~

2. We know each other (really know deep down, not just stupid shit like favorite song or color).

I'm stuck. This is the dumbest fucking idea I've ever had. She's never going to agree to marry me and not Hunter. Hell, I can't even convince *myself* this is a good idea.

<u>Reasons Tabs and I are a great match.</u>

1. The sex is fucking fantastic.

2. ~~We get along.~~

2. ~~Compatibility~~

2. ~~Sexual compatibility~~

2. We know each other (really know deep down, not just stupid shit like favorite song or color).

3. I love her and promise to spend the rest of my life bringing a smile to her face every day.

This is the best I can come up with. If this doesn't do it, nothing will, and I was never getting her back anyway. Hopefully the ring will push her over the edge to my side.

Three ten p.m.

I start walking back to the ferry terminal. The ring is not in the safe deposit box. I have no fucking idea where it is. I try to play a game with my brain and think of another place it could possibly be with each step I take. By the time I reach the block where the terminal is, I'm still coming up empty. I'm sure I would have put it back in the box, and then put the box somewhere meaningful . . .

Fuck. My. Life.

I remember where it is.

I was upset when she gave it back to me. To say the least. I had saved a lot of money for that ring, to make sure it would make a statement in Hollywood. At least as big a statement as I could afford. I used part cash and then spread the rest across three credit cards. I hadn't even finished paying it off when we divorced. So, one night after copious amounts of alcohol, I had the bright idea of putting it somewhere I would never want to unearth it from. I wrapped the ring in plastic and buried it in a pile of the neighbor's dog's poo. Then quadruple bagged the poo and stuck it in the back of my freezer. Which, at the time, was the most meaning I could give any representation of our prior union.

How could I forget about that?

Idiot.

Not that it would have thawed in time.

I can't tell her where it is.

I have to do this without a ring.

Three twenty-five p.m.

I make it back to the ferry terminal with five minutes to spare, and jog down the gateway to enter.

"Invitation, please?" A guy with a clipboard stands at the ferry entrance, holding out his hand.

"You mean my ticket?" I ask.

"No, your wedding invitation. Tickets have been taken care of."

"Oh, I don't have an invitation. I just need to get to the island."

"Can't take this ferry without an invitation."

"What do you mean I can't take this ferry? It's a public ferry. You can't stop me from taking it."

He points to a big sign I had failed to notice prior.

Today's Three-Thirty Ferry Reserved for Private Event. Invitation Required.

Fuck!

"When's the next ferry?"

"Four o'clock."

"I can't wait until four. That's too late. I need to get there before four."

"Sorry, sir, I can't help you. Please step aside, a line is forming behind you."

I turn and see that a few people are waiting behind me. All have invitations with them.

Shit!

I walk to the end of the line and slide in next to two women, both pretty, one tall and one not. "You ladies wouldn't want to take me to this wedding, would you?"

"What?" the tall one asks.

"Do you want to take me to this wedding? I can be a fun date."

The line advances. And it wasn't long to begin with. They are now third from the invitation checker.

"Why would we do that," the short one asks.

"It's extremely important that I get there before it starts."

"Isn't everyone supposed to be there before it starts?" the tall one asks, laughing.

"Well, yes." I look down at my feet and shake my head, advancing with them in the line to second from the invitation checker. "Listen," I start. "There is a woman who will be there, and it's imperative that I talk to her."

"Why don't you just talk to her after?" the short one asks.

We are next in line.

"That will be too late," I say, taking a deep breath and an even deeper chance. "It's the bride I need to see. I have to tell her I love her before she makes the biggest mistake of her life."

"Ohmigod, that's so sweet," both girls enthuse. "How romantic."

We make it to the invitation checker. The tall girl hands over their invitation.

"Identification, please," the invitation checker asks.

What? How did I miss that? He checks the IDs of both girls and ushers them through.

"He's with us," the short one says as they pass. I pull out my ID and hand it to him. He flips through his pages and hands it back to me.

"You aren't on the list, sorry." He looks up. "And you don't have an invitation. I already told you, buddy. Get lost."

"You don't understand," I start to say, just as the ferry whistle booms and the vessel begins to move away from us. The girls wave to me from the departing ferry.

"Good luck," one of them yells.

I'm tempted to do one of those running jumps, but there doesn't seem to be much of a landing pad on the other side.

The invitation checker looks at me, points back to the private event sign, and says, "You can go at four o'clock."

I immediately call Gregor to tell him what's happened. I may need him to intervene for me.

Straight to voicemail.

I text him.

ME: Call me. 9-1-1.

27

TABATHA

I haven't heard from Hunter all day. Which surprises me and doesn't at the same time. I thought for sure he would have responded to my text about the roses. It was such a romantic and thoughtful gesture on his part. I expected it would reopen the lines of communication between us. But now, with only fifteen minutes before the ceremony, I know that I won't talk to him until I meet him at the end of the aisle.

Which I've determined I am okay with.

The girls and I have had a fantastic day and I'm still feeling positive about everything. We relaxed most of the morning with mimosas and massages. Maisey joined us in the early afternoon when we all ate a light lunch with salads and cucumber water, then a little more champagne. Not so much that we were drunk, or even close, but just enough to keep the edge off.

We all look amazing, thanks to Maisey, who just left to go downstairs to look for Gregor. I check my reflection one more time in the mirror to make sure everything is in place. My hair is in a semi-loose updo, with a few strands falling down around my face, and the rest looking almost like it's about to fall down. Even though it's not going anywhere, because Maisey is a genius. She weaved some light gold thread pieces through my hair that glint in the light and match the dress.

My makeup is a fresh and natural kind of dewy look, with some gold highlighting to complement the dress. A soft pink gloss on my lips and just enough on my eyes to make them pop. The overall look is a glam boho-chic. In truth, I've never felt more beautiful.

"You look incredible," Crystal says.

"Thank you, I feel good in this dress." I turn to look at both Crystal and Angela. "Oh, you guys look so beautiful!"

"Yeah, I'm pretty sure I didn't look this good on my own wedding day," Crystal says, turning from the side to front and back again in the full-length mirror, checking her entire reflection out.

"You ready for this?" Angela asks.

There's a quick knock on the door, and it opens before I can say anything. Liza pokes her head in. "Ladies, are we ready to head down?"

I ignore the lead ball that drops in my stomach and nod in response.

"I'll see you down there in five," she says as she backs away and closes the door.

I take a deep breath to calm my insides. I've felt good about this all day, I'm not going to let some last-minute jitters get the best of me. Hunter has made—is making—a huge effort, and I appreciate that more than I can say. The least I can do is respond in kind.

I grab my clutch and make sure everything I will need for the day is inside—compact, blotting tissues, lip gloss, mints—and make a snap decision to leave my phone in the room. Because what could I possibly need it for? Everyone I would ever need to call will be with me.

Angela picks up my bouquet and hers, and Crystal helps with my train. We make our way down the long hall to the elevator. Everything is quiet. I'm not sure why I expected otherwise. The silence is calming.

The attendant is working the elevator again. And, like last night, it works smoothly with no issues at all.

Amazing.

I shake my head, thinking of when Pax and I got stuck in it all those weeks ago. A pang shoots through my heart. If the divorce didn't cement that Pax and I will never have a future together again, today certainly will. I'm moving on. Marrying someone else. I probably wouldn't even be thinking about Pax if it weren't for the whole Matthew Hanhauser debacle.

Would I?

I won't lie, there are definitely times I wish things had worked out between the two of us.

"What'd you say?" Crystal asks, leaning around my right shoulder from behind, where she's still holding the train of my dress so it doesn't drag.

"Who me? Nothing," I say, craning my head back to see her.

Her brow furrows. "Really? I could have sworn you said something about *Pax*." She whispers his name when she says it, but everything else at a normal volume.

"Nope." I shake my head. Because, no way did I say that out loud.

"Are you relieved he won't be here?" she whispers back.

"Why are you whispering?" I ask, since she and Angela know pretty much everything there is to know about me and Pax. As well as me and Hunter.

Crystal jerks her head toward the elevator attendant, who I doubt is paying us any attention. I nod in response anyway and whisper back, "I am glad he won't be here." Even though I'm not one hundred percent sure that's true. "I would have felt self-conscious saying my vows to Hunter in front of him."

That part is absolutely true.

The elevator (finally) reaches the floor where the ceremony and reception will take place and the attendant opens the gate first and then door, stepping to the side and motioning us through with his arm. "Ladies." He nods in acknowledgement.

"Here, let me help with the train," Angela says. She takes half from Crystal and we move as one unit through the elevator door opening, only to hear—

Rip.

I turn suddenly and hear it again.

Rip.

"Ohmigod! Ohmigod! Tabby don't move! Your dress is stuck on the gate," Angela cries.

I freeze.

My dress is stuck on the gate.

My dress is stuck on the gate!

Between them, Angela and Crystal get it unstuck quickly, but the damage is extensive. A long, jagged tear runs through the bottom of the dress, cutting through tulle and the delicate gold floral embroidery. We step into the hall, as far away from the elevator as possible.

That elevator is just plain evil!

Tears burn in my eyes. I try to blink them away, then clear my throat. "Set the train down and see if it's super noticeable."

They lay it down and Crystal fluffs it. I take a few steps forward and the bottom half of the ripped layer drags behind the rest of the dress.

Crystal bites at her nails. Angela covers her eyes and shakes her head.

"I can't walk down the aisle like this!" I cry.

"Can't walk down the aisle like what?" Liza approaches. "What happened?"

Thank god.

"Her dress got stuck on the elevator gate and ripped," Crystal says, her own tears forming.

"Let's see," Liza says. "Maybe it's not so bad."

I walk forward a few steps again so she can see the part that drags behind.

"Not a problem. We prepare for things such as this." Liza's voice is soothing as she speaks, making me feel a little better. "Go sit on the edge of that bench there. We'll prop the dress in the middle, and I'll sew it up."

"You'll sew it?" Angela confirms.

"Yep. It won't be perfect, but it will get her down the aisle."

I nod, tears abating, and settle myself on the bench. Crystal and Angela help to set the ripped part up for Liza to sew. Who, in the meantime, is barking into her headset, "Bridal gown snafu, get us an extra fifteen minutes . . . What do you mean? . . . Well, have you looked? . . . Then do that!"

"What's the matter?" I ask.

"Nothing for you to worry about, I promise. We have every-thing under control." She turns to Crystal. "Maybe you could go get a few glasses of champagne to enjoy while you wait. They have some in the kitchen." She points Crystal in the right direction and turns her attention back to my dress. The thread she's using is clear, almost invisible, and unless you know where to look, I don't think the tear will be noticeable at all.

I breathe a huge sigh of relief just as Crystal returns with the champagne, but still take a large sip of mine. Liza is almost finished sewing the dress. We are only running a few minutes late. Hunter will understand once I explain about the dress.

Everything is going to be okay.

28

PAX

Five minutes past four o'clock.

I mentally propel the ferry forward at a faster pace. Because the speed it's going is practically reverse, it's so slow. I text Gregor again, asking him to call me or text me, even though I don't have cell service in the middle of the sound and these shorter distance ferries don't offer Wi-Fi.

It makes me feel better, like I'm doing something. Then I resume pacing the deck and mentally propelling the vessel.

Four ten p.m.

I try to remember everything involved in a wedding ceremony. The guys walk up to the front, then they seat the family. The bride walks down the aisle . . .

I see two women on a nearby bench and approach them.

"Excuse me, I know this is a weird question, but what are the parts to a wedding ceremony? You know, like, in order?"

"What kind of ceremony?" the one on the right asks.

"What do you mean?" I ask back.

"Is it a Catholic ceremony with a service? Is it Jewish? Non-traditional? Simple with a Justice of the Peace?"

"I don't know," I yell. Then lower my voice to a more respectable level. "I'm not sure. Probably a normal ceremony with not a lot of special stuff thrown in."

The one on the left laughs. "Can I ask why you want to know this? Are you about to perform one and you forgot?" She looks around as though trying to find the service.

"No, I'm just trying to figure out how much time I have if it hasn't started yet."

"Are you late for your own wedding?" the one on the right asks. "You know they'll wait for you, right?" Both women laugh.

"I need to stop a wedding. And I want to make sure I'm not too late," I say, trying to temper my exasperation.

"Ohmigod, that's so romantic," the one on the left says. I'm kind of baffled as to why women think this is so romantic. It's basically an asshole move. Interrupting a sacred event that has nothing to do with you. Completely blindsiding the woman you want to be with you instead of the other guy. Then, if all goes well, force them to waste a fuck-ton of money that's bound to be non-refundable since you—I—waited until the do-or-die moment to take action. And run the risk of becoming a social pariah when the event has over six hundred people in attendance, like this one does.

"Okay," the one on the right starts. "The family gets seated first."

"Right," the one on the left says. "Then the guys walk up to the front, then the bridesmaids."

They tag team the processional and ceremony order until reaching the part where they walk back down the aisle, hand in hand, as man and wife.

"Great," I say. "Thank you." I turn to leave, then pivot back for one more question. "How long does all that usually take?"

They look at each other. "Twenty minutes," the one on the right says, at the same time the one on the left says, "At least half an hour, if not longer."

"Thank you!" I walk to the other end of the ferry. The end that will reach the dock first.

There's got to still be time. There just has to be.

Four seventeen p.m.

We are nearing the island and finally I have service, I dial Gregor again. This time, he answers.

"Dude, I was just about to call you. Where are you?"

"Am I too late?"

"No, it's hasn't even started yet."

"Oh, thank god. Why?"

"I don't know, they haven't told us anything. They walked the family down, and then the quartet just keeps playing music, just not the 'walk down the aisle' kind. The guys aren't even standing up front yet."

"Okay, good. This is gonna work, G. I can feel it!"

"Sending you positive vibes, brother. I gotta get back in. I'll put my phone on silent and try to text you if anything else happens. Damn guy has me up in the front with his family. I don't want to be disrespectful, you know?"

"Gregor, it doesn't matter how you act. You'll never have to see those people again. I am stopping this wedding."

"Okay, man." He laughs. "Whatever you say. See you soon."

I disconnect the call and watch greedily as the island grows closer.

Four twenty-one p.m.

I'm the first one off the ferry and sprinting to the taxi stands.

No taxis.

Okay. Try to catch my breath. No problem. I'll order a Lyft.

I pull up the app. Closest one is ten minutes away. Uber is thirteen minutes. Too long. Way too long.

Fuck.

I look around and see one of those stands where you can rent a motorized scooter through an app to ride around the island.

Perfect.

Four twenty-five p.m.

App is finally downloaded, payment secure, and I am pulling my scooter out of the rack and racing at full speed toward the Cascadian House.

Four twenty-six p.m.

I'm certain those little rascals for senior citizens move faster than these fucking scooters. I lean forward, hoping that will help the momentum.

Check the time. Four twenty-seven. Okay. Ten minutes ago, they hadn't even started the ceremony. So, even if everything began the second G and I hung up, it shouldn't be over yet.

I can do this. I have to be able to do this. There is no way I've gone through everything I have today just to have my plan fail. This is the moment in the movie when things fall magically into place, where the hero makes it in time and gets his girl.

I love Tabatha. We are meant to be together. The universe knows it. I will get there in time. She will agree with me. We will be together.

I swear the little scooter picks up speed just then.

Four thirty-one p.m.

I crash the scooter into the patch of grass in the middle of the circular drive of the Cascadian House and take off at a full sprint toward the front lobby, pausing only to ask the front desk which floor they are on.

"Eight," she says cheerfully. "I think you're a little late though."

I skid to a stop. "What do you mean?" I ask, panting.

"It started at four o'clock," she says.

I stopped for that? She doesn't know. *Jeez*, Pax.

I sprint toward the elevator bay, then remember my experience with Tabs when it stalled on us. I look toward the elevator. Then the stairs. Back at the elevator.

Pick one.

Deciding, I hit the stairs running, taking them two at a time.

29

TABATHA

Liza finishes sewing the bottom of the gown. You can hardly tell the rip is there, even if you look for it. At close inspection, you can see some of the flower halves are off-center, but other than that, it's perfect. And it only took her thirty minutes to do.

"Is Hunter upset?" I ask Liza as Crystal re-fluffs my train behind me, then gathers it again to walk down the hall to the ballroom.

"Upset?" She turns her mouth into her headset and brings her hand up to cover the other side. "Update, now!"

She holds her arm out to stop us at about twenty feet before the ballroom doors. "Uh-huh . . . Right . . . Where is it?"

I look at her questioningly. She doesn't meet my eye.

"What's wrong?" Crystal asks me, her voice low.

"I don't know," I whisper back.

Liza lowers her hand from the headset and looks down at the ground, her expression grim.

"Is everything okay?" I ask.

"Let's just give it a second," she says. Then, after a minute, she continues, "Maybe we should sit down." She gestures to another bench, this one directly across from the ballroom doors.

"Why? Won't that wrinkle my dress?" I ask.

"Probably," she says.

"Okay," I say, drawing the word out.

She clears her throat. "Hunter has a note he'd like you to read before the ceremony."

"Oh, that's sweet," I say.

"One of my assistants has it and is bringing it to us now."

"Okay," I say. "I'll just stay standing."

Liza nods in response, still not meeting my gaze.

Something's wrong.

I can hear someone coming up the marble stairs at a rapid pace, even from here at the other end of the hall, the footsteps are echoing off the stone. I turn and see a young girl racing toward us. She has a cream-colored envelope in her hand, which she passes to Liza once she reaches us.

Liza turns and hands it to me.

My name is scrolled across the front in Hunter's very tiny, very precise, handwriting.

I nudge the flap open with my index finger and pull the note out.

Liza turns away, giving me privacy.

Crystal crowds in to read over my shoulder.

Tabatha,

On what should have been our wedding day, I regret to inform you that I will not be in attendance. The changes to your persona are too numerous and too extreme for me to overlook. I will not spend my life second-guessing which version of you will greet me on a daily basis. Rest assured, I will absorb the expense of the day as originally planned. Since I executed the preparations on my own anyway, that shouldn't be a problem for you. As an aside, the roses from last night were organized prior to the rehearsal dinner. I failed to cancel them in time. They were not an apology, as you falsely assumed. Tell the guests whatever you would like. I will reach out personally to anyone whose impression of the events I see fit to correct.

Best,

Hunter

He will not be in attendance. To our wedding. Not in attendance. How can that be?

What am I feeling?

"Whoa," Crystal whispers.

"What does it say?" Angela asks.

My arm falls to my side, the note floating from my grip to the floor. Angela picks it up to read it herself.

"I'm so sorry, Tabatha," Liza says.

"You knew?" I ask her.

"I knew he was gone. I didn't know about the note until just now."

I'm in shock.

"You fixed my dress knowing he was gone?"

She nods, looking ashamed. "I'm sorry. I didn't know what else to do. I've never had this happen before."

"Neither have I!" I cry.

Angela pulls me into her arms and hugs me. "I'm so sorry, Tabby."

He left me.

Hunter left me.

"He left me," I whisper.

"I know, I'm so sorry, babe," Crystal says, hugging me from the other side, sandwiching me between them. They lead me to lean against the wall between two large potted plants. I hang my head and try to get a grip on the emotions I'm feeling.

I wait to feel heartbreak, but it doesn't come.

I'm not sad.

I feel, I don't know, almost lighter maybe? Is that relief? Am I relieved Hunter called it off? I think I am. As long as he did it, I don't have to. It's the coward's way out, that I know. But it allows me to continue to avoid it. I feel like a fifty-pound weight has been lifted off my shoulders, I could float through the rest of the day with no problem.

"I'll give you a minute," Liza says, heading for the ballroom and pulling the door open slowly. I want to tell her that it's okay. That I'm okay.

"*Stop*!" Heavy footsteps echo down the hall.

I look up, not able to see beyond the plant. Pax races into view, stopping himself with the handle of the closing door, his body swinging just past it, feet skidding on the floor.

"Pax?"

He turns to face me. "Tabs, oh thank god, don't go in there, please." He walks toward me, breathing heavily. "Shit. Give me a second to catch my breath." He hunches over, hands on his knees, gasping for air. "Pax?" I ask again.

He holds one finger up. "Eight flights of stairs," he wheezes.

I look at Crystal. She shrugs, then takes Angela's hand and the two step away to give us privacy. Pax straightens and comes to stand in front of me, taking each of my hands in his.

"I've been thinking about us," he starts.

"Us?"

He nods, then looks me up and down. "Wow. You are stunning. This dress . . . your hair . . . honest to god, Tabs, you take my breath away."

The walls around my heart, constructed to protect me from Pax, begin to crumble.

"He doesn't deserve you."

"He—"

"Hell, Tabs, I don't think I deserve you either, but I woke up this morning knowing that I had to give it one more shot. I had to see if I could convince you not to marry this guy. I want us to try again. You and me, we belong together. I know that deep in my soul. We fit, Tabs. And before, with the divorce, that never should have happened. We were just young and stupid."

I raise my eyebrows at him.

"Okay, I was young and stupid." I smile. He continues, "I should have tried harder to talk to you, to find out what you were feeling, and I should have admitted I let myself get manipulated. And I don't know if it was seeing you again, when you're planning a wedding to someone else, that stirred up long buried emotions and something clicked. But it did, so here I am, asking you to take a chance with me. I think if you open your mind and let the past go for just a minute, you'll realize that you and me, we're right. We're *good*."

I remain silent, waiting to see if he'll continue.

"Here, wait, I made a list." He pats his front pants pockets, then digs in the interior pockets of his suit coat before pulling out a folded piece of paper that looks a lot like a torn piece from a tourism flyer and hands it to me.

I open it.

<u>Reasons Tabs and I are a great match.</u>

1. The sex is fucking fantastic.

2. ~~We get along.~~

2. ~~Compatibility~~

2. ~~Sexual compatibility~~

2. We know each other (really know deep down, not just stupid shit like favorite song or color).

3. I love her and promise to spend the rest of my life bringing a smile to her face every day.

I laugh. I can't help it. He crossed out compatibility. And that we get along. Very honest of him. I raise my eyes to meet his. "Out of curiosity, why did you cross out sexual compatibility?"

"Oh, because it's basically the same as the sex being fucking fantastic and I didn't want the bulk of the list to be just about sex. Because we aren't just about sex, Tabs. We are about so much more, and even if you don't believe me now, just give me a chance to prove it to you, please?"

His eyes wide and pleading, handsome face so hopeful.

Still, I wait a moment before saying anything.

"He isn't coming," I say softly.

"Who isn't coming? What do you mean?"

"Hunter isn't coming. He called it off." I point to the note on the floor, where Angela returned it after reading. Pax looks down in disgust.

"He wrote you a note to tell you he wasn't coming? To call off your wedding?" he asks, confirming what I just told him.

I nod.

"My god, Tabs. Are you okay?" He palms my cheek, his expression full of concern.

I laugh again. "You spend all this effort telling me why he's wrong for me, including making a list, then you ask me if I'm okay that he dumped me?"

Pax runs a hand down the front of his face, his other hand still holding on to mine. "Yeah, I guess that is kind of fucked up. But, yes. I want you to be happy. I just don't think it's going to happen with him."

"For what it's worth, I don't either," I tell him.

His eyes light. "You don't?"

I shake my head. "I had my doubts anyway. Then something happened that I thought changed everything, and it turned out I was wrong. But I knew for sure when I read the note he sent."

I hold his gaze before I share this next part with him, wanting him to see it in my eyes and on my face, so that he knows for certain. "I didn't feel sad after I read the note. My first emotion was relief. After that, it was hurt pride because he left me and not the other way around. I've known for a while that it wasn't going to work, that I didn't feel about him the way I should."

"Why were you going through with it then?" Pax asks.

I let out a deep breath and look away for a moment. "Good question." I meet his eyes. "It wouldn't have lasted long if we had gone through with it. I know that. But I think a part of me figured I had to follow through with my commitment to him. Even though I knew I wasn't in love with him."

"Not your smartest move, Tabs," Pax says, stepping in closer, his arms moving to bracket me on either side. His hips pin me against the wall.

"I know," I say softly.

"You don't love him?"

I shake my head.

"And you aren't sad about it?"

I shake my head again, a small smile playing on my face.

"What do you think about my argument where you and I are concerned?"

"It has merit," I say breathlessly, our faces barely an inch apart, my heart beats rapidly. I can't believe he's here. That he's done this. It's crazy, but incredible. I'm scared and exhilarated. And when I see reflected in his eyes what I know is shining from mine, I realize it's always been Pax. He's always owned my heart, no matter where we've been or what we've done.

His eyes drop to my lips. My tongue darts out to wet them and his pupils dilate.

"I do think we need to know for sure whether that sexual compatibility part still holds true," I say.

"Even though I crossed it out?" he asks.

"It was still a good point."

"It was, wasn't it?"

I nod.

He leans in, his lips ghosting across mine. My breath catches, my head dizzies, knees weaken. I reach up and grasp his lapels to steady myself.

"I still love you," he says, his lips barely moving against mine. "I never stopped."

"Pax," I breathe his name.

"Fuck, Tabs," he groans as he claims my mouth with his. My lips conform to his as though from muscle memory. He moves a hand to the back of my neck, his thumb wrapping around toward the front, holding my head in place as he takes what he needs and gives what I crave. My hands skate across his wide chest and up around his neck, one tangling in his short hair, the other trying to pull myself even closer.

I want to crawl inside him. I can't get enough. I feel like my world has been righted and turned upside down at the same time. His tongue duels with mine, making my head light and my pulse race. My breath mingling with his as he continues to assault my mouth in the very best way. It's been years since I've been kissed like this. The sad truth is that Pax was probably last man to kiss me properly.

His hard length presses against my stomach as he works his knee between my legs, my skirt voluminous but the material thin, so I feel every inch of him. His hand runs lightly down my collarbone, continuing down my side, his fingers grazing against my bare skin, making me shiver.

"Ahem." Someone clears their throat loudly from behind Pax. He slowly separates his lips from mine and takes a step back, looking at me to make sure I'm okay. I nod in response and he moves to the side, his arm snaking around my waist, so we can face this together.

30

PAX

I'm not sure who I thought would be interrupting us, but it wasn't Gregor.

"Sorry to interrupt, man. But people are kinda freaking the fuck out in there. Rumors are flying and I thought maybe I'd come check and see if we should say something? I mean, I'm happy to make any announcement on your behalf. And Liza is pacing at the back of the room, close to tears. So . . ."

"Ohmigod!" Tabby's face turns bright red. "I forgot about the people. Jesus." She turns to me. "What do I say? What do I do? Do I just tell them they can go home? What about the reception? Oh shit. This is such a mess!"

I take her hand in mine and squeeze it. "Hey, don't worry. We got this. I'll go with you to make the announcement. This isn't on you. He's the one who walked out. You didn't cause this, he did. Okay?"

She nods. "Okay." Then she squeezes my hand back, gently.

Gregor opens the ballroom doors for us. Hand in hand, Tabatha and I walk into the massive room, which is much larger than I remember. Or maybe it just feels that way because we are flanked on either side by thirty rows of ten people each, all with eyes glued to us. The string quartet stops playing "Canon in D" and begins to play the wedding march. Gregor, who was returning to his seat via a side aisle, instead goes straight to the musicians and motions for them to stop playing.

The room fills with silence as we make our way down the aisle toward the flower-filled stage where the ceremony was to take place. The aisle seems to go on forever, blanketed by a white runner that crackles under our feet as we go. Huge bouquets of red flowers sit in stands at the ends of each row, in stark contrast with the white covered chairs. Large black bows secure the chair covers at each seat back. And everywhere I look, ten times as many eyes blink back at me.

The closer we get, the tighter Tabatha squeezes my hand. Whispers begin to bounce back and forth, filling the space as the guests try to determine what is happening. At this point, the wedding was supposed to have started forty-five minutes ago. I notice a number of seats at the front on the groom's side are already empty, so he must have told a few close friends.

We climb the steps to the microphone and turn to face the crowd. Tabatha straightens her back and raises her head. I'm so fucking proud of her right now for facing this head-on after Wimpy the DoucheCock left her stranded. It can't be easy.

"What do I say?" she whispers from the side of her mouth.

"We got this," I say. "Okay, just repeat after me."

She nods and then begins to repeat the words that I feed her.

"Thank you all for coming today. I'm sure you're probably wondering why I'm standing up here with this guy and not the other one."

She turns to look at me after she says that, a *what the fuck* look on her face.

"Just go with it," I mumble.

She rolls her eyes and turns back to the guests. "The other guy decided not . . ." she repeats, then faces me again. "I'm not saying that," she hisses to me. "I can use his name and so can you."

Then to the restless onlookers, she says, "Hunter and I have decided not to marry." Gasps ring out through the room.

She holds her hands up in an attempt to silence them and continues to parrot what I say. "I apologize for the inconvenience and the confusion. In an effort to make it up to you, I've decided to marry this guy over here. If anyone wants to stick around for that, services will commence in just a second . . . wait, what?"

She spins to face me. "Pax, what the hell? You can't just highjack my wedding."

"Why not?" I ask.

"Because." Her neck strains with the angle of her head as her eyes bug.

"I think it's the perfect solution," I say. "Everything is already here. I mean, the monograms are all wrong, of course, and I doubt I will like any of the gifts that Simplecock picked out, but I know for certain the cake is good. Wait, he did pick the good cake, right? The one with the—"

"Pax. Stop! Just stop."

"What, babe?" I put my hands on either side of her waist, wanting them to be somewhere on her.

Liza approaches from the side, seeming to have finally gotten herself back together. "Tabatha, would you like me to send people in to the reception?" she asks.

"Yes," I say, answering for her, at the same time Tabatha says, "No!"

"Why not?" I ask at the same time Liza says, "Okay."

A decent chunk of the crowd is still waiting in their seats. They're either wondering what is really going to happen next and if a wedding will indeed take place, or, my guess, if Tabby is going to open the bar.

"Either way, you should open the bar," I tell Tabby.

She waves a hand at Liza. "Fine, open the bar." Liza leaves to do her bidding.

News that the bar is opening races through the crowd and within minutes, the room is empty with the exception of me and Tabby on the stage, Gregor and Maisey still in their second-row seats, and Crystal and Angela standing in the back.

I take her face in my hands. "Tabatha, I want to be with you. Day and night, from here on out. I want to marry you, grow old with you, kiss you until I can't breathe, fight with you, make love to you, all of it. I'm serious about that."

She reaches her hands up and covers mine with hers. "I know you do. And I want that too. I think. But I can't just flip and do that today. An hour ago, I was supposed to be standing up here with another man."

"I never would have let that happen," I tell her.

She laughs.

It wasn't supposed to be funny.

"You said you think you want that too. What do you mean?" I ask.

"I need time to think. I can't just rush from one situation into another."

"I'm not a situation," I argue.

"I know, I didn't mean it in a bad way—"

"What other way would there be?" I ask.

"Please, can we not fight?"

"Tabs, I told you I love you. I want to marry you. We kissed." I turn and point to the hallway. "Right out there, just a few minutes ago. And it was amazing. I know from that kiss that you want the same things. You can't tell me otherwise."

"I know. And that kiss was great. I need to know that I'm not doing this with you just because it's not happening with Hunter. Does that make sense?"

"No!" I'm upset. I'm trying not to be, but I am. Earlier, all I'd thought about was making sure she didn't marry Pimplecock today. But then, as soon as I realized that she and I could just marry here and now, it became all about that for me. A two-fold mission that I'm now desperate to accomplish.

"What are you saying?" I ask. "Do you not want to get married at all?"

"It's not that. It's just . . . look, can I just have some space, please? I need time to think. And I need to do that without you." Her eyes plead with me, tears falling down her cheeks.

"Okay." I nod, my chest thick, my breath shallow. I sound agreeable. But inside I'm dying. I want to beg her not to waste any more time by not being together. I want to shake her and make her realize how wrong she is for wanting space.

She rushes back down the aisle where Crystal and Angela are waiting. They each wrap an arm around her and lead her from the room.

Gregor appears at my side, claps a hand on my shoulder and asks, "You okay, man?"

I clear my throat. "Yup," I say.

He looks at me in disbelief.

"Hey, she didn't say no outright. She just said she needed time. And space. Without me." I sound optimistic. So much so, I think Gregor almost believes me.

So why do I feel so desolate?

31

TABATHA

The girls and I head back to the suite Crystal and I shared last night.

"Wait for me!" I turn and see Maisey coming toward us, a bottle of champagne in each hand. "I thought we could use these," she says, smiling.

We take the elevator down a few floors, again no issues, and settle into the room. I flop face down on the bed, no longer caring if my dress gets wrinkled or not.

"Did I hear right," Crystal starts. "Pax wanted you to marry him right now, using yours and Hunter's wedding?"

"Yes," I groan, my face buried in a pillow.

"That's so romantic," Angela says, pouring us all a glass of champagne and passing them around. She forces me to sit up so I can take my glass. Maisey nods in agreement.

"Really?" I ask. "You don't think it's kind of demented?" I drink down half my glass and hold it out for a refill.

"Not at all," Angela says.

"It's kind of like that movie," Maisey says. "The one with Reese Witherspoon and McDreamy? *Sweet Home Alabama.* Oh, except she was still married to the other guy. He was cute."

"Oh! Maybe you and Pax are still secretly married," Crystal says.

"Mmm, that would be Josh Lucas, the other guy in *Sweet Home Alabama.* He's hot. I'd do him," Angela says.

"You'd do a lot of guys," I tell Angela. "That's not a discriminatory list."

"Touché, bitch," she responds, raising her glass toward me.

I turn to Crystal. "We are definitely not still married," I say, gulping from my now full glass.

"Don't make me sound like a slut, you tramp. And it's not like this is coming out of the blue," Angela says to me. "You guys were married before."

"Takes a tramp to know a tramp," I mumble back to her. "I know we were married before, but I'm not sure that helps." I kick off my shoes and stretch my toes. Angela and I often call each other names. It's a show of endearment and not malicious like it sounds.

"He's still in love with you, you know." Maisey blushes slightly as she sips her champagne. "Gregor told me."

"Pax told me that too." I sigh.

"Do you love him?" Crystal asks, crawling onto the bed with me. We both situate ourselves against the headboard, while

Angela and Maisey take up residence at the foot of the bed. It feels like a slumber party, minus the slumber part.

"I'm not sure I ever stopped," I whisper in response to Crystal's question, tears pooling. Again. I rest my head on her shoulder and she reaches up to stroke my hair. "I don't want to cry about this. I'm being lame. What's wrong with me?"

"Nothing," Maisey says. "And you aren't being lame, you are a woman in charge of her emotions, who isn't afraid to feel them."

"Hoo-rah!" Crystal raises her glass.

"So, what's the problem? If you still love him, you may as well marry him. Big deal." Angela fills all our glasses again. It's a good thing Maisey brought two bottles.

"It's weird!" I fling a hand in the air to enunciate my point. "Right?"

"What's weird about it?" Crystal asks.

"For one, I was supposed to marry someone else today!"

"So?" Angela asks.

"Am I making a big deal out of nothing?" I ask Crystal and Maisey. "Since this one over here"—I gesture to Angela—"seems to think that marrying someone else is no big thing."

Both heads nod back at me.

"So, what do I do?"

"This might just be me, but I say go get your guy," Crystal says.

"Just like that?" I ask.

"Just like that," Angela says.

"Hell, yes," Maisey adds.

Go get my guy. Just like that. Hell, yes. Well, shit, maybe I'm *the only weird thing here.*

I drain my glass. "Okay. How?"

Crystal hands me my phone from the nightstand. "You could start by calling, find out where he's at, and then go talk to him. No pressure, just a conversation."

"Okay." My hands shake as I pull up Pax's number. It used to be first in my favorites list. Now it's buried in the "Bs" under his last name.

I hesitate before hitting the button to connect. "I'm scared."

"Of?" the girls chorus.

"I don't know. Being rejected? Being happy? Having it work out? Having it not?"

"Pfft." Crystal waves a hand in the air. "That's normal. Don't even worry about that. It's called doubt. It's what we mortals feel when making a decision. You fancy pants people wouldn't know of such things." I laugh and hit the button to connect the call. Then hold my breath. It goes straight to voicemail. I disconnect before leaving a message and tell the girls as much.

"I'll call Gregor," Maisey says.

"And say what?" I ask.

"I'll just find out if he knows where Pax is."

I nod in agreement and she makes the call.

"Hey, it's Maisey," she says. Then she giggles. "I was just wondering if you knew where Pax is . . . oh . . . oh no, where? . . . do you think . . . okay . . . thank you."

She turns to us. "Gregor just put him on the ferry back to Seattle. And he thinks Pax is going straight from there to the other ferry that'll take him back to Port Orchard and his house after that. He says that Pax was doing okay, but not great. And that he wanted to be alone."

"Is that good?" I ask.

"I think so," Maisey says. "I mean, he's just going home. You know where that is, right?"

"No," I say. "He bought that place after we divorced and moved back here. I was still living in Los Angeles. I have no idea where he lives."

"Okay," Maisey says. "Coming right up." She calls Gregor again and gets Pax's address for me. We know there isn't another ferry for at least a half an hour, so there's a little time to finish our champagne. Even though part of me wants to go pace on the ferry dock waiting for the next one to depart.

"So, what's the story with Gregor," Angela asks Maisey, who in turn blushes a delightful shade of pink.

"I've never met anyone like him," she gushes. "I mean, he's just so nice."

I almost choke on my champagne at that. But then I remember I'm giving Igor BigJerksy another chance, starting by no longer calling him Igor BigJerksy. And that's in large part due to how happy Gregor seems to make Maisey. Even though it's only been a week.

Maisey keeps talking. "He's completely okay with my daughter. Even though I won't introduce them for a while. And he's funny. Smart. Charming."

"We still talking about Gregor?" I joke.

Maisey laughs. "He said that you guys have a checkered past."

"That's one way to put it," Crystal adds.

"I'm going to have to get along with him if Pax and I get back together," I say.

"Especially if he and I start dating." Maisey blushes. "You and I are friends now, you can't take it back. You're stuck with me."

I smile at her. "I wouldn't have it any other way."

"When you and Pax get back together," Angela says to me.

"Huh?" I ask her.

"You said if you and Pax get back together. I'm saying when you do."

I nod in agreement, grab my wrap and clutch, and put my heels back on. "Is it too early to head to the ferry?"

"Not at all," Crystal says. "If nothing else, it will make us feel like we are doing something productive."

"Will you guys come with me?"

"Of course," Angela says. "But if shit gets all touchy-feely between you two, I'm out of there."

"Ditto," Crystal says.

I laugh.

Maisey gets a text. "Gregor says he'll meet us at the ferry dock if we want, but that he's not telling Pax what you are doing."

"Is it better if it's a surprise?" I ask.

"Yes," the girls say in unison.

And with that, we head out. Three badass chicks and a jilted bride, all dressed to the nines and on a mission to get the guy for the girl.

32

PAX

The ferry ride back to Seattle took a hell of a lot longer than the allotted twenty minutes they claim, I'm sure of it. I'm also certain full years of my life passed before we reached land. Then I still had to wait for the ferry to take me in the other direction to Port Orchard. Fucking waterlogged state with no bridges. Normal places have bridges. Washington has ferries.

I pace the walkway, waiting to dock.

Once we dock, I pace the terminal, waiting to board.

Then I go back to pacing a different walkway, waiting to dock again somewhere else.

Because sometimes life is just one big vicious circle while you try to get to your destination. Not that I have anywhere to be. I don't even have plans for when I get home. I figure I'll sit on my deck with a bottle of Macallan and my camera and see if I can't make sense of things for a while. Or at least until the Macallan dulls life enough to force me to sleep.

It's not like she said no.

This is what I tell myself so I don't jump overboard into the icy waters of the North Pacific Ocean. She said she needed space.

So why am I so distraught over this? It wasn't a no. It was a *not right now*. What kind of man am I that I can't wait a couple of days to see what my woman wants?

She may not be your woman.

Of course she's my woman.

Maybe she's her own woman.

That's bullshit. We belong together.

Doesn't mean she'll come back to you.

I tell myself to fuck off so I can stop the argument ping-ponging back and forth in my head. And spend the rest of the ferry ride reciting Seabirds stats to myself to stay occupied.

10-6-0, 2nd NFC division. Lost Wild Card to Dallas 22-24. 26.8 points. 353.3 yards. 193.3 pass yards. 160 rush yards.

This is bullshit. It doesn't matter what I do to try and keep my brain occupied, underneath it all will still be Tabatha trying to break through to the forefront of my thoughts.

Stay positive.

I'll give her a few days and maybe give her a call, see where she's at with everything.

My phone buzzes with a text.

My heart leaps.

Please be Tabby. Please be Tabby.

It's Gregor.

G-MAN: Hey, Maisey bailed on me to be with the girls. I was thinking I'd come over. Cool?

ME: Me casa es su casa, my friend.

G-MAN: See you soon.

I don't know what I'm going to do when football season starts again. It happens to me every year. I get used to Gregor during the offseason. Then, come August, I lose him for another seven months or so. Now I know how military spouses feel when the other is deployed.

Because G is as close to a wife as you'll ever have again.

Fuck off, self.

I board the ferry to take me to Port Orchard, where I can finally head home. My house isn't far from the ferry terminal. Maybe a ten-minute drive at most. So, before I know it, I'll be home and I can get rid of this monkey suit and indulge in some hardcore self-pity for the evening.

The west-facing side of my house is my favorite. Not only do I have multiple decks that overlook the sound, but on the main level, I have two sliding glass doors that are barely a foot apart and almost act as a disappearing glass wall. An abundance of trees on either side gives me all the privacy I could ever want.

It's a big house, too big for one person, but I love it anyway. The main floor hosts the living, dining, and kitchen spaces on one end, with a big master suite on the other. One floor below are two guest rooms and an office, and just below that, my darkroom and studio. Technically it's three stories, but it doesn't always feel that way because I only bother myself with two floors—the top and the bottom. The whole building is set into a hill making the stories really more like gentle declines with steps. But every floor has a large deck with access to the big backyard below, and a phenomenal view of the sound.

I can usually count on the view to cheer me up when I'm feeling down. But today seems to be the exception, I'm realizing, as I sit on the upper deck, cigar in one hand, scotch in the other. I didn't even change out of my suit, just plopped my ass down and started letting my thoughts wander to random places.

The weather is perfect. I'm guessing the temperature is somewhere in the mid-seventies. A slight breeze whispers through the tree leaves, the rustling sound acting as a perfect complement to the gentle waves lapping at the shore.

Gregor strolls onto the deck.

"Hey," I say. "Pull up a chair. I've got a cigar here for you, we can work our way through this bottle of scotch together."

"That upset, huh?" he asks.

"You know, I think I just got the wind knocked out of my sails, so to speak. I got carried away by the big rush of momentum and emotion and excitement. And Tabby wanted to slow it down. And if I want her, then I have to be okay with that."

He raises his glass toward me in acknowledgment.

"It doesn't mean I'm not going to drown my sorrows in scotch and cigars tonight though," I add.

Gregor sits back in the extra-large deck chair that we special ordered just for him and puffs a few times on his stick. "Okay," he says. "So, you see her again, what do you say?"

I think on it for a moment. "Well, first I apologize for trying to rush things and 'highjack her wedding' as she called it. Then I tell her that I'm willing to wait, as long as it takes. That I want us to avoid making the same mistakes, and I just want to work toward a future with her."

"That's real sweet, man." He smiles big at me.

"Aw, thanks, G." I smile back, feeling good for the first time since I left Tabby at the Cascadian House.

He pats at his jacket pocket, then his pants pocket. "Uh-oh," he says.

"What?"

"I think I left my cell phone in your guest room with my other stuff. I'm supposed to text Maisey."

"Have you guys even been on a real date yet?"

"Nope."

"And she's got you this wrapped around her finger?"

"I'm just being polite," he says defensively. "But, yes, she does have me this wrapped around her finger." He grins sheepishly.

I puff on my cigar. "Are you going to go get it?" I ask, blowing smoke into the air, literally.

"Would you get it for me?"

"Me? Why? You're a grown ass man who, last I checked, is capable of maneuvering his body into spaces to collect things."

"Yeah, I tweaked my knee at the gym earlier this week, PT wants me to avoid stairs when possible."

"Oh shit, man, I didn't know." I stand. "Sorry. You going to be okay for the start of the season?"

"Oh yeah." He waves his hand dismissively. "I just have to rest it for a while."

"I'll get it for you, G. No sweat, be right back."

I head into the house and down the stairs to the guest room with the king bed, as that's the one Gregor usually stays in. I open the door, and head for the nightstand, where I'm assuming his phone will be. Empty. I check the other nightstand, but it too is empty. In fact, I don't see any of his things in here. I turn to go check the other guest room and watch in shock as Tabatha comes in and shuts the door behind her.

"Tabs? What are you doing here?" I swallow thickly, my throat suddenly dry as fuck. She looks amazing. She's still in her wedding dress, but her shoes are off and in her hand. Her hair still mostly up, her makeup intact, but her eyes are red-rimmed.

"I was hoping we could talk for a minute."

"Okay. Of course. Sure. Have a seat." I gesture to the foot of the bed next to where I sit down. Her gown rustles slightly as she moves toward me and settles in, sitting close enough that our thighs are touching.

"I'm sorry," she starts.

"You have nothing to be sorry for," I say.

"I ruined it because I was being stupid."

"You weren't." I caress her cheek and hold her gaze in mine. "Not even a little bit. I was impatient and anxious."

"You were romantic."

"Agree to disagree," I say, smiling.

She reaches up to run her fingers along the scruff on the side of my face. "I want us to be together. Starting now. If you still want that too."

"More than anything," I say.

"Kiss me?"

I lean in and touch my lips to hers. Not soft, but not hard either. I want to remember this moment when she agreed to once again be mine and I was able to touch her freely. I move to take the kiss deeper but stop at a knock on the door.

"This better be good," I groan to Tabs then say louder, "Yeah?"

The door opens and Gregor pops his head in. "Uh, hey man, I found my phone. Oh, hi, Tabatha." He waves and smiles. She does the same. I have a feeling he already knew she was here and the phone request was just a ruse to get me downstairs. "So, the girls are here too, we're gonna run to the store and grab some steaks to grill for dinner. I'm gonna use your car." He holds up my keys and jingles them. "Should be gone half an hour?" He looks at me when he says this, one brow raised as though it's a question.

I chuckle. "You could be gone as long as forty-five minutes to an hour," I say. He gives me a thumbs up in return and closes the door behind him.

Tabatha giggles. "What do you think you need an hour for?"

"This."

33

TABATHA

Pax pulls me onto his lap and together we attempt to situate my dress so it's not *so* in the way. He leans forward to touch his forehead to mine. "Hi," he says.

"Hi." I smile. I can smell the cigar and scotch on him. Even though I'm not a scotch drinker, I love the taste of scotch on Pax's tongue. Always have. Especially after he smokes a cigar.

His eyes hold mine and I'm caught in his stare. I want so badly to kiss him and at the same time I want this moment—right before the kiss, where I know it's going to happen and everything in my life is about to change and the anticipation drives me wild—to last forever. Because I remember what it's like to kiss Pax. The brief interlude at the Cascadian House aside, he has a way of moving his lips against mine that makes me want to keep them interlocked incessantly.

He runs his nose along the side of mine, breathing me in, and I whimper in response. "Fucking love the sounds that come from your mouth." His voice is low and gravelly, making me wiggle against him, searching out that hard length that I know is beneath our layers of clothing. Finally, his lips whisper across mine for a second before claiming them in a kiss both soft and loving, yet hard and unforgiving.

His tongue seeks entrance, punishing in its pursuit as my body melts into his.

More.

I need more, want more. Pushing at his suit coat, I'm trying to get it off so I can rip at his shirt. I miss his hands on me the minute he moves them to help me remove his clothes. But at last I have his bare chest in front of me. His beautiful bronze chest that belies his profession, making him appear more like an athlete.

I run my hands across his skin, fascinated by the muscles quivering underneath my fingertips. He pushes the straps to my gown down my arms, I shake them off and the top falls to my waist. My nipples harden as his chest hair brushes against them. My panties flood. I need the skirt away from my body.

Now.

"Help," I say. "Help me with the zipper."

Pax reaches behind me and tugs it down, we stand so I can push it off. He removes his shoes and slacks at the same time, then pulls a condom from his wallet and quickly puts it on, his hands shaking as he moves. Until, finally, we are bare in front of one another. I drink him in—tall, lean, muscled, beautiful. His long, thick cock stands at attention, pointing toward the sky. I want it in me. My pussy, my mouth, my hands. I reach for him, but he stops me.

His gaze scorches my body as it travels up and down. "My god, Tabs. You are so beautiful. I just want to look at you. I've missed you. I've missed this." He reaches up with both hands and they travel slowly down the sides of my head to my shoulders, down my arms, to my thighs and back up again. "I want to worship every inch of you." He leans down and plants a kiss atop my right breast, then my left, his hands still touching me everywhere at once. I can't help but shiver. I'm scared and excited, turned on more than I've ever been.

"Please, Pax," I moan.

He pulls me against his body and we come together in a war of arms and legs, lips and tongues, moans and cries. Forced against the wall, I wrap my legs around his waist, instinct taking over as he grinds his hips against mine. His length slides back and forth against my clit, my own juices acting as lubrication. He's so hard and the friction dizzying. I use his shoulders as leverage and twist my hands in his hair, the pressure building until I explode. Burying my cries in his neck, biting down hard when the pleasure becomes too intense, clutching at him to keep me from melting to the floor.

My body lax and muscles spent, I drop my head to his chest as he works his hand under my ass from behind, pushing a finger inside of me. Excitement rears anew.

"Oh god, Pax. That's so good."

He sinks another finger in, scissoring, readying me for his cock. Blood roars through my body, my brain a fusion of hyperactivity and enamor. I've missed this more than I want to admit. This. Him. The feeling of losing control and not being able to stop it. Knowing he wants me so much, that he's wild for me, is intoxicating.

I want to whimper at the loss when he pulls them out, but the promise of more closely follows. "I can't wait, Tabs." He aligns the tip of his cock with my core and plunges inside me with one thrust.

"Oh shit," I cry out. "Pax!" My eyes roll to the back of my head. I'm going to die from sexual pleasure. It's that good. Pax fills me in a way I've not experienced since him. Sensually, emotionally, physically. The feel of his balls slapping against me as he sinks all the way in. I want to thank the universe for bringing him back to me.

He pauses for a moment to let me adjust to his size.

I don't want to adjust.

I want to be fucked.

"I need you to move. Please," I beg.

"What, baby? Like this?" He pulls out to the tip, then thrusts into me again, fast and hard, his fingers digging into my ass as he holds me in place. "Is that what you want?" he asks, grunting.

I nod, unable to speak. He does it again. And again. I'm so close to coming all I can do is cry out with every thrust. It's so hot. I'm so turned on, I have no choice but to climax again. A long and all-encompassing orgasm that just keeps going and going. As though my body has been starved for release and it's finally being served. Everything he does—the way he touches me, how he knows exactly what I need right as I need it, the ferocity with which he needs to possess me—is overwhelming.

"Jesus, Pax." I exhale. But he isn't done.

He pounds into me, mercilessly, pulling out completely and driving back in, over and over. I wrap my arms around his neck, trailing kisses from one side to the other. Breathing him in, my body comes back to life with each beautiful thrust between us.

How have I lived without this? Without him? I can't go without him again.

"I love you," I whisper in his ear.

"Fuuuck!" He draws the word out and comes with a roar. "My god, Tabs. I love you. I love you so much." His forehead rests against mine and we try to catch our breath.

Slowly, I lower my legs to the ground, my stance still shaky. He brings me over to the bed and we lay down, him pulling me into his arms. I hook one leg over his thigh and an arm across his chest, my head over his heart. His pulse is still racing, his breathing still deep. I wipe the sweat from my brow, and notice belatedly, that I'm still wearing Hunter's ring.

I wait for the shame to fill me as I remember today was the day I was promising myself to someone else. But it doesn't come.

"Is it wrong that I don't feel bad about today?"

"Which part?" Pax asks, turning and kissing my temple.

"All of it. Hunter leaving, ditching the wedding, sleeping with you."

"You shouldn't feel bad about any of that, baby. Life is messy, we can't control it. And you can't blame yourself for things you can't control."

I wiggle my fingers in front of his face, showing him the ring.

"You're lucky I'm still reeling from the best fucking orgasm of my life, woman. Otherwise, I might take offense at you still wearing the other guy's ring still."

I pull it off and toss it over onto the nightstand. "I'm sorry. I forgot it was on. I was so intent on finding you, and then—"

He puts his finger against my lips to silence me. "It's okay. I'm not upset. I know what was supposed to go down today, why that ring was on your finger, why that dress is on the floor. I don't care about any of that. I've got what I want right here in my arms. The rest of it? Yeah, it's going to be difficult and trying to deal with. You've got baggage, babe. But when we tackle it together? Tabs, we are unstoppable." He kisses my temple and pulls me tighter to him. And in that moment, I do feel unstoppable. Invincible.

And yeah, it's not ideal that Hunter left me at the altar, or that I left all those people at the Cascadian House. I don't know what will happen with the fallout of this, but I do know that one day I will thank Hunter for leaving me today. For having the guts to do what I couldn't, for ending a bad match before it began. Whatever his reasons.

"If we get married again—"

"When we get married again," Pax interrupts.

"Does it still count as twice if it's the same person? Like, have we still been divorced once before?"

"Pfft, no. There's a statute of limitations on it. As long as you marry the same person again within, like, nine years and six months and three days, you're okay to just say you were married once."

"Really?" I ask, smiling and trying to factor the dates in my head, even though I'm sure today would end up being that deadline.

"So, you want to avoid that stigma, babe, we best be getting hitched right about now."

"Okay." I sigh, then disentangle myself from his embrace to sit up, a huge smile on my face. "Well, what are we waiting for?"

34

EPILOGUE

PAX

I would love to tell you that we rushed off and got married that night. But we didn't. Instead, we had a great dinner prepared by Gregor, with Maisey, Crystal, and her husband Michael in attendance. Angela skipped dinner to go back to the Cascadian House to collect Tabby's things for her, including the luggage and clothing for the three-week honeymoon that wouldn't be happening, and bring them back to her.

Tabby and I were alone again within a few hours and I took full advantage of the remainder of the night by fucking her, making love to her, then fucking her again.

Besides, the next flight to Vegas wasn't until morning.

~

TABATHA - ONE YEAR LATER

Maisey puts the finishing touches on my makeup. I'm nervous as hell, but at least I look good. Walking the red carpet while five months pregnant is not my ideal. We weren't even really planning on having kids, but now that I'm pregnant, I'm liking the idea more and more. Pax is beyond excited. And with the prospect of one on the way, he's now decided he wants four total. I told him he needs to spend more time at Crystal's with the twins if he thinks he wants four.

"You look stunning," Maisey says, smiling at me.

"It's all because of you," I tell her.

Pax comes up behind me and runs his hands down the sides of my arms, then takes my hands in his and pulls each up to kiss the backs, before also kissing the top of my head. "It's all you, Tabs."

I look up at him and smile.

Pregnancy has not been easy for me. Especially after obsessing about my weight for so long. Where everyone else sees pregnant, I see fat. But I'm working on it, I know it's a process. I make healthy choices for myself and my baby and hope for the best. The worst part aside from that is the chronic heartburn, an ailment I thought had left me along with Hunter. So, hopefully that doesn't mean the baby will stress me out as much as Hunter did.

I'm kidding.

Sort of.

Motherhood scares me. But it should, right? I mean, it's a huge responsibility. Pax takes it all in stride, which is good for me, and I rely heavily on that positivity. If he says we can do it, then we can.

Now I just have to get through tonight. The other most nerve-wracking thing in my life so far. The Industry Awards. I'm up for best-actress in a leading role for the mini-series I did before Hunter and I split.

Maisey leaves us and Pax helps me out to the limo. I want to get to the theater a bit early so I can circumvent the mad rush of the red carpet before showtime. My dress hides most of the pregnancy, even though we've already announced it to the world. But I am not as svelte a figure, especially not in pictures. And pictures last forever.

Pax spends the ride to the venue talking me up, boosting my confidence, soothing my angst. Which he continues throughout the entire walk down the carpet, and during the cocktail reception before the show starts. I hadn't realized how tense I was, how necessary that was from him until I my name is called and I walk up to accept the award. He squeezes my hand and kisses me on the cheek, then stands when I do to help me with the stairs leading to the stage.

I take the first step and turn back to him. "You are my every-thing." I take his face in my hands and give him a short, but intense kiss. He has tears in his eyes when I step away. I take that with me, that pride as strength as I stride across the stage to collect my accolade.

"I'd like to thank the industry for this honor," I start. "And my agent, Angela. Without you, this never would have been an option. You fought for me when no one else would, knowing I could do it even before I did. Thank you. The crew, thank you for your constant support. Maisey, especially you." I take a deep breath before starting the next part. "This last year has been a whirlwind for me, as some of you know. If you follow the news at all." The crowd laughs, as I knew they would.

Because instead of mine and Hunter's breakup remaining private, his mother decided to sue me, on his behalf, for the cost of the wedding. Even though Hunter was the one who left me at the altar. In the end, the judge threw out the case since Hunter stated he'd pay for it all in his "Dear Tabatha" note he left me on what was supposed to be our wedding day. It was public and ugly and written about extensively in the gossip rags. Combined with the quickie marriage to Pax, and rumors of an affair, our faces were everywhere. Now with me pregnant, and the industry nomination, the publicity has not stopped.

"This role was a gamble for me, but it paid off. And I am so very grateful to have been given the opportunity. I don't know what the future brings, but I know it can't be any crazier than the past, am I right?" Laughter sounds through the room. "I wouldn't have been able to do anything I've accomplished without that man, right there." I point to Pax, sitting in the front row.

"Not only did he knock me up, but he propped me up when things got sticky. With a simple reminder that life is messy, we can't control it. And you can't blame yourself for things you can't control. I take those words with me daily as I slog through both the ugly and the beautiful, appreciating every moment, taking life one day at a time, and remaining grateful for all the wonderful things that happen in this crazy world. Thank you!"

Hey Reader,

Now that you've finished this book, please consider leaving a review. I'll be your best friend if you do.

XOXO, Denise

THANK YOU FOR READING!

If you enjoyed this book, please consider leaving a review. Hell, even if you didn't enjoy it please consider leaving one. That way I'll know what to change for next time.

If you want to know more about my books and new releases, join my newsletter!

POUR DECISIONS - SNEAK PEEK

Chapter One

My eyes have a hard time opening. Last night's mascara holds my lashes together, making them stick like glue. I use my fingers to pry open the right, blinking rapidly to adjust to the light. It's dim, but still an intrusion from the black void of a moment ago. My head raises and my left eye mimics the right. My vision blurred and hazy. A sea of white surrounds me, accompanied by the faint smell of sex, sweat, and bleach.

I'm not good with mornings. I don't like them; they don't like me. As though in testament to such, my stomach protests as I sit up slowly. Could be that its morning, could also result from too much alcohol and not enough food last night. My head spins as I take in the surrounding room. I'm in a hotel room, that much I remember. It's a nice one, spacious and well furnished. One of those with separate bedroom and living room areas. A ceiling fan rotates above my head. I can't recall ever seeing a ceiling fan in a hotel bedroom before.

Blackout curtains cover the window while the faint hum of the air conditioning dances around my ears. A quick peek under the sheets shows my naked body glaring back at me while snippets of last night's festivities pepper through my mind. My girlfriend's and I venturing out to the Villa Royale hotel for drinks. What started as a low-key happy hour stretched into four, then five. Or was it six?

Dancing. Oh god, so much dancing my legs ache.

I'd gotten word early afternoon about my nomination for the West Coast Winemaker's Association (WCWA) Innovation Competition (WCWAIC). My friends Tess and Megan thought it would be a good idea to take me out for drinks and we came to the same hotel that is hosting the WCWAIC starting tonight. My face grins at the memories, my body stretches languorously, and my throat groans at how good it feels. All the parts working independently, yet simultaneously, while—

Oh. Wait.

My legs aren't the only part of me that aches.

I trail my fingers down between my legs and push gently at the sore, swollen tissue, remembering how thoroughly and completely that delicious man fucked me last night. Multiple times if the condom wrappers on the nightstand are any sign.

Wait again.

The man.

I glance to the other side of the bed, relieved to find it empty. My sleep-addled brain finally catching up to the fact that the only light in the room is filtering through the cracked bathroom door, where the shower is running. And all the pieces come together in a linear fashion.

The competition.

My nomination.

Tess, Megan, and me celebrating.

Copious amounts of drinks.

The gorgeous guy.

All that dancing.

Fantastic sex.

Aw, fuck!

I need to go now before the guy gets out of the shower and we have to do that awkward morning after thing that everyone talks about. Where you don't know if you should go to breakfast, maybe have sex again, trade numbers, or avert your eyes and go your separate ways. Not that I would know. This is my first one-night stand ever. But I've heard enough stories to be frightened.

I scramble from the bed and begin the hunt for my clothes. The room isn't cluttered, far from it, but I'm still having a hard time identifying things. I grab my fishnet stockings and try to pull them on while standing.

Oh, they're ripped.

Wow, really ripped.

Especially in the crotch.

Nicely done, Morgan.

I mentally pat myself on the back, before realizing I didn't need them on anyway. What better way to make the proverbial walk of shame look even more embarrassing than by wearing the ripped stockings from the night before

I shove them along with my bra into my purse. Searching for my underwear while trying to zip the back of my dress at the same time. Right arm over my right shoulder, left arm bent behind my lower back and moving up from the bottom. Both trying in vain to reach the zipper pull or each other. Clearly, dresses were designed by sadist contortionists with no concern for how normal people dress in short amounts of time or otherwise.

Grabbing my shoes and purse in one hand, all the while holding the front of my dress to my chest, I quietly slip out the door into the hallway. Then toe on my shoes as I hit the elevator call button and continue to try unsuccessfully to zip my dress. The telltale ding signals the elevator car and the doors open to reveal a tall blonde woman in gym clothes, toweling non-existent sweat off her face, just as I'm pushing my heel into my shoe.

I nod my head as I enter, and give her a small smile, trying to pretend everything is normal. My dress isn't half hanging off my body, and I'm not—

OHMIGOD!

The reflection in the mirrored walls of the elevator car show someone who can't possibly be me. I mean, it's my dress, but no way is that nest of tangles and disarray my hair. And the raccoon eyed face with streaked eye makeup belongs to a stranger.

I can't help but gasp once I see myself. My free hand flies to my hair as I attempt to pat it down before licking my finger and running it under my eyes to get the smudge under control.

"Crazy night, huh?" the girl asks. She looks nice when she smiles at me.

"You have no idea." I smile back, a feeling of camaraderie developing, as though we're sharing in a sisterhood of sorts.

"Want me to zip your dress?"

"Oh, god, would you," I breathe. "Thank you so much." I turn my back to her, shivering slightly as her icy hands graze my skin.

"Looks like you had a good time." She gestures to my neck.

I lean in closer to the mirror, inspecting the number of hickeys on my neck.

My first one-night stand.

My first hickey on other parts of my body that aren't my neck.

"I did." I smile, pivoting to face the front. A flyer announcing the WCWAIC competition hangs from a bulletin box above the button controls and snags my attention. My heart does a little flip knowing that starting tonight, I'll be a part of that. And a competition like this one, where innovations in the wine industry are judged and awarded, could make a career for someone as small-time as me.

The car stops and the doors open, I make my way out to the lobby. Feeling proud for stepping out of my comfort zone and doing something so ordinarily out of character. Both in submitting to the competition and in a one-night stand.

"Bye," I say to the girl as we part ways; she in the direction of the juice bar and me toward the exit. But as proud as I may feel in that moment, I still wait until I'm a block away before pulling up an app and ordering a car to come and take me home.

Chapter Two

I pull up the messages on my phone to send a text to my best friend, Tess, and see all the pictures that she and Megan sent me the night before. Dozens of pictures of me on the dance floor with the guy from the hotel. And almost every single one they took is flattering. If it weren't for the fact the girl in the photos is wearing the same dress I am, I might not believe it's me.

This girl looks . . . hot.

Confident.

Sexy.

I'm not any of those things in my everyday life. Look up shy, mousy, and wallflower with social anxiety in the dictionary and there I will be. Which often makes me wonder how different my life would be if I were confident and sexy. Would I have a boyfriend? A better career? Might I have finally moved out of my mom and grandma's house to live on my own?

Cause none of those things are true now.

I'm working on the career part though. This award will help that along. If I win, that is.

Tess' words from last night ring through my mind.

When.

Not *if.*

When I win this competition, the recognition will help to further my career. The WCWAIC award is for showing innovation in wine making and selling techniques. Coming up with something that benefits the end user, i.e. the wine drinker, in a way that's not been done before. It's rare that a competition like this comes up, where the primary goal isn't focused on something more traditional, like "Best Cabernet Sauvignon" or something along those lines. There's just this one for the west coast, and then I think one of the big wine magazines has a national one.

Winning should mean more sales, which means more money, which is all I need to get a place of my own. While I may love my mom and grandmother, I don't need to be living with them any longer. I'm going to be thirty years old next year, I should have been out of their house six years ago. But they live where my grapevines live and I really love my vines.

I flip through more of the pictures with me and the guy who is so totally out of my league. As he kisses my neck, grabs my hips, laughs at whatever I'm saying. This girl has him captivated. How did I do it?

I dial Tess, hoping she's awake.

"Toot, toot, and beep, beep," she answers in a sing-song voice.

"What?" I ask, laughing.

"Bad girl. Talking 'bout the bad girl, yeah," she sings the Donna Summer song from seventies into the phone.

"I am not a bad girl, take it back!"

"I will not take it back. Last night was awesome! I've never seen you cut loose like that. You were having so much fun! Did you spend the night with him? Was the sex good? What did he say this morning? Did you exchange numbers? Are you doing the LYFT of shame home right now? Are you going to see him again?" She rattles off questions.

"Um, let me see." I tap my finger on my lips, pretending to think, even though she can't see me. "Yes. Yes. Nothing. No. Yes. And I doubt it."

"Nooo! Why?"

"Which of those responses are you asking why to?"

"Exchanging numbers. Seeing him again. Did you say anything to him?"

"No! I snuck out while he was in the shower."

"Morgan!"

"Tess!"

"Come on. Really? This has got to be your first one-stand in—"

"Ever," I interrupt.

"No," she gasps.

"Yes," I affirm, nodding.

She's silent for a moment. "I guess you're right. Well then, all the more reason why you should have embraced it. Jumped in the shower with him. Left your number in his wallet, a lipstick print on his boxers."

"I don't think so," I say.

"Spoil sport. Fine, let's get back to the sex then. You said it was good?"

"Better than," I whisper into the phone. I catch the LYFT driver's eye in the rear-view mirror and turn my head to the side, covering my mouth with my other hand. "Mind blowing." I lower my voice, not wanting him to hear.

"What?"

"Mind blowing. Like what we see in movies," I mumble.

"You guys watched a movie? Like porn?"

"No," I sigh. "I said like what we see in movies."

"Wow, like porn movies?"

"No, just normal movies. Or, I don't know, maybe porn," I giggle. This time when the driver looks back at me through the mirror, I meet his gaze and stare hard. Screw him for listening in. It's my conversation, not his. And it's private. Though, I probably shouldn't be having it in *his* car then, but whatever.

"I knew the sex would be great. He was so good looking!" Tess enthuses.

"Is that all it takes?"

"Pretty much. The better looking they are, the more sex they've had. And the more sex they've had, the better they are at it."

"What about that whole *average-guys-try-harder-in-bed* theory you had before?"

"Morgan, let's face it, anytime you get the opportunity to sleep with a hot guy over an average guy, you need to take the hot one. You never know when you'll get a chance again."

"Gee, thanks. You're quite the ego booster this morning."

"Oh, you know what I mean. Things like that don't happen to girls like us."

"Who are girls like us?"

"You know, average girls. We're cute, smart, successful, but there's nothing crazy extraordinary about us."

"And the ego boosts just keep coming," I say drily.

"Says the girl who just left the hot guy's bed."

"There is that," I say, tempted to blow on my fingernails, then shine them on the chest of my dress. Last night was like a coup for ordinary girls everywhere. Because the guy wasn't that drunk.

Riggs.

That's his first name. I didn't ask for his last. Even his name is sexy. I shiver at the memories of his hands roaming my body, his lips murmuring beautiful words, his eyes worshiping in their quest to see everything about me at once, yet still retain each detail. I should be on cloud nine after last night. And part of me is. But the part of me that didn't leave my number, or get his, and who snuck out while he was in the shower, that part of me knows I'll never change.

Always preferring the sidelines to center stage; the wall to the middle of the room; the backseat to the driver. Probably because my mom and grandmother are such drivers. There's not room enough for three of us in the same house. It's barely tolerable with the two of them. Which reminds me, I never did text my mom or grandma to say I wouldn't be home. Not that I have a curfew or anything, I'm a grown woman. But they worry when they don't know where I am or what I'm doing.

The driver turns onto the long dirt drive leading to our house. It's impressive when you don't realize that we're at the tiny square house to the west and not the multi-level chalet straight ahead. But that's a story for another time. Right now I've got to square my shoulders and prepare myself for the onslaught of questions the two pains in my neck are going to shower me with the minute I walk in the door.

"Hey, we're pulling up to the house, I'll call you back in a bit," I tell Tess.

"Later, bad girl."

I chuckle as I click to end the call and gather my purse, looking around to make sure I haven't left anything in the back seat. "I can tip through the app, right?" I ask the driver, even though I already know the answer to that.

"Yep," he nods once as he answers. It's a dumb question but I don't know of another way to let the driver know I plan to tip them. I don't want them driving away thinking I stiffed them until later when they get their paycheck or whatever and realize I did tip them. I mean, by then they may not even remember who I am or what day it was they drove me.

This way they have it on their mind, hopefully for a couple days, and then make the connection that I'm the girl who left the tip. Not that I'll ever see them again, but that's not the point. I want them to have the instant gratification of knowing I appreciated them and the service they provided, and that I plan to reward them financially.

I slip inside the front door as quietly as possible in hopes my mom and grandmother are still asleep or at the very least, preoccupied somewhere else. Which turns out to be futile. The familiar voices of the cohosts for a popular morning show are already echoing through the room, followed swiftly by the tenors of my mother and grandmother as they argue the points of the story that just aired. It won't matter what it was about, they will never see it from the same point of view. Even if one of them has to argue against their personal beliefs, they will over agreeing with the other. It's not something I understand or even try to.

"There you are!" my grandmother exclaims. "Come here right now, young lady."

I bow my head slightly and walk toward them, ready to be shamed for staying out all night without calling and then walking in looking like . . . well looking like a hot guy fucked me hard all night long.

"Morning, Grandma." I lean in to give her a kiss on the cheek. She smiles, but it's fast, and her face turns hard again.

I brace myself for whatever punishment is about to verbally rain down.

"You tell your mother that Tom Selleck's mustache is real. That man does not need to use a hair growth treatment on his face. He is all man. A real man. And real men can grow a proper mustache."

"It's too lush, Morgan. Look at it, no one has hair like that, facial or otherwise. He's got to be using extensions or some sort of potion. And it's definitely dyed."

I look back and forth between the two of them, not quite believing what I've walked into. They've rewound the program and have it paused on the man in question. I have to admit, his mustache looks lush, and very dark. Almost too dark. I squint at the screen, trying to see if anything looks amiss. But Tom Selleck looks just as he should, otherworldly handsome with all that thick, dark hair above his lip and atop his head.

Both women lean toward me from their chairs, waiting to hear my answer. As though this will be the time I will produce a tie breaker. I won't. I never have, and I probably never will.

"Hasn't it always looked like that?" I ask, trying to take the middle road. "Lush and full? Like, since he was young."

"Ha," they both say, even though I've proven neither point.

"Okay, well, I've got to go get ready for my day and plan out tonight." I wave over my shoulder as I head down the hall. Still wondering why no one said a word about my appearance or the fact that I was out all night.

Get your copy of Pour Decisions now!

ACKNOWLEDGMENTS

Every time I finish a book I realize there's no way I could have done it without a ton of help. And then—since no one edits my acknowledgments and I don't write them until the very end—I spend hours worrying I've misspelled something or my grammar is incorrect.

That said, in no particular order, I want to thank:

Rachel Radner, Author - You know how dependent I am on you, but I'm not sure anyone else does. So here is my public declaration - no way in hell could I ever finish a book without you, Rachel. You are amazing.

Shannon Myers - my new critique partner and MC Romance writer extraordinaire. Thank you for the feedback and I look forward to many more pages together.

Stephie Walls - You are what I aspire to as a writer. Thank you for your friendship and support. I heart you big, BFF.

Linda Russell - Foreword PR - You slow the swirling vortex of craziness and indecision that is my brain. And talk me down off every ledge. Thank you. Thank you. Thank you.

Cassie, Opulent Designs - I love the cover. Just love it. Thank you.

Missy Borucki - OMG, woman. I have no words. You make me better with each book. So, I guess I have those words. Oh, and these: Thank you so, so much!

Jenn Wood - Thank you for taking a chance on me (again.) You are awesome!

My Dirty Darlings - Life would be so boring without you all to bounce ideas off of and fuck around with online day after day. Plus, I could never make it through without your encouragement. Never.

Gabriella Scavella-Bell, Jaime Reynolds, Rochelle West, Susan Henn - Your support means everything. I'm humbled by the time and energy that you give me. I can't thank you all enough.

Remi-licious - You may not read my books, or even remember what most are about, but you're still the bestest friend a girl could ask for. I love you!

While I'm at it, I'm going to thank **Daniel Sobieray** for being such a hunk. Or maybe I should thank his parents for passing along such good genes. Anyway, he's the guy in (most of) my teasers and the perfect visual inspiration for romance novels, including this one. Totally go follow him on social media, his pics are hot. Plus, he pretty much made my day/week/year/life when he followed me on Instagram and xoxo'd me on Facebook. It's the little things.

Speaking of hunks: **my hunk-a-hunk of burning love, BW**. The one on which all my semi-flawed/alpha-esque/charismatic male characters are based, topic of plenty-o-FB conversations—which he hates—and the best decision I ever made. Hands down, dude, you make me a much better me than I could ever be on my own. Thank you for being mine. I love you.

ABOUT THE AUTHOR

Denise has been reading since before she could talk. And to this day, escaping into a book is her go-to activity before anything else.

She likes to write about sassy women and semi-flawed alpha-esque men (hard on the outside and just a little soft on the inside.) Denise's female characters always have strong friendships, potty mouths, and like to drink—a lot.

Denise is loyal to a fault, a bit too sarcastic, blindingly opti-mistic, and pretty freakin' happy with life overall. If she couldn't be a writer, she'd be a singer in a classic rock band. Right after she learned to carry a tune. She has more purses than days in the month, an obsession with colored ink pens, and a slightly unhealthy bracelet habit.

Home is in the Pacific Northwest where she lives with six special needs Siberian Huskies and a husband (BW) who has the patience and tolerance of a saint. And, lest she forget, Denise also lives with too many to count characters inside her head, who will eventually have their stories told.

For more about Denise visit her website at: www. DeniseWells.com

Or follow her on any of the social media sites below.

ALSO BY DENISE WELLS

Loving Lexie, a steamy cowboy enemies to lovers romance

Seducing Sadie, a steamy firefighter romance

Trusting Tenley, an emotional second-chance at love romance

<u>ANTHOLOGIES</u>

High EX-Pectations, a romantic comedy short in the **Imperfect Date Anthology**

CAUGHT UNDER THE MISTLETOE - A Holiday Affair to Remember, a romantic comedy holiday short

STORYBOOK PUB CHRISTMAS WISHES - Mistle Oh-No, a romantic comedy holiday short

STORYBOOK PUB - Breezy Like Sunday Morning, a romantic comedy short

<u>LIMITED RELEASES</u>

GIRLS JUST WANNA HAVE FUNDAMENTAL RIGHTS - Charity Anthology

SEEDS OF LOVE A Charity Romance Anthology to benefit Ukraine - Charity Anthology

HOT AS F$#K SUMMER ROMANCE ANTHOLOGY - SULTRY SUMMER NIGHTS

LOCKED AND LOVED: An Isolated Romance Collection

SUMMER WITH YOU: Summer Shorts Collection

JUST A LICK Collection

LOVE LETTERS Collection

STOCKING STUFFERS Anthology

PRAISE FOR HOW TO RUIN YOUR EX'S WEDDING

Just read this!! If you are looking for an addictive and quirky romance then this is for you.

— GOODREADS READER

I have no words! Honestly, what is there to say but read/enjoy/devour this book.

— GOODREADS READER

I laughed so hard about the mustache!!! This book was perfection!

— GOODREADS READER